SISTER
OF
STARLIT
SEAS

SISTER OF STARLIT SEAS

TERRY BROOKS

NEW YORK

Published in the United States by Del Rey,
an imprint of Random House, a division of
Penguin Random House LLC, New York.

DEL REY and the CIRCLE colophon are registered trademarks of
Penguin Random House LLC.

Title-page art: © Tatiana Prihnenko-stock.adobe.com
Chapter-opener art: © Zhanna Varanetskaya-stock.adobe.com
Map illustrator: Jared Blando

Library of Congress Cataloging-in-Publication Data
Names: Brooks, Terry, author.
Title: Sister of starlit seas / Terry Brooks.
Description: First edition. | New York: Del Rey, 2023. |
Series: Viridian deep
Identifiers: LCCN 2023035728 (print) | LCCN 2023035729 (ebook) |
ISBN 9780593129777 (hardcover; acid-free paper) |
ISBN 9780593129784 (ebook)
Subjects: LCGFT: Fantasy fiction. | Novels.
Classification: LCC PS3552.R6596 S47 2023 (print) |
LCC PS3552.R6596 (ebook) | DDC 813/.54—dc23/eng/20230817
LC record available at https://lccn.loc.gov/2023035728
LC ebook record available at https://lccn.loc.gov/2023035729

Printed in the United States of America on acid-free paper

randomhousebooks.com

2 4 6 8 9 7 5 3 1

First Edition

Book design by Edwin A. Vazquez

For my two irreplaceable Annes,
who know how to keep my feet to the fire

Lands of the Fey

Ghoul Hives

Fey Border

Dragon Hive

Skyscrape

Mountains

Rampellion

Aerkling Hives

Water Sprite
Islands

The
Fishing Ponds

Viridian Deep

Spawn Ridge

Strewlin
Swamp

Cressidon Woods

n

Human Border

BONNINGHAM WOOD

HARBOR'S END

THE WASTELANDS

GOBLIN CHAINS

Roughlin Wake

GOBLIN PRISONS

THE LANDS OF MEN

BLANDO

SISTER
OF
STARLIT
SEAS

ONE

IN THE LATE-NIGHT HOURS OF THE SECOND DAY OF THE FULL MOON, I slip from my concealment to begin my latest mission. I will be instantly visible should I leave the shadows, so I stay close within their cover, my thoughts on my intended rescue and the importance of its success. I am young still—I know this—yet I am much more capable than my seventeen years might suggest. Well seasoned by three years of hard living and perilous adventures, I can now do what many others cannot.

When I left Viridian Deep, I was considered little more than a wayward and somewhat difficult child: Charlayne—known by all as Char—the youngest daughter of Ancrow the Magnificent. (My bitter appellation for a mother I never really knew and have come to resent.) I had three other sisters and a brother who were all so much more accomplished and well regarded than I was. So I was bold and careless and ready to risk my life on every occasion just to gain some attention, and was therefore considered a needless risk-taker.

But to me, it never felt needless. There was always something in me that drove me to recklessness, as if there was a part of my being that lay undiscovered and unfulfilled. And if I could just locate that part, then I would finally be able to settle down instead of always searching around the next corner for whatever adventure or revelation might await.

I have not yet found what I am searching for, but my restless wandering has led me to Jagged Reach, a large island in the Helles—a warmer and more tropical sea than the one that bordered my homeland. There I joined a pirate crew—and in the peril and risk and freedom of life on the open seas, I almost found what I was looking for.

Better yet, I have finally fallen in love.

And if that love is to have a future, I remind myself sternly, then I had better get on with what I am doing.

The docks are layered with dew from a midnight fog, not to mention scattered raindrops and the constant swell of brine. The dampness makes the wooden slats underfoot slick and treacherous, but I have no fear. I never have. It is what makes me such a good pirate.

I tread carefully in the blanketing darkness, stepping slowly, carefully, and purposefully. I am a warrior, a paladin, an archangel of fire and fury. I carry my weapons strapped across my thighs, down my back, and about my waist, and I wear my heart on my sleeve—for I am all that stands between death and my intended. Without me, he will surely perish—and that I cannot allow.

And perhaps—perhaps!—this rescue will finally prove how much he needs me.

With a surge of hope, I continue on. I have a destination, and I need to reach it before sunrise.

The way forward is clear. It is late, and those who work these docks are mostly asleep. There are night watchmen on patrol, but I know their ways and can avoid them. Also, each ship keeps a nighttime watch, though the sailors assigned mostly only come out on the half hour for a quick look around, then hastily retreat back into the warmth of their cabins. There are dangers in the dockland world, to be sure, but while death has nodded my way more than a few times, it has never come as close to me as it has to others.

Down the shore, the oyster catchers are readying their craft to enter the adjoining rivers that feed into the Helles. I can hear their stays being tightened and their anchors being raised. Men's deep voices rise up in the dark, intermingled now and then with the higher-pitched shouts of women. Fishing is an equal-opportunity endeavor, where both sexes work together. Not all professions are so balanced, but fishing requires a closeness—a trust and a sharing—that some types of work do not. Duties are shared, and earnings are spread out equally. I could have chosen this work once, back when I first came to the island of Jagged Reach and the city of Pressia. But I chose another way—a better way, which shares many of the same advantages—and I am not one to look back.

I have never been, and never will be.

I slip past the oyster piers and continue on to where the warehouses loom in huge dark blocks of timber and stone. Here the docks are longer and more heavily timbered, to handle the ocean-going freighters and monstrous haulers. Here the heavy-laden carriers must load and unload their goods—everything from timber and steel to woolens and appliances. Yet what comes here is not what goes out, because their services benefit two worlds. This island lies between the Fae lands and the Human provinces, so the bonds of trade—some of it illegal—bind our two peoples in ways that transcend both worlds. In most places, there is a defined separation—a refusal of the one world to even believe in the presence of the other. But on these islands, in the safety of the waters of the Helles, it is possible for each to engage with the other. Here the wards that separate the two worlds have weakened sufficiently to allow for Fae and Human to interact and coexist on a different and more productive scale.

It surprised me at first, this forbidden intermingling of Fae and Human. I had been taught it was an impossibility—that the wards of the Fae forbade it from happening. But as with so many things we are taught in our childhood, there are exceptions to every rule. And Jagged Reach has been one such exception for a thousand years. Yes, there are rules governing the exchanges between Human and Fae, and yes, some restrictions still apply. But people, no matter their origins, gravitate toward one another, and the more you interact, the harder it becomes to see your neighbor as all that different from yourself.

It is one of the things I have come to love most about my life in Jagged Reach, how I see around me every day a multiplicity of people, all different from me, amid which my own green skin and leafy hair stand out not a bit. Besides, how else can you explain my having fallen in love as I have? How else can you explain my willingness to risk so much for a Human—someone who is considered by most of the Fae as an impossible match?

I slide along the walls of the nearest warehouse, deep within the shadows, looking hard at what lies about me. Discovery now would be disastrous, so I cannot make a wrong move at this point. My eyes shift from one docking site to another, from one vessel to a second, from one worn plankway filled with movement to a score of others so that nothing escapes my notice.

I spy the dock lookout as he approaches from some distance ahead of me, well out in the bright exposure of the moonlight, his attention fixed on the piers. I know him instantly. He is a mean piece of work we call Crouch for his tendency to walk with a bent, lurching gait, his head lowered. He shambles rather than walks, but his strength is enormous. I have seen him brutalize more than one unhappy soul in the supposed pursuit of his duties. Mostly, I think, he enjoys hurting others—especially when so many he encounters are smaller and weaker than he is. I once watched him kill a man by twisting his head about and dumping his lifeless body aside like so much garbage.

I don't want anything to do with him, but he is not near enough to see me yet, so I must hide before he gets much closer and let him pass. He carries a triad staff, the better to employ the *inish* he commands. I do not fear him, but I do not underestimate him, either. He does not command the *inish* power of a Watcher, as Harrow does, but then neither do I. So I must not engage him.

I settle into the relative concealment of a warehouse entry where the shadows are deep. With his eyes fully exposed to the moonlight, Crouch's vision will be severely limited. He will pass me by unknowingly, and I will be little more than another piece of the shadows that hide me. All I need to do is remain still and make no sound—something I am immensely good at these days.

I wait patiently for his passage, already frozen in place. Favor smiles on me, for he passes me by without a look and goes on down the dock without glancing back.

I wait until he is out of sight and proceed once more, easing my way toward the Faraway Trades Company's Warehouse #3, where I will find what I am looking for. Gulls perch on pilings and abandoned wharf ends, resting in huddled groups. A few calls ring out, shrill and somewhat chilling, but none move or startle as I pass. From farther back, cranes draw in heavy ropes, and chains clank in an endless clatter, as the unloading of a heavy cross-channel freighter commences. I welcome the disruption of these sounds, which draw attention away from me. I give them a few moments of continued activity, then push on.

Time is passing. I feel it slipping away.

I move more quickly now, sliding along the warehouse fronts, counting off the piers projecting out into the water, their lengths littered with machinery. Cranes for heavy pallets and boxcars. Lifts for fishing gear and light surplus. Spans for drying and cleaning nets and harpoons. Bins for fish before they are washed and prepared for sale. Racks for weapons and light armor. Tubs for gear that will need cleaning and drying.

I give it all a careful look as I pass. There are too many hooks and gaffs for my taste. Too many blades and spears. Too many ways to bring things to ground that wish only to be free.

I reach Warehouse #3 of the Faraway Trades Company and halt once more, this time in the relative safety of the building next door, deep in the shadows of an overhang. The building is dark and quiet, though the world about it rustles and clangs with the tonnage being moved from the ships anchored along the row of docks I've left behind. Warehouse #3 is almost at the far end of the harbor, and down here activity is minimal. It could be because business is down or shipping is slow, or it could be because these units are mostly for storage. But I know better. I know these warehouses are owned by Humans and manned by Goblins. You seldom see the latter, of course—Goblins are not appreciated anywhere in Fae country. But those who work here are kept safely tucked away within a bevy of storerooms by their Human overseers, who employ them for a particularly vile purpose.

For Warehouse #3 is the hub of the Faraway Trades Company's illegal sideline—a business that is known to exist, but never openly acknowledged: slavery. Here the Human representatives of the Ministry are involved in the imprisonment, sale, and shipping of both Humans and Fae to countries that will use them as forced labor for the remainder of their lives. Even though widely decried in the Human world—and anathema to most Fae—it is secretly allowed. And I should know. I have worked hard to put a stop to it, as a part of my new pirate life on the Helles.

When we are not smuggling or reappropriating goods, we are engaged in actively destroying the slave trade. And the Faraway Trades Company is well known to us as the worst of the worst. Apart from such warehouses, which can contain their living merchandise on their way from one port to another, rumor has it that it maintains several secret slave colonies for more long-term storage of its "goods." We have been searching for such a colony for as long as I have been part of the crew but have yet to find one. Faraway Trades is primarily a shipping company, so these colonies must be somewhere near water. But for all we have searched among the more remote islands in the Helles, we have still found no sign of them.

Yes, I am a thief and a pirate, and have definitely operated on the shady side of the law. (After all, crusaders need some way to earn a living.) But for all that, I have never thought to enslave another creature. In the world of the Fae, we believe that our people are born free and entitled to stay that way. But the Humans tend to view things differently—especially when it comes to workers for their salt and iron mines, rock and ore extractors, and reef skimmers. For those are hard jobs that few would voluntarily choose.

The Faraway Trades Company provides workers for the jobs that no one in their right mind wants to do. So to fill those positions, it scavenges and steals, and it does so with the tacit permission of authorities who do not care to involve themselves in the darkness that such undertakings necessarily require.

I learned most of this from my intended—a pirate and a brigand, but a good man nevertheless, who is hunted relentlessly by those he plagues with his endless war against slavery. With his ship and his loyal crew, he hunts these fiends across the waters, and when he finds them, he brings them down.

I should know. He has been my captain for almost three years now. He told me of his purpose, explained his intentions, and shared his vision for a better future. He brought me out of the darkness of my ignorance and into the light of his own knowledge.

And I love him enough that I will now risk my life to save his.

I look back at Warehouse #3. He is locked within, waiting to be executed and guarded by a small army of Goblins—any one of which is twice my size.

I stand almost no chance of saving him. Yet I must try.

I am Char, daughter of Ancrow, sister of Auris, Harrow, Ronden, and Ramey, and I am brave enough to take the risks that await me.

I step forth from my hiding place and advance.

TWO

I MOVE SWIFTLY TO WHERE MY INTENDED IS IMPRISONED, WORKING my way over planks worn and ragged from years of exposure to both work and weather. I am conscious of only him and nothing else.

You might think it odd that I constantly refer to him as my intended, and you would be right to do so, as he neither sees nor refers to himself in such terms—or even believes that we share any more intimate relationship than captain and crewmate. I am merely a friend and ally, a girl he found in a dockside bar working the counter, illegally employed. I earned my money however I could in those days, and often that required lying to prospective employers to persuade them to take me on. I look and sound older than I am, which gives me an advantage, and I am wiser in the ways of the world than most girls my age. I am in many respects a chameleon, and I take advantage of that to keep others guessing.

But back to my intended.

I call him that because—to me—that is who he was from the first moment I met him. I call him that to remind myself that there will come a day—perhaps this very day—when he sees me with new eyes. To him, I am just the little inland girl who took to sea life like a fish to water, and who never seems more at home than when out on the waves. And indeed, this is how I see myself. I am a girl born to live near the sea. The ocean draws me. I ride the waves like an old sailor, at peace in the strongest of swells. Storms do not scare me, no matter how strong, and the waters cradle me as they would a child of their own. I can swim and dive with the best of them, much as I did back home with my best friend Florin, a Water Sprite.

The young captain they call the Silver Blade—born Brecklin Craile—believed in me right from the start. But to him, I am just a fledgling crewmember he has trained to the pirate life. He does not see me as a potential partner yet, much as I long for that.

What was it that drew me to him? That he saved me, yes. But also something more intense, complex, and deep. I felt it right away when I heard his voice and saw his face. It was like the scent of nectar wafting from a flower. It was a mix of face and body—his long, narrow visage combined with his startling blue eyes and that lean, rangy torso, full of leashed energy.

But it was his presence, too. Calm and collected, constantly at ease but always at the ready, never hurried or rushed. It was the certainty he conveyed—the difficult-to-define but undeniable confidence that, whatever happened, he was ready for it.

As I slink toward Warehouse #3, I remember once more how it all began, as clear as if it were yesterday.

I was working out of the Boat Hook, down toward the end of the docks, where the dregs of the nautical trade always drifted. There were rules and at least a pretense of proper behavior in most places in Pressia . . . but not at the Boat Hook. I was working at a place where life was cheap and perilous, and keeping a blade close was always necessary. I had learned early how to wield blades of all sorts, so I took to carrying at least two or three on a constant basis, both for emergency and for appearance. Seldom was I challenged after the first few times I was tested, because word got around of my skill. Yet, as I have said, there are exceptions to every rule, and the same applied here.

Because Delph Ruan never did learn when to quit.

He made his intentions clear right from the start. He wanted a warm body at night and a worker by day to carry out his wishes and improve his situation. Not a wife, you understand. A wife was out of the question; no sucker for love or commitment was he. But a partner would do, if she possessed certain skills and attributes.

I brushed him off, but he persisted. He was loud, imposing, and endlessly rude, declaring early on that he wanted me, though I was firm in telling him no.

It was not enough to discourage him. At first, he was nothing more than a temporary nuisance. But then he began harassing anyone who showed an interest in me. He knifed one man—didn't kill him but left his mark—and once he even challenged me to a one-handed knife fight: a match where combatants tie one arm behind their backs while the other, knife in fist, is bound to their opponent with a three-foot length of rope. He seemed surprised when I accepted—though I did so only because I'd had enough and wanted an end to his pursuit. He thought he had me at his mercy, but he was like that—always thinking things that weren't true.

His plan was to yank me off my feet, bring me down, and with his knife at my throat offer to spare my life if I gifted him with a night or two of special favors, which he was sure would win me over for good. He even bragged aloud of his intentions to those who would listen.

When the fight began, we were ringed by barflies and other low-life scum. He yanked me toward him straightaway, foolish man—and found himself flying over top of me to land flat on his back. I was on him instantly, quick as lightning, and it was my knife that ended up at his throat and my voice offering to spare his life if he made a sacred promise to never come at me again.

I thought that would be the end of it, but it wasn't. Not in the least.

Several weeks passed, then one busy night he caught me coming in from the washroom out back, where I had gone to clean up. He grabbed me from behind, pinning my arms to my sides, snatching up two of my three knives, and dragging me backward along the hallway with a sack thrown over my head. I tried to reach for my third knife, but he found it first and cast it away.

"Time to pay the price of admission," he hissed as he dragged me out the back doors of the Boat Hook and into a cluster of storage bins near the water. Without a word, he yanked off the sack, cast me down, and fell atop me. He was big enough that I was pinned fast. I tried biting and scratching, but he only laughed and said he liked his women wild. I screamed, but the noise from inside drowned out my cries. I yelled that I was only fifteen—which at the time was true, though barely—but he did not care about that, either.

Then suddenly he froze in place, still holding me fast, but gone as still as could be.

"What mischief is this, Delph?" a voice said from behind him, a sword point prodding his exposed rear end. "Are there no grown women who consider you worthy?"

"Leave me be," my attacker snarled. "This is my business."

A boot to the stomach kicked him off me. He lay sprawled on the dock, his face a mask of rage. "I'll have your innards scattered along the piers from one end to the other for this!"

"Will you, now?"

I looked up at my rescuer and knew him at once. Everyone on the docks did. He was the Silver Blade. His skills with weapons were astonishing, and even at his young age—maybe as young as early twenties—he was the stuff of legends. I had never met him, never done more than glance his way momentarily, another figure in the crowd. He was too . . . what? Too impossible for someone like me, too far out of reach, too important to even consider me. I was a runaway with no real future, and nothing to recommend me.

"Would you like to stand up, Little Scrapper?" he asked me.

I scrambled up and faced him, brushing back my leafy green hair self-consciously. "I would. And my thanks."

He laughed. "Most welcome. Now then." He shifted his blade

from Delph's rear to his front, pressing a bit harder. "I think we need this one permanently gone, don't you?"

I was inclined to agree, but Delph was helpless and there was terror in his eyes. And I knew the Blade's reputation: Take no prisoners; grant no favors. "I would like that. But not this way. Release him. If I ever see him again, I will geld him myself."

Brecklin Craile lifted his blade and sheathed it, adding a final kick to Delph Ruan's backside. My attacker scrambled to his feet.

"This isn't finished, you stunted little tree!" he screamed at me as he raced away.

With the Silver Blade standing next to me, I watched the beaten man flee, my emotions in turmoil.

"Charming," the Blade said quietly. "Yet he is dangerous, that one. You must be careful."

He caught my eye, and I forced myself to meet his gaze. "I can take care of myself," I declared stoutly.

He grinned. "I have no doubt you can, Little Scrapper. So then, what would you say if I offered you a place on my crew?"

I knew what he meant, because everyone on the docks knew what he was. He was asking if I wanted to become a pirate.

"Why would you want me?" I asked.

"Because you have a pirate's soul and a warrior's heart. Because I can already tell from having watched you over the past two weeks that you were born to the profession. Because you are already halfway there, in case you hadn't noticed. And because you are fierce and wild, and I like what I see."

He paused. "But mostly because I like your imperious thatch of emerald-green hair." Another pause. A smile. "Your very *leafy* green hair. I know of no one else who can boast of such a fine mantle of Fae-dom."

In that moment, with his words already an unforgettable echo in my mind, the look in his eyes would have been enough to make me do anything he wanted.

"What say you?" he pressed. "Care to join up?"

"I would like that," I whispered. "Very much."

THOUGH ALMOST THREE YEARS GONE, STILL THE MEMORY BURNS within me. I will never forget it.

Which is why I continue on to reach Warehouse #3 of the Far-away Trades Company and stand fixed in place, facing the walls. I am here through a stroke of good luck. Brecklin was taken on the streets as I went to meet him, ringed about in seconds by a dozen cloaked figures—taken, thrown down, secured, and hauled away. Had I not been close enough to witness his abduction, I would never have known. As it was, I had no time to act, and I was too far away to make any difference. I would have been seized myself or cut down before I could do him any good. But I was able to follow his captors, to see where it was they took him.

So now is my chance to give him back his freedom. I know I can do it.

I creep along the side of the warehouse, staying well away from the huge front doors where larger deliveries come in, searching for a smaller entry. I find one quickly enough, well down one side of the building: ironclad, sealed, and locked. I test the latches, find them secure, and fish through my pockets for the picks I was given by another thief I worked with awhile back: one who took a liking to me as—and I quote—"a snot-nosed possibility." But I appreciated the thought behind the backhanded compliment, if not the word-ing. The picks were good ones, strong and sturdy, and they have never failed me. They do not fail me now, and in spite of the double locks I am through the door in seconds and inside the warehouse with no one the wiser.

The air is stale, the sound muffled, and my instincts provide a feeling of utter emptiness. The interior is faintly illuminated by docking lights that spray through windows high up on the three-story walls to shed muted glimmerings into the deep shadows of the interior. The light is weak, but it is sufficient to see by. I am standing in a hallway that runs down the length of the building in a narrow corridor. A series of closed doors decorate its empty length. These doors likely open into interior rooms, and I must find the one that matters.

I begin walking, testing each door I pass, finding all of them locked tight, hearing nothing from within when I press my ear to them. By the time I reach the front of the building, I am discouraged and frustrated, but still I peer cautiously around the corner to discover what lies beyond. To my surprise, I find a pair of Goblins positioned to either side of the huge doorways leading to the exterior, their backs to the wall.

So this warehouse is where Brecklin is being held, I quickly decide. What other reason could there be for the presence of guards? But now I have to come up with a plan, not only to determine in which room the Blade is imprisoned but also how to subdue the Goblins. A frontal attack is tempting but would be insanely risky. Anything that gives them more than a brief look at me before I am on them is foolhardy. Yet do I have another choice? I am not like the other members of my family, blessed with formidable *inish*. I am capable enough in my own way, but all the skills and tricks of magic that have been gifted to my brother and older sisters have been denied to me.

Auris is the most accomplished in the use of magic; that is why I admire her so much. She came to us a stranger, unaware of the kinship we shared, for all of that had been withheld by Ancrow, secreted away in so many layers of deception that it took months for her to uncover the truth. But she was Ancrow's only natural child and the most skilled of all of us in the uses of magic. Her *inish* was— and continues to be—something of a legend. Half Fae and half Human, she can do things that no one else is capable of, now that our mother is gone. It was not a choice she made, but a condition that her breeding imposed on her.

Harrow and Ronden are skilled in the use of magic as well, but not to the same extent as Auris. After our mother was gone and Auris had returned from her confrontation with the treacherous Barghast, we had all found ourselves wondering just what determined the extent of the *inish* allotted to each of us.

We have yet to find an answer.

Still, Auris—Ancrow's only natural child, born of a flagrant violation of our mother by an immensely cruel Human in the name of science—is the most powerful of us, the one for whom the *inish* runs strongest and the magic deepest. But why, when she carries only half the Fae blood as the rest of us? Still, something in her makeup—be it the mix of species or the depth of life drawn from her mother—makes her seem almost invincible.

Ronden and Harrow are full Fae, Sylvan-born and -raised, and have lived their lives as Ancrow's children. She made them hers from the first—conducted their training and taught them how to master their magic. Both were wedded early to her ways, and both have followed in her footsteps to become Sylvan Watchers. For them, the training was hard and constant, and their magic runs deep.

Ramey, of course, has no combat skills or *inish* magic, either. But she doesn't count, for she has no interest in possessing either. Ramey's skills are of the mind, and her talents lie in her ability to reason things through. I think she prefers it that way. She is the most stable, the most centered, of us, and for her, magic is a tool she does not care to acquire. She likes her life simple and straightforward, and now, given her growing relationship with Atholis, settled into hearth and home, mostly ignoring what *inish* she can access.

I don't even have that much to rely on—or at least not to the degree that my brother and sisters do. I have sought the use of my *inish* with a determination that is frightening, and yet so little of it has ever surfaced. I, too, am adopted, though my history is unknown and my abilities—if I have any that are magic-related—remain concealed from me.

Admittedly, the same had happened to Auris for a time, which for years gave me hope, but eventually I had to come to terms with the fact that I would have no sudden flowering of magic, as she had. And my failings in that area are in large part responsible for my leaving home. My inabilities haunted me, making me always feel less than my siblings. I am not like my brother and sisters, and I know now that I never will be.

For just a second, the old bitterness surfaces. As the youngest I have always been the least capable, the most vulnerable, the highest risk to myself because I am perpetually taking risks I shouldn't. Or, at least, that was how my family saw me, and that was what spurred my flight from Viridian Deep in the first place. Well, along with that nebulous sense that there was something out there I still needed to find, something that remained hidden from me.

Still, even without *inish*, I have my own way of dealing with challenges.

I look ahead, through shadows and crates, to where the pair of Goblin guards stand watch, and craft my plan. Then I tighten my resolve and carefully remove from my pockets a steel ball and two razor-sharp daggers, the latter each no more than four inches long. I place the ball in my right hand and the daggers in my left. Standing just at the corner of the conjoined passageways, I heft the steel ball in my open palm and think through my plan one final time.

Then I dart around the corner and heave the ball over the guards and down the corridor, to where it strikes against the floor and clatters on down into the shadows.

The Goblins act immediately. Burly heads turn to source the noise—and even as they do so, I am out of hiding and racing to reach them. Heads turned away, their attention still fixed on the steel ball, the Goblins do not turn. I run quickly and silently, my flexible boots allowing me to avoid detection. Then I am on top of them, daggers in hand, one right and one left, before they fully realize I am there. I jam the first dagger into the thigh of one guard and, skidding to my knees, plant the other dagger into his companion.

Both grunt in annoyance and surprise, barely aware even now of what I have done to them. But the powerful sedatives that coat the blades quickly run their course, and both Goblins are rendered senseless.

Together they collapse, motionless, on the concrete floor while I sprawl nearby, smiling.

Old Windy—teller of tales, seeress, and drug maven—taught me this trick. The Seers of my old life would have liked her. Together they could have created an incredible amount of mischief.

I search the pockets of the unconscious guards on the off chance they might contain something useful, like keys. But they do not. I stand up and look about in disgust.

Where is Brecklin?

I start searching the corridors once more. The Goblins I drugged will be asleep for at least an hour, so they will cause no trouble. I have time enough. I just have to figure out where I need to be to save my intended. My love. My future.

With more time on my hands now, I pick open one lock after another, but my hopes steadily dwindle as my options are reduced. If he isn't here, I don't know where to go next. Those who control Faraway Trades might have taken him anywhere. This was where they brought him yesterday, but they could have moved him by now. However, the Humans who operate this business are not particularly clever or inventive, so I cannot think why they would change their habits now.

Then it occurs to me that perhaps I am missing something. I know what goes on in this warehouse complex, but I have never been inside before. Perhaps I am looking in the wrong places.

I look up toward the ceiling and see the dock lights revealing the roofing timbers. Nothing there. So how about looking down? I had not imagined there would be chambers below the waterline, but perhaps those who control the company are cleverer than I had thought.

I circle the corridors once more, knowing that time is fast running out. Eventually, I find what I am looking for, but it is not what I thought it would be. It isn't a trapdoor, hidden in the flooring, that opens onto stairs. Instead it is an elevator. I only find the door that opens onto it because I hear it begin to operate as I pass by.

I am a Forest Sylvan, so I know little about machinery and cannot be certain what it is I am looking at. But I station myself to one side of the sealed doorway to discover what is happening. After all, I have no other choices left to me at this point.

The door slides open, and a single man appears. Not a Goblin, but a Human. I don't recognize him, but he is obviously someone of importance. He is too well dressed for the docks and exudes an obvious air of confidence. I am behind him with my knife blade pressed against his throat before he knows I am there, locking his arm behind him to keep him still.

"Where is the Blade?"

He doesn't respond. I press the knife a bit tighter against his skin. "I didn't hear you."

"I don't know!"

I cut him, sliding the blade of the knife just enough into his neck that the skin breaks and blood seeps from the cut. "Where is he?"

"Down below! But you can't help him."

"Let's find out. Back into the elevator. No tricks."

We board the device, my knife still at his throat, his arm locked in place behind his back.

"This won't help," he says.

He gasps as I cut him a little deeper, and now the blood is running freely down his neck. "Don't talk. Just do what I say."

He presses a button on a panel, and the elevator starts down. I note the numbers as we descend. We go ten floors below the harbor before the elevator stops.

When the door opens, it reveals a room filled with what appear to be medical equipment and supplies. There are strange implements and machines all over—tables and cots, racks with equipment of all sorts, and screens that blink and scroll to serve some mysterious purpose. I don't waste time on any of it. I am here for something else entirely.

I find my intended chained to a wall at the back of the room. He has been beaten but seems to still be conscious. A pair of Humans sit at a small table, paying no attention to him. Instead they appear to be eating. One of them glances up and sees me, and stands up instantly.

"Inspector Alcoin!" he gasps, and I tighten my grip and nudge my prisoner anew with my knife.

"Tell them to sit down."

My prisoner does so, and together we edge across the room. The Blade has lifted his head far enough that he can see me, and I note the surprise and shock in his eyes. He did not expect me to come for him. Foolish man. As if I would do anything less! I keep my concentration on my prisoner, edging steadily closer to the pair at the table, both of whom are seated anew.

One of them reaches for a communication device. "Don't!" I snap angrily, and he puts the device down again.

"Inspector . . ." One of them starts to address my prisoner once more, but I hiss at him in warning, and he quiets down at once. Both men can see my knife and the blood leaking from the wound in my prisoner's neck, so they know how things stand.

As we draw closer, I lean in toward my captive's ear. "Don't even breathe," I warn him. "Just tell them to release the Blade right now."

He does so, and the men rise, unchain Brecklin, and let him slump to the floor. He remains there for a few moments in something of a daze, then straightens and rises and comes to me. His eyes find mine and he smiles. "Hello . . . Little Scrapper."

I almost cry at the sound of his voice, but there is no time for it. We need to get out of here, and the quicker the better.

But it is already too late.

Behind me, faintly audible in the near silence, the machines that operate the elevator begin to whine. Someone else is coming down.

THREE

I AM SUDDENLY LOST IN A MORASS OF DOUBT AND FEAR, BUT THE Silver Blade is there to help.

"Elevator," he gasps, staggering toward the doors as if reaching them quickly is the only solution.

I follow a bit more slowly because I am still dragging my Human prisoner along as a shield. With the knife still pressed against his throat, he responds as I wish him to and does not struggle to get free. The other two men stare at us in confusion, uncertain about whether or not to act.

"Stay back!" I shout at them, and that seems to do the job. Neither moves to follow.

Brecklin, stumbling and lurching, nevertheless manages to reach his goal and paste himself to the wall on one side of the elevator, waiting for me. I notice that he is wielding an iron bar that he has managed to pick up somewhere along the way.

As weak and worn as he looks, he still has some fight in him, and he has no intention of being taken again. I am heartened anew by his spirit and determination. We will get out of this mess, I am certain. I reach him as quickly as I can and take up position on the other side of the elevator doors, already knowing what he wants me to do. I give him a nod and a smile of encouragement, and he nods back.

When the doors open, another pair of men enter the room, already engaged in whatever it is that brought them here in the first place. I let them advance two steps past the doors, then shove my prisoner at them with as much force as I can muster. The man goes stumbling into them, sending all three tumbling to the floor. Then Brecklin and I are through the doors and into the elevator, the Blade stabbing his fingers at the buttons to take us up, me standing at the rapidly closing entrance to keep everyone else out.

I succeed. The doors close and the elevator begins to ascend. I do not fool myself about what we have achieved. The men we have left behind still have the use of communication devices and will be calling for help. The most we have is a few minutes of grace before others are on top of us. We have to act quickly if we want to remain free.

For a moment I stand there just staring at Brecklin, and then I throw myself at him and clasp him in my arms, hugging him to me as if I will never let him go. If I could make that happen, I would. But even the few moments we have instill me with fresh resolve.

"Whoa, Scrapper . . . whoa," he gasps, as if I have hurt him. Perhaps I have. I have no real idea how badly wounded he is from his beating. I loosen my death grip on him and back away.

"I'm just so glad to see you. I was afraid that . . ."

I can't finish, breaking into tears, and I am immediately ashamed of myself. I look weak and helpless, and I sound like a fool.

But Brecklin grins in response. "I'm very glad . . . to see you, too. I can't believe you've come . . . but I guess I should not be surprised . . . You're . . . built that way. You never give up."

I wish he would embrace me, kiss me. I had been hoping this bold rescue would make him realize how much he wants and needs me. But he seems distracted.

"How badly hurt are you?" I ask. "Is anything broken?"

"Not that . . . I can tell. I just got knocked . . . around a bit. I can . . . make it . . . now that you're here."

I smile back, all out of things to say, still struggling with relief and happiness at finding him alive and well enough to aid in our escape.

"We have to hurry once we reach the ground floor," I warn. "They will have called for help. We'll have to find someplace safe."

"I know," he says, that familiar smile breaking my heart all over again. "We will."

I am less certain of our chances than he appears to be, but I take heart from the strength that resonates from him. Speed and good guesswork will serve us well, but what we need most is good luck, and I have always had plenty of that.

We reach the ground floor, and the doors open. No enemies in sight. We exit and move for the doors leading out of the building, but at the last minute I pull him back and turn him down the corridor leading to the side entry. Better that we choose the more obscure, less obvious route. Stay in the shadows; stay out of the light. Get down the docks far enough that we won't be seen out in the open and can find a place to hide. I am already thinking ahead to places I know where shelter and concealment can be found. I wish I could reach the other members of our little band, but it's hard to tell what happened to them once they learned that their leader had been taken.

Harder still, at this point, to track them down.

With Brecklin in tow, I reach the side exit through which I gained entry earlier. No one has appeared to stop us. No one has appeared for any reason whatsoever. I am beginning to think we are going to escape this place easily, and the thought makes me nervous. Nothing is ever this easy. I pause at the door and peer outside. No one in sight. We slip through the doorway onto the side dock, and make our way toward the next building. The dawn I have been fearing all night is coming, the sky starting to lighten as the moon sets. I step carefully and turn back to help Brecklin when he loses his footing in a stumble.

Still, there is no sign of the reinforcements that we both anticipated were coming.

We are two buildings away when things abruptly change. We have rounded a corner onto the main boardwalk when an entire batch of men appear behind us. Shouts rise up and the men charge toward us, even as we sprint for safety. My own movements are sufficient to gain me my freedom, but Brecklin is considerably slowed by his injuries and struggling to keep up. We gain a measure of space when a huge loader rumbles across our path, and we manage to dodge around it before it blocks the pursuers behind us.

I spy one of my favorite hiding places just ahead—a loading hatch in a tavern that leads into a basement and can be secured from within. But instead of taking advantage of it myself, I grab Brecklin and practically drag him over to it.

"In here!" I order him, heaving open the lid. "I'll come back for you!"

He doesn't argue with me. He knows better. He knows, too, that he is holding me up—that my chances of escaping will be stronger if I can go on alone. He slides inside, and I close the lid and listen for the lock to engage. Then I am off again, rushing for safety.

I make it another two buildings down, away from the Faraway Trades warehouses and my pursuers, when I am abruptly tackled by someone who was hiding in the shadows to one side.

I am pinned to the planks, unable to move as shouts go up. "Hey, hey, over here. She's over here! Come on, mates, she's down and out!"

I recognize the voice. Delph Ruan, my nemesis, come back to haunt me anew.

I thrash to break free, but he has me trapped in a position where I can gain no traction. In a matter of what feels like seconds, my Faraway Trades pursuers are all around me, pulling me to my feet and binding my hands behind my back.

"See there, that's her, ain't it?" Delph is back on his feet and waving his arms triumphantly. "Thinks she's so smart, but ain't no one smarter than the Delph. What's she done, anyway? I knew it was something bad, the way she was running. She steal something? Is there some kind of reward for catching her?"

One of the men in the party—the one I assume to be the leader—nods to a couple of men with heavy iron rods. They close on Delph Ruan instantly and, without hesitation, beat him to death with their weapons. It happens so fast I can scarcely believe what I am seeing. They use those pipes as if they have done so many times before, and the man barely has time to gasp once or twice before he is gone, nothing more than another discarded corpse on the docks. Another man in the party walks over, grabs Delph's legs, drags him to the side of the pier, and pushes him over.

I did not like Delph and will not miss him an ounce, but no one deserves a death like this. I glare at the leader, who ignores me as he says, "You see what happens to those who cause us trouble?"

"Is that your plan for me?" I spit back at him.

The man's head turns my way, and he regards me coldly and dispassionately. "I don't think so. But the decision isn't mine."

His gaze shifts to the others. "Bring her."

To me, he says, "Behave, and we won't have to gag you. Otherwise, we will."

And so I am dragged away, back toward the Faraway Trades warehouse, where I am to be dealt with in whatever dark way my captors wish.

But at least I have saved my intended.

I AM RETURNED TO WAREHOUSE #3 AND LOCKED INTO AN EMPTY upstairs room by myself. I am not bound or chained or otherwise incapacitated, but instead left alone to ponder whatever fate awaits me as a result of my efforts to free Brecklin. It is a pitiful end to my heroics, and likely a sad capstone to my almost eighteen-year-old life. Whoever is behind this—likely members of the leadership of Faraway Trades—will look to make an example of me, I am sure.

I am given plenty of time to consider what they intend, as I am left alone for long hours with no visitors, no food or water, no bathroom, and no explanations. I should have been turned over to the constabulary of the city of Pressia, but instead I am wrongfully detained by those deep in the slave trade. I can expect no mercy. I can anticipate no reasonable end to my detention.

I consider ways to escape. It is in my blood to do so, and I have never been content to just wait and see. I am the finder of my own fate. However, I have no weapons; all were stripped from me save a tiny dagger sewn into my belt on the backside of my waist. I don't even have my precious throwing stars, those razor-sharp missiles with which I am so skilled. I have my paltry *inish*, but it is nothing like that wielded by my sisters or Harrow.

So, with no weapons save a miniature dagger, and no physical attributes that I can rely on to free me from my present situation, I will have to depend solely on my instincts and foresight and quick thinking—all of which I have discovered and mastered over the years. For all that I lack of Auris's *inish*, my instincts are every bit on par with hers, and I have repeatedly relied on those instincts to save me. They were there when the Goblins came for Auris and I sensed their presence and rushed to her aid, and when Malik first appeared and took me prisoner. They were there when I saved Florin from the sea, when she fell while we were climbing a forbidden cliff and was knocked unconscious.

But how can they help me here when I am sealed up, locked away and helpless?

My captors come for me after night has fallen once more. I have slept some, and I feel myself equal to whatever is coming. I feel strong and confident. I feel determined. Brecklin is free, and I do not care what happens to me so long as he is safe; I love him that much. Admittedly, he does not know this and probably does not love me in the same way, but I know this can change.

I am marched out of the room, down various hallways, and out onto the docks. Night has settled in fully, and the day's activities have mostly died away. I am brought to and left standing on a dock that is tucked away between two Faraway Trades warehouses, and screened further by cargo boxes that hide me away from the main boardwalk. A strange iron rack, flat and affixed with locks and chains, sits nearby. Four men hold me, and the man I took prisoner earlier in my efforts to find and free Brecklin stands before me. The day is calm and surprisingly warm, and the air smells of fish and the ocean.

The man—Inspector Alcoin, if I remember correctly—steps forward and looks at me. "You have one chance. Tell me where the Silver Blade is hiding and I will let you go. Otherwise, you are of no further use to me."

I don't know where Brecklin is by now, but I wouldn't tell in any case. I shake my head.

Alcoin nods, smiles. "Bind her."

I know at once what is coming. I begin to take deep breaths.

The men holding me force me down upon the rack and lock me in place, faceup. The rack is lifted to an upright position, and I hang from its bonds helplessly. Alcoin makes a gesture, and the device and I are dragged to the dock's edge. I am praying to the Fates of the Fae, but I am doing so silently. I will not break down.

"The water beneath these docks is a hundred feet deep, and the currents are strong. If the chains give way, you will be swept out to sea. I will give you a taste of your fate and then haul you back up again. It might be wise if you answer my questions at that point. If you don't, then down you go again. You will be lowered and raised over and over until you tell me what I want or until you drown. So be smart. Talk to me right now."

Stubbornly, I shake my head once more.

Alcoin shrugs. He nods to the men holding me.

Then the rack—with my body firmly attached—is shoved off the pier and into the water.

FOUR

I AM SINKING.

Instantly.

Me and the iron rack to which I am bound.

I have sufficient presence of mind to take a last, deep breath before I am in the water. The shock of the ocean's bitter cold is almost enough to make me gasp, but I manage not to. That I am actually in the water, secured to this huge weight and rendered helpless, is terrifying.

I am sinking still.

Sinking faster.

Sinking helplessly.

I hold on to my courage with an iron will and begin trying to free myself from my bonds, but I can tell in seconds that my efforts are hopeless. I cannot begin to loosen the chains that hold me in place. Still, I keep trying, because getting free is the only way I will manage to stay alive. If I breathe in even once, it is over. I am surprised that my Faraway Trades captors have chosen torture over death, but I suppose recapturing Brecklin is their first priority, and I am the only one who knows where he is—or was. So here I am.

Abruptly, I am hauled back to the surface, left hanging on the iron rack gasping much-needed breaths as Alcoin calls out to me. "How's the water, Fae girl? Deep enough for you? Feel like telling me how to find the pirate now?"

I shake my head once more, and back down I go.

I open my eyes for the first time in the murky waters and watch the surface darken slowly as the rack drags me down, the light disappearing and the world falling away. I am a good swimmer and can hold my breath for almost two minutes, but I am not immune to drowning once that time is gone. Is it possible Brecklin will come for me? Is it at all likely he has been watching and has seen what is being done to me and will throw all caution to the winds and hurtle himself into the Helles after me?

In a fairy tale? Sure. Here and now, in the real world? Not so much. I am as likely to be saved by a passing whale buoying me on its back to the surface.

I am hauled to the surface once more, but they have left me down there longer this time. I choke out water and gasp for air, in much worse condition by now. Again and again, they demand answers. Again and again, I refuse.

Again and again, I am lowered back into the waters, and each time allowed to sink much deeper. And each time come up in worse condition, gasping and choking.

I sense they are at the limits of their patience, and the next time I go down, I feel it will be my last. Each time the rack goes under the water, I have been searching for a weakness in my bonds, but I cannot find one. Now I am so weak I cannot even bring my fingers to bear, cannot use them to loosen the chains. I am pinned fast to this piece of iron, and this time I sense we are both going down to the bottom of the bay, and that will be the end for me.

I cast about for something—anything—that might help me. But the water is so dark and empty there is nothing to be found. If only there were something I could latch onto: a bit of old ship hull or mainmast, a smokestack or a winch. Anything that would slow my descent. Why aren't there rock formations or varying levels of sea-floor? Why is it so empty down here, so desolate? It is growing harder to hold my breath, harder to resist the urge to draw in the much-needed oxygen that would save me. It is getting difficult to concentrate, my mind wandering and my awareness growing darker. I catch sight of something moving below me, swimming circles as I descend. Sharks, I think. But I wonder nevertheless if they might be something else. I have no idea how much time has passed, but I am aware of how quickly the last of my breath is diminishing.

I am young and strong, but it isn't enough.

I . . .

Am . . .

Sinking . . .

Faster . . .

The iron rack settles on the ocean floor, the force of its landing abrupt and jarring. But at least I am resting on top of it and not pinned beneath. Still, no hope is in sight. I am secured to the immovable rack and lack any reasonable way to get free.

The air in my lungs grows thin and stale, and my hopes turn as dark as the water that surrounds me. I take another quick look around for any signs of help and find nothing. I am done. No help is coming; no source of freedom is available. I think about Auris and Harrow and Ronden and Ramey. Will they find out what has happened to me? Will they mourn my passing? I have a few more seconds at best. I close my eyes and steady myself as best I can for what I know is coming.

I hold my breath until the pain of it is too much and then I open my mouth and let the water in. I feel it rush into my mouth and down my throat. I am trying hard not to give way to the darkness that is closing about me, but my strength is failing fast.

In those final moments, I feel my body doing something odd. It is almost as if it is . . . readjusting in some way, changing from what it was to . . . something new. I cannot track its source or determine its effect. I can only tell that it is happening. My instincts—always better than those of almost anyone else—tell me to just relax. Stay calm. Believe in myself. But there is no reason for me to do any of this. After all, I am drowning. Still, the feeling persists. And so, as my breath runs out and my consciousness closes down, I give myself over to doing what my always wise and knowing instincts tell me to do. I settle into a state of peacefulness that nothing happening to me warrants.

I experience a final moment or two of awareness, and then abruptly everything goes black.

I disappear into a mix of memories and dreams.

I AM NO LONGER WITHIN MY BODY.

I drift, untethered. I have moved beyond my corporeal parts and gone far beyond, into unexplored territory.

Within that realm of uncertainty, I am in no pain and I am possessed by a calmness different from anything I have ever known. The water has hold of me, both inside and outside. It is all around me and all through me. It is a pervasive presence that shouldn't feel the way it does because it is foreign to my being. I am not a creature of water and waves; I am a creature of air and earth. I am a Sylvan Fae, and water is not our habitat.

And yet . . .

Somehow . . .

Memories surface in my mind like little tadpoles seeking a home, and I am taken back to where I once was and wish I were again. Back home . . .

I HAVE ALWAYS BEEN, AS HUMANS SOMETIMES CALL THEIR MORE unpredictable offspring, a wild child. With my tangle of greenish, leafy hair curling hither and yon, my unusually dark-green skin, and my profound, almost ethereal connection with nature and her creatures, I am clearly a Fae girl right from the beginning.

Yet nothing defines me quite so well as that appellation: Wild Child.

I am that, through and through. I am prone to reckless behavior, likely to react more quickly than I am to think. Since my earliest years, I am quick to go to the aid of others—my siblings especially—when I feel them threatened. And so I end up diving into dangerous circumstances a more reasonable person would hesitate to confront and perhaps even turn away from, giving me a reputation for being both hopelessly naïve and impossibly brash. Whether it be an eight-foot metal juggernaut, or a dragon of forty tons, or an encampment of a hundred Goblins confronting me, I do what my instincts tell me I must do and push aside my doubts. Several times I have rushed to the aid of my beloved half sister, Auris. I fought for my brother Harrow when he was incapacitated by a creature so terrible that I can barely speak of it, even now. I risk myself for my sisters Ronden and Ramey constantly. My behavior was tolerated when I was young and callow, but it is disparaged and criticized the older I get.

And yet I cannot help it. Who are we in this world and this life if we are not true to ourselves? My actions are unpredictable and seemingly without thought, but I am always reacting to situations where my course of action seems clear to me and the threats I face seem not to matter. If you love someone, you do what your love dictates is necessary to save them. You do not stop to think through the risks you take. You do not pause to consider if there might be a better way. I do not understand or accept the idea of consideration as an alternative to action. We do not achieve through standing about and considering. When those we love are threatened, we need to respond rather than debate.

I have never apologized for responding instinctively to what I view as a threat. I have never reconsidered coming to the aid of others when they are in need. When I was younger, I was considered impetuous and foolish, but charming for my courage. But as I grew, this behavior began to grate on my siblings. Even Ramey, whom I loved so much. Even Auris, who loved me more than anyone. They fussed and worried and tried hard to contain me—to persuade me to think more carefully about my actions and abandon my predilection for throwing myself into situations in a way they found entirely too impulsive.

But when old Soffie fell into the river during a windstorm, I gave no thought to the wildness of the rain or the surging waters. I only knew that I must go into the river after her or she would drown. Did I call for help? No. Did I search for aid? No. There was no time. There was no other reasonable choice save to go after her.

When Squinch climbed a tree so rotted that its limbs were prone to breaking off under even the slightest of weights, I climbed up to where she was crying and brought her down. How could I not?

When Auris and Harrow were attacked by Goblins not once but several times right in their own home, I did not think about calling for help from others. This was my new sister and my older brother, and I loved them, so doing anything other than rushing to their aid had never occurred to me.

The stories go on, and all of them are much the same—all of them involving risk to me that I mostly ignored. I was not unaware, but I was not deterred, either. I was compelled to act on the spur of the moment, and I did not hesitate.

Still, all was well until I reached my thirteenth year and Auris decided she would become my new mother. My real mother—at least, the mother who had adopted me from the Protective Leaf Orphanage—was gone, and Auris, five years into her partnership with Harrow and three years after the birth of her son, decided I needed a stronger hand. She seemed to think it was her obligation to put me on a more appropriate path. This was annoying in the extreme at first, but it soon became intolerable. So I did what my conscience said I must and rebelled. I pointed out that our relationship did not allow her to instruct me in how I should behave. By then, even Ramey was telling me not to be so difficult—although, by then, Ramey was also in love with Atholis and no longer the quiet, wise sister with whom I had been so close. Instead, she was infused with an independent streak that was gradually separating us in palpable ways.

I do understand the reasons that all of my once close siblings chose to become instructors and advisers instead. I know they cared about me and were trying to do their best to help me learn better and wiser ways to act. But their constant interference was intolerable. I never sought their counsel, and they did not have the right to use their advanced age and their supposedly greater wisdom to dominate me. Just because I was the youngest does not mean I needed correction and criticism at every turn.

And then there was my growing sense of something missing from my life—something I would never find at home.

The result of all these changes was that I began to drift away from my family in very noticeable ways. Before long, I was traveling more and more frequently to the country of the Water Sprites, to visit with my true other self, Zedlin's younger sister, Florin. Florin was a revelation to me. A Water Sprite two years older than me, she was even more brash and impulsive. She and her brother were true orphans, without even an adoptive parent between them, and she stood up to her brother at every turn, openly declaring that she was grown up enough to make decisions for herself. She violated rules without heed of the consequences or punishments. She was adept at manipulating and cajoling any authority figure who confronted her. I studied how she managed to avoid being tamed or subdued, and it was illuminating. It was clear from the first day we met that she was in control of her life far more than I have ever been.

It was inevitable that we should become friends, and the recklessness of each of us fed off the other.

All of which eventually led to my decision to ask her to help me when I decided to leave home a month before my fifteenth birthday.

I STIR, SLEEPY AND DAZED, NOW BACK WITHIN MY SKIN. I REGAIN MY senses slowly, but even so things seem markedly wrong. My eyesight is somehow altered. I can see clearly—more so than ever before—and the scope of my vision has broadened noticeably. My body doesn't feel right, either. It feels longer and more supple—but also rather disproportionate. It is not uncomfortable or bothersome exactly. Just . . . different.

And my breathing!

Fates of the Fae, what's going on with my *breathing*? I am entirely surrounded by water, totally immersed in it. Not just outside my skin, but inside, as well—as though I am consumed by it. And I am breathing—but not in any way I recognize. I reach for my face to see what is happening, but I am still chained to the iron rack I was fastened to before being dumped in the bay.

I react to this forced imprisonment as anyone would. I stretch and strain and struggle to break free of it. As I heave about, I realize that something is different. My body is longer and more powerful. Already, I can feel the chains that bind me beginning to break apart. I thrash even harder, straining to break my bonds, determined to get free. Within seconds, the links start to give way. My legs have somehow become joined together from their bonding, but my thrashing is so powerful that they snap free of their shackles. As one hand wrenches free, I use it to reach up and break the other free as well.

My eyes are drawn to the iron rack, which is suddenly being drawn back toward the surface of the ocean waters. I stare at it, wondering what my captors will think when I fail to resurface with it. Likely, they will think the ocean currents broke me free and carried me away. They will give me no further thought.

My throat moves instinctively to swallow the water I feel clogging it, and I realize something else odd is happening. I am breathing, but my nose and throat are filled with water, and what I feel going in and out of me is all liquid. And it doesn't go through my nose and mouth as my breath once did. No. Now it feels as if it is passing through my neck!

But how can that be?

I reach down instinctively and feel the serrations on either side of my throat—vertical lines that open and close.

I am completely confused and more than a little frightened by this. I suddenly wonder why I am even still alive. I was drowning only minutes earlier and yet here I am . . .

Here I am, what? Alive, yes—or have I evolved or transformed into something else?

To add to my growing distress, I realize there are shadows moving all around me. Large shadows. Elongated shadows. Right away,

I think of sharks, or other water predators, come to feed on my body. I thrash some more, terrified by what might be happening. I stare through the water as the shadows circle around me and wish that the light was better so I could tell what they were. But I am deep under the surface of the ocean, and here everything is shadowy and obscured. It must still be night, high overhead.

I experience a very distinct rush of panic, along with a deep sense of confusion and suspicion. I thrash in response, and the shadows flit away, frightened or at least made nervous by my movements. I tire quickly, though, so close my eyes and try to think things through. Somehow, I am still alive in spite of almost certainly having drowned. And somehow, I am changed, too. I feel it. I sense it. I am not who or what I was, and I am not at all sure what I have become.

Suddenly, I miss Brecklin terribly—his presence, his reassurance, his support. His ridiculous confidence. His guidance was something I could usually rely on, but now he is gone—along with my family and my former life. I am trapped beneath the ocean, alive but struggling to discover what has been done to me. Because holding my breath has long since ceased to be a concern, I try to voice my feelings, but it is hard to form words underwater.

The creatures swimming around me move closer. When they are near enough that the murk and shadows do not entirely mask their appearance, I get a good, close look at them, and my surprise approaches astonishment. They are not sharks or fish of any kind. They are something out of legend, something born of fairy tales and myth.

They are Mermaids.

Or at least, this is how they appear to me. They have human bodies above their waists and supple fish tails below, and my first reaction on seeing them is to decide I am hallucinating—or at least mistaking what I am seeing. There are no Mermaids. Water Sprites are the closest living thing we have to such creatures, and—save for their gills—they are almost entirely human.

So . . . Mermaids?

I study them just as thoroughly as they are studying me. We are different species studying each other for what is perhaps the first time for them, and certainly the first time for me. I am not at all sure about them; I do not have any experience I can draw on that would inform me of the proper way to react. So perhaps how I feel now is something akin to how I felt when first encountering Malik, back when he was mostly a machine. But really! Mermaids? How do I even begin to accept that they might be something more than a myth?

I try to speak the word. "Mermaids?"

Again, vocal speech is mangled and I cannot make myself understood.

A pause follows. Then one of these creatures says something into my mind: *Merrow.*

I don't know what that is. Another word for Mermaids? I shake my head. The shadows disperse and then reassemble, hovering all about me. My eyesight has changed enough that I can make out their expressions and the specifics of their features. But having a conversation with a people that are half human and half fish is not easy. I keep wanting them to change into something else, or to reveal that they are somehow in disguise. But the ease with which they maneuver their bodies, and the relaxed way in which they shift and turn, suggests how they look is exactly what they are. There is no disguise, no dissembling, nothing but what I am seeing.

They regard me for a time, then one of them swims closer. A woman. She regards me carefully, shifts her gaze, and then—of all things—smiles. After a moment, she touches my arms, stroking them gently.

I should be reassured by the welcoming gesture. I think I might have been if not for the fact that the next thing I notice, when I reach out to touch my new friend back, is that, like the creatures who swim about me, I have a fish tail, too. More to the point, *I have no legs.*

My clothing below my waist has disappeared, and what remains is a long, supple, and attractive fish tail that I can twist about and position as easily as if it had always been a part of me. My tail is colored—appropriately enough—in veridian tones, matching my still-green skin and hair, and has attractive, almost leafy, patterns woven all through it. Even more astonishing is the fact that my body now appears to be somewhere around nine or ten feet long! Yet even in the midst of my shock and near panic, I remind myself that, whatever I am and however I look, at least I am still alive.

I attempt a few motions intended to convey my gratitude, and then this bevy of fish people are closing about me as if we were old friends, hands fastening on me as they guide me away to an unknown destination.

FIVE

TIME PASSES. WEEKS, MAYBE MONTHS. I CAN'T BE SURE. THERE IS no measure of time under the water, save for charting the passage of days into nights and back again.

I am no longer who I was. Not physically and not mentally. I have left that life and entered another. I have become someone else. I still have my memories of my family and my past, but my current life as a Merrow feels worlds and eons away.

I am not at all comfortable with my strange transformation in the beginning, but with time I adapt. I have always been curious, and I know so little of this world. I know so little of who and what I now know I am. But I am anxious to learn and smart enough to remember once I do.

The people who have adopted me—who saved me and brought me to their home—refer to themselves as Merfolk, and more specifically as Merrow. They tell me it is an ancient term that they have carried with them through countless generations. I am under the impression that the Merrow consider themselves a distinct species, which suggests there are other forms of Merfolk in other regions of our world of which I know nothing. And likely never will, for these creatures are territorial in the extreme and will not cross into one another's regions. Nor is there any interbreeding—for the most part. Because in the time-honored tradition of exceptions to the rules . . . there is clearly me. And what am I if not a half-breed of some sort?

Because I do look different from them, with my green Sylvan coloring, which I can tell intrigues them. Most of them—skin, hair, and tails—mimic the colors of a coral reef: pale pinks and oranges, yellows and aquas. Their tails likewise sport flowing patterns, which mimic branching corals, or the whorls of shells.

Despite my once weak *inish*, I find myself instantly fluent in the mental Merrow language—which surprises me. But with my transformation, I also feel a new flowing of magic within me, so perhaps it is the change that has finally unlocked it. I learn quickly that my hostess—whose skin, hair, and tail are a pale, seafoam green—is Winnis, and her young daughter—a light-aqua streak of joy—is Douse. The senior female Merrow of her household, whose coloration must once have been like Winnis's but has now faded almost to white, is Lagos. Her partner is Pash.

Their community is fairly large; there are hundreds of Merrow here, of all ages, sizes, and abilities.

Their primary methods of survival are not what I expect. I am thinking they are farmers from the way they have embedded their community deep within the fertile, shallow reefs that front the shoreline some miles south of Pressia, but I quickly discover that I am wrong. These Fae are trappers and hunters, who employ food-seeded traps and springdoor cages to snare various feeders that serve as their main food source. In addition, they employ sand snares and plows to unearth various forms of sea life that dwell in large numbers beneath the reef surfaces and shallow seafloors.

I miss this entirely at first, but after noting the hunters at work foraging and ensnaring, I begin to understand how they survive.

They think me a fascinating creature, though I am never quite sure why. It could be because, as a people, they tend to stay away from air-breathers and surface folk in the way I might keep clear of snakes. They dislike both Humans and Fae, and refer to them as ground-dwellers.

At first, most of their care is devoted to making sure I am healthy and well. We are all, I think, a bit astonished to learn what I am. All these years I have thought myself a Forest Sylvan, but now it turns out I am a hybrid. It seems most likely that I had a Fae mother and a Merrow father, brought together in some mysterious way I may never discover. Though Lagos tells me that, under rare circumstances, a Merrow can be born with a longing for land, and the ability to shift shapes at will, from water-dweller to land-dweller and back. But the more the Merrow avoided land people, the more their isolation grew, the less this trait began appearing. The last one born to their group had been a girl named Carlindallin—but she had vanished onto the land over fifty years ago and had never returned. And no more had been born since.

Still, along with my outward Fae appearance, it seems I was born with a large chunk of inner Merrow, which only emerged when I was cast into the ocean and on the verge of drowning. When it was clear my Fae body was failing, what had been hiding inside me took over. My air-breathing abilities shut down. Gills erupted along both sides of my neck, my legs morphed into my powerful new fish tail, and I transformed into a Merrow. I cannot remember the particulars of any of this, because by then I was unconscious and thought I was dying. But really what I was doing was changing to adapt to my new circumstances.

My rescuers told me later that they watched it happen, uncertain at first if I was simply a drowning Human or something more. They suspected the latter when I did not die at once but seemed to fall into a deep sleep—after which I was transformed.

Understand, I am not at all convinced that this is a good thing. After all, even though the change has saved my life, what is to become of me? What do I know of living underwater, for Fae's sake? I am alive, yes. But at what price? I have become something that I have believed for my whole life to be nothing but a myth. And the transformation is so complete, I'm not even sure I can return to my Fae form again. What would my family say if they could see me now? What would Brecklin think? How can I ever function again in a world of air and earth after this?

Am I now a Merrow for the rest of my life, or is the change only temporary?

I don't know yet. To discover the truth, I will have to return to the surface and see what happens, but I am not yet ready for that. There is too much here to learn, to explore. I am endlessly fascinated by these people, who now see themselves as my community, my friends.

As well, I am still learning more about how this community survives in these waters, so close to Fae lands and yet still undiscovered. Winnis helps explain. To avoid detection, the Fae in her community collectively grow and distribute various forms of seaweed and entangling water foliage that clogs the propellers of boat motors attempting to pass through. The staging of these traps is assigned to the younger males and females—those out of childhood but not yet treated as adults, with adult responsibilities. And because of the vegetation, ships for the most part avoid these waters.

Still, that does not guarantee their safety, for there can be dangers from beneath the water as well. Winnis lost her partner—Douse's father—to a razorbill several years back, while he and some other members of their tribe were hunting. A venture into a place that should have been left alone, a momentary glance away from the dark, and a partner and father is lost.

It is a lesson I do not forget.

In the meantime, I am still evolving. Just two days ago, I became aware of webbing forming between the fingers of my hands. Moreover, there are indications of additional webbing forming beneath my arms, where they attach to my shoulders. Most distracting of all, my gills are now expanding to allow for greater and easier access to the waters that give me life.

My instincts tell me to let it happen as it will. I am in no danger from these changes. I am simply going through a period of adjustment.

All of which brings me back to that matter of why the Merrow have chosen to save me when they could have simply let me die—indeed, under normal circumstances, this is exactly what they would have done. They do not associate with land creatures of any kind, and if one of us happens to fall off our ship and drown . . . well, it isn't their responsibility to keep us safe. Or even in their best interests. If anything, they regard both Fae and Humans as dangerous. Too much of what we do causes damage to the Merrow homelands—which for them is defined as everything that lies beneath the surface of the water.

My new caregiver, Winnis, speaking to me in her soft Merrow voice, explained it to me early in our relationship.

Land people hunt, kill, and destroy. Entire parts of the ocean are ruined, and many fish are killed needlessly. They take away so much—which is why we hide. If the land people knew we existed, they would hunt us, too. So we choose to have nothing to do with them.

She paused as I nodded my understanding. After all, I saw the same thing on land that she did underwater.

What about me? I asked.

You are Merrow. She gestured at my body. *Tail, gills, eyes, ears.* (I forgot: My ears have started to become pointed.) *How you look and swim.*

One webbed hand lifted in warning. *Had you not changed to Merrow, we would have let you drown.*

That made my fate very clear to me, and I was grateful that I changed when I did.

I understand, I told her.

Then ten-year-old Douse was quick to add, in her high-pitched, child's voice: *But we love you as Merrow, always. Good Merrow girls are always welcome. You are good, aren't you?*

It made me smile, hearing her follow-up laughter before quickly darting away—as if she had managed to summon great courage by daring to speak to me. She doesn't talk much, and she is very young, but she reminds me of myself at her age. Even though we are not entirely the same, there is enough familiarity between us for me to think of her as I would a sister.

And after all, this is my new family for as long as I choose to stay, and my excitement at a new world to explore, coupled with my fears for what awaits me back in Jagged Reach, keeps me from pushing harder for a return to the surface.

Yes, I do worry over Brecklin's fate, but the Silver Blade is clever and resourceful and survived for years without me, so I sense he will be fine. I do find it ironic that—for almost the first time in my life— my vaunted instincts persuade me to take my time and not rush into anything. How my sisters would laugh! But my new family is eager to teach me what it means to be one of the Merrow, and there is still much to learn about who and what I have become.

Even so, my thoughts turn to the rest of my absent family, wondering what they would think of their little Char now. I think especially of Auris, who underwent her own transformation after she discovered Viridian Deep. What would she say if she could see me now? I do know that Auris and her son—as well as Harrow, Ronden, Ramey, and all my friends from Viridian Deep—must miss me, as I miss them. It has been almost three years now since I have seen my homeland and my family.

Sometimes—I am not making this up—I can sense one or more of my family or friends looking for me, likely with the aid of the Seers. I try reaching back to answer each time, but never succeed. Yet the Merrow have informed me that, should the Seers attempt to find me now, they will likely fail, because no one will be looking for who or what I am now. Which makes me feel more isolated than ever.

They will wait for you, Sharri, Douse assures me, always the positive voice in any conversation. *They will always wait.*

I smile and nod in agreement. But I wonder.

———

ONE DAY, SEVERAL MONTHS INTO MY STAY, WINNIS OFFERS TO TAKE me someplace new. Off the coast of Jagged Reach, but well away from the ports and the land people, are uninhabited islands and atolls where things swim that few have ever seen. Would I like to have a look? Would I ever! A place to which I have never been and seascapes I have never seen?

So, on a day filled with sunshine, soft waves, and gentle weather, she and I set out with Douse in tow. Douse is still young enough that she lacks the physical strength to make the journey without stopping, and I find myself grateful for that. Though I consider myself strong and resourceful, I do not have the Merrow familiarity with the ocean, and know I need the accommodation as much as Douse.

Still, we reach our destination with relatively few problems. Winnis takes us to the outer reaches of the islands, down through the deep waters of the Helles, until we feel safe enough to swim up to the shallow coral reefs and sandbars where all the promised fish and other sea life congregate.

There are sea turtles the size of flatbed wagons, hovering in the midst of waving seagrasses and strange floral plants colored and fringed. The turtles pay us almost no attention, their efforts concentrated on feeding and nesting. There are mothers sharing space with small ones who were once their young but now swim free; there are fathers so big I think that, should they be so inclined, they could swallow me whole.

There are huge groupers with throats that suggest landlocked mining shafts. Giant eels prowl the rock crevices of the shell clusters and rock formations that decorate the ocean floor. Rays of all shapes and sizes, their cloaklike forms decorated in all kinds of patterns and colors, swim in pods as they feed. Some of the fish are much smaller, but their colors are magnificently bright. Because Douse is wearing a brilliant-red halter top, many of the similarly colored fish are attracted to her. Some fish are tentacled and searching the rocks for snacks. Some have needles for noses and threaten us in the manner of swordsmen.

At one point, we encounter enormous tiger sharks, their giant mouths a mass of razor-sharp teeth and their eyes alert as they track potential prey with clear intent. Working their way toward schools of fish, they show little interest in the three of us. We are not their first choice for dinner, Winnis assures me. While Douse is the smallest of the three of us—she tracks at almost six feet from top of head to tip of tail fin—we are all of us as supple and quick as almost anything out there, including sharks. Unless they are in attack mode, we do not need to fear them. But I keep close watch nevertheless; sharks do not seem the sort of animal I should ever trust.

Then we dive deeper, to where the giant clams yawn their huge jaws in greeting, inviting us to come inside for a closer look. But Douse and I have been schooled at length in what to worry about, what to avoid, and what to beware of, so we do nothing to risk ourselves during our quest. We know to stay clear of the stingrays and the lionfish, the reef stonefish and the moray eels, and slow crawlers and Stokes Seasnakes that would paralyze us with a single nip or sting.

It is all amazing, but just when I think we have exhausted our adventure, Winnis tells us there are a few more things we need to see and something she would like to get. She leads us down farther into the ocean depths, and I think again about her earlier assurances that the depths that affect Fae and Humans will not affect us. Nature constructed the Merrow so that they can survive at all levels, and there is nothing for us to fear from the deep.

I am not convinced of this.

Nevertheless, I swim down.

We are several hours into our excursion when Winnis takes us to the deepest point in our adventures yet, leading us to a set of massive caverns that link one into the other and contain thousands of fish and other creatures that glimmer as if lit from within and radiate flashing light and glowing tentacles. Swarms of crustaceans crawl the floors of these caves, a living carpet that undulates across the sands and rocks in perfect rhythm, interwoven and interlinked. They fill vast spaces and move as one, all of them keeping the same pace as they navigate. There, too, are thousands of fleeting, pale threads of mobile worms that make their way from one place to another.

All of them are harmless, I have been assured. Only one significant predator roams these spaces, and there are only a handful of these, and they are seldom seen. The worst are called Bar Slinks, and they are huge and very mobile. They navigate these caves as elongated, sinuous serpents that sometimes actively hunt their prey and other times simply sink and wait for it to come to them. They hunt and eat almost everything. Douse has seen only one in her young life, but she is quick to describe it in a way that gives me chills. The one she saw was about twenty feet in length, but they can grow to twice that if well fed. Their appetite is enormous, and their ability to take down larger creatures is immense. They might not be able to seize and devour a massive whale, Douse explains, but can take down almost anything else and will not hesitate to do so.

I am pleased to hear from Winnis that we are not likely to encounter one, but I intend to keep a watchful eye out in any case. I know how the ocean works well enough by now to never misjudge what a predator might do.

Which is fortunate for all of us.

We are deep into the caverns, maybe an hour's journey in, when I see my first Slink. I am so surprised that I think for a moment I must be mistaken. The Slink is just lying there, so quiet and unobtrusive. But its shape is unusual enough that I spot it right away, even though it is perfectly still. It rests squarely on the cavern floor, close by where one of the moving crab carpets scuttles slowly over the rocks. I feel a sudden rush of excitement. To see something this rare all at once is astonishing. I am across the way, well on the other side of the cavern. Winnis has gone on ahead, as usual, and is high up against the ceiling, scavenging some sort of shellfish—probably the reason for our trip down here—so she hasn't seen anything.

But Douse is swimming right into the Bar Slink's view and doesn't realize it is there.

My instinctual warnings activate instantly. My *inish* screams at me from deep within: *Do something!*

I don't hesitate. Even though I am instantly terrified, my fear is all for Douse and not myself. In a rush of need and determination, I use my powerful fish tail to propel myself across that cavern so quickly I am all the way over to the other side in a flash of sheer power, pouncing on Douse, scooping her up like a toy, and hauling her away. I do not look back; I simply swim as hard as I can with the young girl in my arms until I have her safely clear.

It all happens so quickly. Yet when I look back, I can see the full length of the Bar Slink plastered against the wall from which I have just retrieved Douse, hanging fully visible now, jaws snapping as if still searching for the food I have denied it. It cannot seem to believe it doesn't have Douse's small body in its possession.

I am shaking as I huddle against the wall across from it, unable to believe what I just did. I did not realize I could act so quickly. I had no idea a Merrow could harness such power, such strength! I glance at Douse, who is petrified, give her a reassuring smile, and swim with her over to her mother as the Bar Slink sinks back to quiescence again.

Together, the three of us retreat through the caverns and out into the open waters once more before making our way back to the surface. All the way, I look for the Bar Slink to be sure it isn't following, though I suspect this one is too big to escape from its caverns. And all the way I bless my new physical form for being able to do what it did. I may not be Auris, but I now possess a power that she does not.

We all surface briefly, then swim on to gather in the small lagoon of an isolated island. Winnis hugs Douse as if she might never let go, then turns to hug me, as well.

Thank you, Sharri, thank you! So much. I saw it all. I was too far away! She pauses to lock eyes with mine. *But . . . you were too far away, too. You shouldn't have been able to do what you did.*

I feel a shock go through me at her words. If I have not just accessed a normal Merrow's speed, as I had assumed, but instead tapped into something else, then what was it? How could I, a Merrow newly formed, do what Merrow born to the sea could not?

I think again of Auris, how her half-Human blood seemed to make her a better, stronger Fae. Could the same thing be happening here, with my Fae heritage somehow enhancing my Merrow half?

Unaware of my spiral of thoughts, Winnis is continuing. *You were so quick! Thanks be to the tides and the ocean's swift swells.*

I am embarrassed, but proud, too. I have done something of use. I have proved my value. I have done something to pay back what was given to me when I was freed.

Though a part of me still wonders.

I don't know how I did it, I admit.

Winnis embraces me anew. *How doesn't matter. You did it. I will never forget. Never!*

Me, either! a familiar voice trills.

Douse is quickly in my arms, and we are all laughing and crying and holding one another close, and it makes me feel like I have truly found a new home.

SIX

T HINGS ARE QUIET FOR ABOUT A WEEK AFTER OUR RETURN FROM the islands, and life goes on much as it has for several months now. I make friends within my new community, and I play with an eager Douse at every opportunity. I am her new hero, and she cannot spend enough time with me.

Then, abruptly, I get sick.

Very sick.

It happens overnight. I go to sleep feeling fine and wake wishing I were dead. I hurt all over. I cannot move at all without pain. I hurt even when I just lie there. Winnis and Lagos are instantly concerned, and give me medicines that render me so exhausted I cannot stay awake. They use grasses and herbs from the ocean, plants and other sorts of growths I know nothing about, to help my body heal. I have a common ocean-bred sickness called Trichron, they advise me, and I will overcome it in time. They do not say how much time, but after three days of constant suffering I cannot imagine that it will end before I simply give up trying to fight it off.

Mostly what I do—other than attempting to make myself forget my discomfort—is dream.

The dreams come often and unbidden—as well as broken and fragmentary. And all of them are about my past and the ways in which I have squandered it. All highlight my failings and my fruitless attempts at making something useful of my life.

A few are about Brecklin, and the ways in which even my great love has fallen flat. But most are about my lost family—Auris, Harrow, Ronden, Ramey, and myself—demonstrating my failure to appreciate what I had, what I could have made of it, and how I let it all slip away.

I thrash and turn during these dreams, aware of both the physical pain my movement causes me and the emotional pain aroused by these revelations. It is all real; it has all happened. And I groan at what I have let slip away.

More and more—and much as I have grown fond of my Merrow hosts—I find myself wishing it were Auris who was tending me, or Ramey or Ronden or Harrow. Their absence is a pain inside me, a void that cannot be filled.

I am woken often by Winnis, and sometimes by Lagos and Pash, each time wishing I were somewhere and someone else.

I am told Trichron is normally a disease restricted to younger Merrow, and it is unusual for someone my age to experience it. Perhaps I have contracted it because I am a halfling and not a fullblooded Merrow. Or perhaps it is simply because I have never been exposed to the pathogen before now. It is impossible to be sure. But I can sense Winnis and Lagos's worry, because of both my age and my half-Fae blood. Has the disease somehow changed to affect me, and could this change how it impacts the community?

Douse, who has already had Trichron, keeps trying to sneak into my room, only to be deflected by her careful parents. I understand their concerns, though I find myself missing Douse's cheerful good humor.

But eventually the sickness passes, and I find myself feeling better day by day. Until one morning I wake with the pain almost gone and feel a new energy coursing through me. It is time, I decide, to do something I have been putting off for far too long. I have to return to the surface to discover if my Merrow self can readapt to life on land. I have to find out what sort of limits my physical transformation has placed on me.

I have to find out what sort of hybrid I really am, and if I can ever return to the family I found myself missing so badly when I was ill.

So, shortly afterward—when I am feeling myself once more—I prepare to risk everything to discover the truth.

I TELL ONLY WINNIS OF MY PLANS.

I explain my reasons, and ask her to tell her parents and Douse and the other Merrow with whom I have become close that I have decided to leave long enough to figure out just what my hybrid body is capable of. But I assure her that I will return. It is simply that I must know what abilities I retain from my old life before I can decide how I will live my new one.

Winnis is not as supportive as I had hoped. She warns me of the risks, of the clear dangers of leaving the water under any circumstances, of the damage I can do to myself if my body refuses to readjust and my land self cannot be restored. The Merrow cannot breathe out of water, and should I not revert, I will die. Plus, I am still too weak, she insists. I need more time to recover from my illness. I am not ready for the pressures of changing my physical self this soon after my recovery.

She means well, I know. And she is my closest friend in this new world. But she sees me as weaker than I am. She thinks of me as a newborn, still largely ignorant of the ways of the Merrow. She is not wrong—not entirely. But she is underestimating my endurance and determination.

Do not do this, Sharri, she begs me. *Think it through more carefully. Give yourself more time to heal.*

I will do nothing to endanger myself, I insist. *I will be very careful. I know what I risk, but I think that risk is necessary if I am ever to be at peace with myself. I have to know all of what I can or cannot do. I have to find out where I belong.*

She replies at once, without hesitation. *You belong here, with us.*

But I also belong back in my old world, Winnis. And I miss my family. All those fever dreams I experienced reminded me of that. I need to know if I can ever see them again.

If you go, you will not come back, she insists.

She is wrong, but I cannot change her mind. So I instead promise to think about it some more. It is not quite a lie—the time is not yet right for me to leave—but when it is, I will go. My instincts are scratching at me with an urgency I cannot ignore.

More days pass as I go about my business, but on the first night of the new moon, when everything is darkest, I make my escape. I leave in the deepest hours of the night, slipping away from my new family and friends, abandoning my refuge and swimming back toward the shores of Jagged Reach. I will find an appropriate spot to beach myself and then see how being back on the land affects me. If it threatens my health and safety, I will quickly return to my new home. If I can manage to survive, I will then have to make a decision about what is best for me going forward. I do not pretend I know the answers to this dilemma. I only know I must find the extent of my limitations and abilities before making any firm decisions.

I do not deceive myself. There is no reason to think I can go back. Again, I think of Auris. Once she became completely Fae in appearance, she never again reverted to her Human form, even though she reentered the Human world on multiple occasions, when looking like them would have been an advantage. So yes, there is every reason to think that what I am now is what I will remain—a Merrow creature. And it is very possible that this is the identity I must embrace. I am prepared to accept this . . . I think.

But then again, Auris never had to contend with life or death in quite the same way. The Fae I was could not breathe underwater, and the Merrow I am now cannot breathe on land. Perhaps the difference here will be the distance my body will go to keep me alive.

But I cannot know which direction this will go until I try.

I gain the surface and poke the top of my head out of the water, casting about for direction. With my gills still underwater, the breathing question remains moot, but my eyes are not so quick to adjust. The sharpness of vision I enjoyed as a land-dweller is gone, and my eyes are still adapted to seeing underwater. Still, the lights of Pressia are wavering in the distance, so I resubmerge and begin to swim to shore. I am feeling strong and capable, and ready to accept whatever truths I discover.

I swim submerged for the entire distance that it requires for me to gain the shores of Jagged Reach, then I turn southward and swim the shoreline, looking for a likely place to test myself. I need a shallow shore, a place where I can easily roll back into the water if this all goes badly. I find it quickly enough. A small bay opens off the heavier swells of Helles Sound, and I find myself in relatively shallow waters with easy access to the shoreline. Ahead of me, perhaps a hundred yards inland, settled amid a heavy stand of spruce and pines, sits a darkened cottage. There are a few outbuildings and a fishing boat docked at the water's edge, and I swim away from all of it to find a quieter, more deserted spot to climb ashore.

But when I find the perfect spot, I still hesitate. How badly do I want to know if I can be a land creature once more? How much do I want to risk possible damage to my body—or even death—to find out? I stretch out in the shallows and consider, then steel myself and edge onto the woodsy banks. Because I am now saddled with my fish tail and have no legs, I have to crawl up the banks with my arms. With my gills now fully out of water, the time has come to test my breathing. But it is as I feared. I cannot take air into my lungs—assuming I still have lungs—because my body wants the water that has kept me alive for months. I work at making myself breathe but feel myself weaken and thrash back into the waters once more.

A failure.

I inhale the ocean waters, steady myself, and try once more. I tell myself to relax, to stay calm, not to push or wrestle with what my body is telling me, but rather to try to convince it to adapt to what I want. Which is the ability to once more breathe the air and know I can exist on land without suffocating.

I close my eyes and force myself to be calm, stretched out amid the tall grasses, letting my body do what it wants. For several moments, it demonstrates very clearly that it wants the water out of which I have just crawled. But I resist the pull, waiting for something more to happen—maybe for my body to give me a sign of some sort. Maybe for some sort of readaptation.

Instead, my vision starts to gray, so back into the water I go. But now I am both irritated and determined. I will not settle for this answer, I decide. I will not give up. I will keep trying for as long as I am able to move, and maybe I will yet find a way to regain my former self. If I could change one way, I should be able to change back again—providing my life is at risk. I just have to be willing to embrace the reminder of how close I am to dying. This reasoning is a bit delusional, I admit, but I cling to it as I would a lifeline. I miss my family. I want to assure them I am okay, show them what I can do. Ironically, it was the knowledge that I might be trapped in this form forever and never be able to see them again that made me realize how desperately I want to return.

If there was one thing the dreams made clear to me, it is that my family and Viridian Deep hold meaning for me, and I do not want to leave them behind. Everything I cared about was yanked away from me when I was tied to that iron rack and dipped into the ocean. I lost it all in a matter of minutes, and while I have been fortunate enough to gain something new and special—something I value deeply—how can I accept never seeing my brother and sisters again?

Besides, I very much need to find out about Brecklin and my friends and shipmates back in Pressia. How can I abandon Brecklin

Craile, whom I tell myself I still love as much as ever? How can I just let it all go and try to pretend it never existed?

I can't. I know I can't. I don't even want to pretend that I can. I know myself too well. I have to find a way to return.

So back up onto the land I go, to lie in the grasses and wait for the borders of death to save me. The problem is, it is not death I am seeking, but life. I stay until my body is screaming for air, my vision again starting to gray, then scramble back into the water once more, defeated. I don't know what else to do. I don't know how to make this change happen. I still cannot find a way to make myself breathe air again. I am angry and frustrated and a little desperate by now. Am I deceiving myself with false hopes?

Stubborn as always, I try over and over. But after at least two dozen attempts I collapse in the grasses, exhausted, and pass out.

I SHOULD HAVE DIED. I SHOULD HAVE SUFFOCATED ONCE I LOST CONsciousness and lay there in the open air, exposed. But I didn't.

I wake suddenly, abruptly, from the black, empty space into which I have descended, fighting to regain my senses, unaware at first of where I am or what has happened. I see darkness turn to starlit night and the silhouettes of clouds, then I blink and remember. I am on land. I am breathing air, with lungs.

I draw in a deep breath and exhale, tears of joy filling my eyes. I am breathing again! I am taking in and exhaling gulps of air and no longer choking. Somehow, I am restored.

And . . . I concentrate, and find myself able to wiggle what seem to be my toes. Do I have legs again?

I lift my head to glance down, and find myself held fast. I am ensnared in lines that tie me in place, and that in turn have been fastened to iron spikes.

My heart plummets. I am a prisoner once more. And from the breeze over my body, I also seem to be naked from the waist down.

The night and its surroundings are silent, but I scan about quickly, searching for whoever or whatever has done this to me. I cannot quite believe I have gone from being a prisoner on land to being cast to my death, only to find myself back where I started.

"Yah, lass, no struggles, if'n ye please. Them ties are only so's ye don' hurt yerself."

I look over to where the voice is coming from and find a shadowed figure sitting cross-legged in the grasses, looking at me. It is hard to tell much else. There is a tangled mass of long hair and twig-like limbs clothed in ragged garb, and boots. Bangles and beads glitter faintly from wrists, ankles, and neck in the weak starlight from high above us. A quick assessment tells me this is a woman.

"Are ye well enough now?" the other asks me. "Does ye have yer aches and stretches all settled from yer sleepin' time?"

"Well enough," I answer. I am vaguely aware that I am speaking aloud, in the common language of the ports once more.

"Ye be a water and land creature both for sure, I well know," the other says. She still hasn't moved. "Born of two worlds, with two lives."

I stare at her. "Can you untie me, please? I don't intend to cause you any harm."

"Might do, but are yer words real or false?"

"I am not lying. I have no reason to cause you harm. I am just trying to find my way home."

"Then ye must come from land but can live in water. Right enough, sure, but seldom so. Lest ye have the means—the magic. Witch girls are rare. Not seen another in fifty years."

Witch girl? I don't like the sound of that, but I stay calm. "I was born on land and only discovered I could live in water a few months ago. It's a long story."

"Well and good. Must have much to tell, much to share. Will ye do so for an old lady-kin? I be of this world, but know something of t'other. Of the Merrow-born. Ye be one of them, am I right?

I nod. "You are. Can you please free me now?"

"If ye promises me I'll not be harmed or dragged into the seas and drowned. Yer word?"

"My word. No harm to you. No dragging anyone into the water and drowning them."

"Aye, well. Yer voice says you speak true. Let's see what yer eyes got to say."

I watch as she seems to untangle and rise, her limbs getting longer and more scarecrow-like than I would have thought possible. She hobbles as she walks toward me, coming close and bending down again. She is frail clear through, and seems lacking in substance and life both—a wisp of something once human but now substantially reduced. Her tangled hair is woven through with strands of grasses and brightly colored ribbons, left to grow wild and long.

She peers at me, her strange greenish eyes studying me closely as she tracks me from my head to my feet.

Feet!

I grin. Toes and all, returned. My fish tail is gone and my legs are back. Even as she watches, I scan my new body to find the Merrow parts vanished and the Fae parts restored. I am essentially back to who I was.

"Ye finding yer other self, no? True witch girl, ye are, I can see. Sea witch of the rarest sort. Almost none of 'em left. But yer like the one I once knew, girl. Able to be not only one sort, but both—land and sea in turn. Fae and Merrow."

I wonder if she means Carlindallin, the girl Lagos told me about. Or maybe someone more recent? Someone who could possibly have been my mother? My heart starts to beat faster in excitement, but she seems oblivious.

"My, my, what a treasure," she continues. "Look at me. Let me see yer eyes meet mine. Look at me, now. Look close."

I do as she asks, and after a long moment, she nods. "Young ye be, but true of heart and honest. Aye, it is as ye say. It's there in the way yer eyes reflect yer soul."

She reaches down, removes the netting, and begins to unstrap the bindings that hold me in place. I find myself overwhelmed with emotions. It feels odd, how quickly the Merrow part has vanished. I am overjoyed at being my Fae self once more, but at the same time saddened that my Merrow self has gone. It is what I was searching for, but is it really what I want?

"Thar ye be, witchling," the old woman says, releasing the last of the ties that bind me. "Ye must forgive me my fears, but thar's those that would harm an oldster like me who dared even to touch 'em. Some Merrow-kind are hard and mean and want no part of land-folk. Of them sort, I must be cautious. But ye are not of that kind."

"I would not want to be," I say.

"Naw, ye are of my sort. Live and let live. Take yer friendship where ye finds a place and let it to be as it should."

She collapses more than settles next to me, her ancient eyes bright, her spindly limbs interlocking to hold her in place.

"Here I be, then. Name's Portallis—as in the dockings I makes my home and my studies. Yers?"

"Char," I answer, giving her a quick smile. "I am a Sylvan Fae. My home is in Viridian Deep."

"Knows of it, but never went. Never really gone much farther than here, along these shores. Belongs here, I do. My space and my world. So, now then. Yer story. Tell it t'me, witch girl. All ye have to share. No judgments do I intend. Only perhaps an observation or two. So, now. Speak."

I glance down once more at my naked body, fish tail gone, legs returned.

"Yes, but . . . first, can you give me something to wear?"

She laughs at my discomfort and wanders off to find me a pair of pants.

seven

HUDDLED IN THE DARKNESS SOMEWHERE ON THE SHORES OF the Helles, lulled by the lapping of the ocean waters and the soft brush of the winds, Portallis and I talk until the sky begins to lighten. We are strangers met by some fate we don't yet fully understand, but we become friends quickly and with an odd sense of kinship. Portallis is a woman cast adrift by the world's disinterest and by a personal choice made years ago. So she now lives alone in her shabby hut amid the trees she loves and the ocean she worships, a recluse and hermit with no particular direction in her life and few regrets for whatever she might have missed because of it.

I am a foundling she has saved—or at least, so she sees me, and tells me so. I have been brought to these shores and into her life because fate intended for us to meet—or so she insists. I am both a conundrum and a fascination, a Fae become a Merrow and then reverted through magic and genetics. She sees me as someone who could have been her daughter under different circumstances, she says, and for that she is grateful. She has lived alone for so long— she tells me this several times over—and has been praying someone would come to ease her loneliness. She does not hunger for love, but she does miss the sense of belonging to a family. I ask of her friends and neighbors, of the rest of her family, but she only shakes her head and says she is all there is, and that she is mostly content to have it that way.

"Tell me, now," she says finally, as the sun crests the horizon, "what ye intends, now that ye be land-born agin. Have a plan, do ye?"

We are sipping tea from cups—an oddly thick liquid she has brewed from an unknown mix of herbs and spices. The drink is a bit startling and clearly intoxicating, and after the first few sips I am very aware of the need not to overindulge.

"First, I need to find the friends I had before I became Merrow and learn what has happened to them. And to one in particular— a man I have considered joining in partnership with."

"Ah! A man! Well, now. Best watch yourself, Char of the dual lives. Men are fine, but not to be trusted too far. Still, ya look capable enough. I trust ye are schooled in the ways of t'other sex?"

I don't know about that, but I smile and nod anyway. "He is a close friend and I trust him to protect me. I care deeply for him, and I would not feel right walking away from him now, after all he has done for me. He has guided me well these past few years, since I left home, and I must let him know what has become of me."

But even as I speak the words, I wonder how much of what I am assuming is true. I've been gone from Brecklin's life for months. Likely, he presumes me dead. Realistically, how can I think otherwise? Moreover, if I put my emotional attachment aside and face the situation straight up, how much have things changed? I am now a different person in so many ways and uncertain about not only my present life but everything that might happen in the future.

"And will ye then go back to yer birth home, lass?" Portallis asks. "To yer real family? Will ye seek out the truths that had been kept from ye or lost in time?"

I do want to go home, more than anything. But I doubt my family will know anything more of my strange dual nature than I do.

Ancrow adopted me from the Protective Leaf Orphanage, so the staff and Ancrow are the only ones who might know anything about my background. As Ancrow is dead, that leaves only the staff, and enough years have passed that I wonder if anyone is still employed there who remembers those days. I wish *I* remembered those days, but I suppose I left there young enough that I recall nothing of that time. Ancrow, Harrow, Ronden, and Ramey are the only existence I recall.

"I'll go to Pressia first, to find Brecklin. I'm thinking maybe he can sail me home." Though I wonder if he will even be there. With the Faraway Trades Company hunting for him, he must have gotten far from the city for a while—unless they captured him again, and he is now dead. But either way, I have to find out.

" 'Brecklin,' is it? That be yer lad's name? A good strong one. But be careful, girl. Do not risk yerself needlessly. Stay clear of those Humans that pollute the seas and lands both—those dark-cloaked snakes that make slaves of t'others."

I am not sure exactly who she is talking about, but I can make a good guess. "I will."

"Fate brought ye to me, and all such meetings happen fer a purpose. And I ken this be one t'do with who ye now know yerself to be. Part of one species, part of t'other. Rare and special, that. Feel it yerself, don' ye?"

I nod. I do. I have felt that way from the moment I first changed without knowing what I was doing, and I am reaffirmed in that belief thanks to this strange woman.

She takes a strong drink of her tea. She is already on her second cup, and I wonder that she is still sitting upright, given the potency of the brew. But she seems unaffected, and I gather she must have built up a resistance to its power.

"By rules of fate and laws of species far and wide, yer not of a sort one encounters reg'arly," she continues. "Knows that, don' ye?"

"I guess I do—though it is still a mystery to me. I have no memories of my birth parents or their kin. The only ones I know are the people who took me and raised me: my sisters and brother. And for a brief time, the woman who called herself my mother."

"P'haps they can tell ye somet'in 'bout it all, then."

"I doubt they know anything more than I do. The only ones who might have known are my real and adoptive mothers, and both are now dead. Or maybe the people at the orphanage from which I was adopted." I shake my head. "This is all so new and strange, and I am quite different than I have always believed. But you said you have seen this before?"

"Once, long back. Fifty years, p'haps. A girl, she were—one like yerself. Never told me her name. A Merrow, but with a yearning for a Human life. She was fleeing somet'in, and wouldn't tell me what. Looking fer her freedom, I'd guessed. Came here, and I sheltered her for a few days. Then she was gone again. Left one night, just like that. Never saw her agin, ever. Odd and lonely and lost, she was."

This accords with what Lagos had told me, and I find myself wondering if maybe my mother was one such as this. I had always assumed that my birth mother was Sylvan . . . but what if she wasn't? What if she, too, was one of those rare Merrow who could transform at will?

Portallis is silent for a moment, then shakes her head. "Don' know what become of her after that. Never have. She was just gone."

Like me, I think, when I fled my family and home and came here. Vanished into the night to be somewhere else—to be *someone* else. I wonder if she found either in her flight.

I feel a sudden urge to find answers to all the questions my circumstances raise.

"I am grateful for your care and patience and kindness," I tell Portallis. "But it is time for me to go, to find my own answers."

"Sure 'nuff, sea witch, but draw it in a bit now." She gives me a crooked smile and gestures. "Morning comes, but is that when ye should show yerself, or might'n it not be better to wait fer another nightfall? Ye seem wary, for all that ye are recovered and such, so maybe hold back a bit?"

"I am well enough."

"Ye see it so, do ye? Have you slept well and eaten and rested? Sure, ye are brave, but mebbe not ready yet. Stay on this comin' day. Sleep as long as ye like, eat some food and take some drink, rest and strengthen a bit. Then go."

I see the sense of what she is telling me, and she is right about my need for sleep. As soon as she mentions it, I feel how exhausted I am.

"Fine, I'll stay," I agree. "If it is no trouble for you to have me here."

"None." She rises. "Come back up under the trees where the shade will cool ye in the heat of the day. I kin bring ye out a fresh wrap and see ye settled. I kin keep watch. I kin keep ye safe."

She does as she says and fetches a blanket and a pad for my head and selects a place back within the shelter of the trees and out of direct view of the waters of the Helles and any shoreline walkers who might pass by. She lays me down and wraps me, and for just a moment touches my cheek as my mother once did when I was a girl.

Then my eyes close, and I sleep.

THE DAY PASSES, THE DAYLIGHT WANES, AND I WAKE AT DUSK TO EAT porridge and drink a cup of that toxic but heartening tea Portallis loves. I feel stronger and more able by now, and my body familiar once more.

When I am ready to depart, Portallis and I exchange promises to see each other again soon. Something about her attracts me in a way I cannot explain, and I know there is more about her than what she has told me. I want to know what it is.

I set out walking along the shoreline toward the distant, shadowed rooflines of the port city of Pressia, dressed anew in garments with which my strange benefactor has supplied me—found or gathered up from who-knows-where, but comfortable enough. I have boots and pants and a jacket, and a headscarf that hides my identity better than I would have thought. She also gave me earrings and a necklace, and a belt formed of silver links.

The falling night is pleasant enough, the evening breeze cool and welcome, so I make good time as I head toward my destination. I am unfamiliar with the outskirts of Pressia, but it is simple enough to follow the shoreline. I am already thinking through my options, considering who I must see first. Some—perhaps many—will think me dead. And some will be wondering what has happened to keep me away for so long.

Right away, I tell myself, I must seek out Brecklin and my crewmates and reveal what has happened to me.

In part, at least.

Because I am not so sure that telling anyone I am Merrow as well as Fae is a particularly good idea.

I push on into the edges of the city and make my way along backstreets and alleys and little-used passageways to find the portion of the waterfront I seek. I am cautious in the extreme, knowing my new clothing is an insufficient disguise, given my green skin. I am carrying a blade that Portallis gave me for protection: a wicked curved thing that is as sharp as broken glass and as strong as iron. It makes me feel safe, but I won't let it lure me into thinking I really am.

I discover quickly enough that secrecy is pointless. I am stopped at every turn by people I don't know but who nonetheless recognize me. Questions abound, and I must force my way past the questioners—even those who mention that the Silver Blade has been looking for me. Apparently, the search he conducted was vast and seemingly endless while he remained in port. But he is gone by now, if the rumors are true.

I come down to the water's edge on the portion of the docks where the waste disposal ships lie. Gulls are visible in endless numbers, occupying every spare upright, roof, wind line, and eave for as far as the eye can see. Hundreds feed on food debris and garbage, much of which they have freed from its former containers. They cry out regularly to one another—shrill, chilling calls that echo in the night air.

I ignore them and continue down the walkway, eyes on the darker places that lie ahead, wondering how smart it is for me to be searching for the Blade so openly. Even if he is indeed still in port—which seems unlikely, given the nature of the Faraway Trades men who might still be hunting him—I will be opening myself up to the same people who took us both captive earlier. So won't Brecklin likely be elsewhere by now, and his crew with him? He mostly spends his time salvaging wrecks, or doing midnight runs of contraband, ferrying it from thieves to dealers. He surely will be on his ship right now, along with all those who might know how to find him.

But I have to try something.

Just thinking of seeing Brecklin again excites me sufficiently that I cast my doubts aside and continue my search. What will he say when I appear? It has been months since my seizure, and word will have spread of my supposed fate. I smile to myself, thinking of the look on his face when I materialize in front of him. Perhaps it is this that will make him realize how important I am to him, and we can become partners in truth.

I blush with expectation as I imagine of what it would be like to have this happen. I am vaguely aware of my foolishness, but I give in to it nevertheless.

Still, aware of the danger, I scan for suspicious or unfriendly faces and I find them everywhere. I slip through the darkness into the drinking and gambling sectors of Pressia, for it is there I will find what I am looking for, and again I am besieged by men and women asking after me and wanting to know where I have been and what I have been doing.

When I reach the Boat Hook tavern, I step inside for a look around. There are dockworkers, old sailors, cargo men, pirates, pleasure girls, dealers, and players of all sorts crowding about, drifting from tables to bar and back again, their voices loud and boisterous, filling the air with the smell of their grog and liquor-infused breath. I drift slowly over to the serving bar, which gives me a chance to look about, but I see none of the Blade's crewmen. I hang around for a bit, speaking to this customer and that before moving on, but I learn nothing new.

I then visit the Wench's Waist, Half-Moon Full, Deep Wave, Oyster Treasure, and even Scorpion's Sting, similarly with no success. There is no sign of my crewmates or of Brecklin, and no one seems to know where he is other than gone. On more than a few occasions, I am warned that there are people looking for me, so I start looking over my shoulder more frequently.

As a last resort, I visit the Black Spot. Normally, I would avoid this hellhole of a grog den like I would a boneyard, but I am out of options, so I have to risk a foray into a place I would not usually go. Unfortunately, it sits quite close to the Faraway Trades warehouses, but those people—or at least the ones who are not Goblins—would never be caught dead in a slovenly pit like the Spot. In any case, I am willing to take a chance. But I will not stay longer than required for a quick look around.

I enter, and the stench is a suffocating blanket that threatens to gag me. A mixture of vomit, piss, spilled alcohol, and body odor arises from the wooden floor and threatens to overpower me. I have to move quickly to where the working girls loiter at the bar, trying to keep from being manhandled. I know one or two, and perhaps a quick word with them will reveal something of use. Everyone knows that if there is something worthwhile to be learned, the Black Spot is one likely place to learn it.

I am unique enough in appearance that almost everyone here recognizes me and asks the same familiar questions. A few tell me that the Blade is definitely at sea and has been for weeks. The crowd shifts and turns as I proceed, choosing my path for me, and suddenly I find myself standing in front of a table with an old man sitting at it—a wayfarer if ever I saw one, a huge fellow, sailor-dressed, but not sailor-able I think, his one good eye regarding me judgmentally.

For just a moment, I think I know him. I think perhaps we have met before.

"Use some company, could you?" he asks me. "Buy you a drink, maybe?"

It has been a long, thirsty night, and this is the best offer I have gotten so far. My instincts tell me he is safe, so instead of moving away I sit down. "Aren't I a little young for you?"

He laughs. "Everyone's too young for me. Besides which, that wasn't what I was offering. Just thought it would be good to visit with someone who might actually know something. I heard you asking questions about the Blade."

"I'll accept your offer, then, if you'll tell me what you know."

He eyes me suspiciously. "What sort of poison would one such as yourself be willing to purchase for an old fellow like myself? Hard or soft, rich or bitter, full or drained?"

I don't know what he is talking about, so I shrug. "You make the choice."

He gestures for a serving girl and orders ale for both of us, which appears almost instantly. "There now," he declares, lifting his glass to clink against mine before taking a drink. I sip as well—but only sip.

"Know of any ships bound for Fae lands and seeking an able crewman, someone who's used to making runs of any sort?" I ask.

The old man shakes his head, and his gray hair takes on the look of a broom's end. "Not I."

"I take it you're not a man for night business, then?"

"Not these days, given my age. I stay dockside and safe."

"So tell me, what do you know of the Blade? Have you seen him about? Or heard something, maybe?"

He smiles. "Now, why should I tell you? Why would you even care?"

"I sailed with him, a few months back."

"Ah. Didn't take you with him this time, I gather?"

"He's out then?"

"Been gone two weeks or so, rumor has it."

No more than what anyone else has told me. Brecklin isn't here.

"Well, I'll have to wait until next time to share a run with him, I guess." I manage a shrug. "He's back when, do you think?"

"Rumors say a few weeks. Though I might tell you more if you'd buy me a pint for the information."

I smile and shrug. "No coins, at present."

He shakes his head and orders on his own. I continue to sit there with him while he slugs his order down, trying to think what to do next. So, no Brecklin. No happy reunion for me—at least not for a while.

"Bit of advice, youngling?" my elderly companion says, wiping his mouth dry with the sleeve of his shirt.

I nod. "Always."

"You might want to work on hiding your identity better. Or keep more of a weather eye out. There's a pair of dark cloaks off to your left who seem to have their gaze fixed on you like a fisherman on a trout."

I risk a casual glance, careful to do so without seeming to. I instantly note the two men he means, black-clad and hooded, heads lowered as they quietly converse. Both bear the insignia of the Faraway Trades Company. The head and eyes of one momentarily drift my way.

I give the old man a nod. "They must have recognized me. Time for me to go."

"I wondered. Their interest is obvious. So, go. But not as you came. Go around the end of the bar, past the ladies that provide the service, then out the back door. Turn left into the alley. Go quick enough, and you can lose them easily."

"What's your name, Grandfather?" I ask, smiling.

"Glad Jack."

I risk a smile. "I'm Char."

"I figured. Word gets around about someone of your sort. You're well thought of, you know. It's been a solid pleasure, young Char. Be careful now. You might be plenty tough for a girl, but the Black Spot's no place for you."

I shrug. "I'm having some trouble finding a place that is," I admit.

He leans close. "I'm always here. I'll end my days here. Lived most of my life by now, so I'm just marking time. If you ever need help, just ask. You can find me here anytime, should you ever need to."

"Maybe I'll get back for another visit soon. And thanks for the offer."

He glances over at the black-cloaked men. "You take care, now. Be quick and go fast."

I am up and moving instantly, easing through the crowds and down the bar, past the servers who barely give me a glance, behind the bar and along the hall, and finally out the door and into the night—all in what feels like no more than an instant. I remember old Jack's advice and make a left turn down the alley and scurry along a narrow corridor between two buildings. When I glance back, I find myself alone.

Out in the open air of the docks, I turn back the way I have come, staying in the shadows, keeping watch. I am alone and bereft of friends, chances, and ideas.

What am I going to do now?

I really don't know.

But it won't be the first time, and I will find a way.

EIGHT

ALKING IS EASY WHEN YOU HAVE NO DESTINATION IN MIND,
no time limit, and not much of a schedule to keep. I had so
been hoping that Brecklin would be here, waiting for me, but that
was not to be. It was gratifying to hear how hard he searched for me
before he left, but with the Faraway Trades people still after him,
absenting himself made sense.

That the same people might also be keeping watch for me is a
possibility—although why would they bother if they thought they
had killed me? Yet there were clearly two of them sitting together at
the Black Spot, looking over at me, and Glad Jack had warned me
they had been keeping watch, so I might want to think about getting out of Pressia for a time.

Which again seems to point me toward Viridian Deep. But how
to get there? Is there a vessel bound for there that will take me on as
crew? Or is it best to wait until Brecklin returns and go from there?

I walk the docks, weighing my options. Certainly, I can wait
around for Brecklin's return. He has to come back at some point,
and I can probably manage to stay hidden until he surfaces.

But waiting around for someone else to make my decisions is

foolish, and wandering around on the docks by myself is dangerous. I need to come up with a better plan. I have to find something to do and somewhere to go until I can rejoin Brecklin and my crewmates. I wonder what sort of run they are making. Are they doing a delivery or a pickup? How long will they be gone? Glad Jack said a few weeks, but what makes him an expert? Who else can I talk to who might know?

Momentarily distracted by a wooden placard with a painted bulletin seeking crew for the *Bucking Board*—an old tri-masted frigate I once considered sailing and now wouldn't waste time on—I am suddenly aware of another presence. I am being watched.

Without giving any signs of awareness, I glance back the way I have come and see two black-cloaked figures loitering several dozen yards away, their eyes on a tow-rig but their attention clearly on me. So, the Faraway Trades men that were watching me in the tavern have followed me.

I am suddenly afraid. It is late at night and the docks are virtually deserted. And even if there were anyone present, they'd be unlikely to offer help. Whatever happens next, I am on my own.

I start ambling down the central boardwalk once more, deliberately taking my time. No need to alert those who follow me that I am aware of their presence. Nor do I think fleeing is a good idea. Fleeing indicates fear, and fear feeds the hunger of those who pursue me. These cloaked and hooded Trades men are nothing compared with the Goblins I have tangled with on more than one occasion. Well . . . never more than one Goblin at a time perhaps, but still.

The whole business irritates me. How is it that I am barely one day back and already under the eyes of my former captors? What purpose does it serve to be keeping watch for me? What sort of Fates are allowing this to happen now?

I start walking again, aware of the booted footsteps that follow mine, wondering what this pair intends. One of them must have recognized me. Or perhaps they just decided I looked suspicious and needed to be checked out. Or maybe they are some of the men from

Warehouse #3, come to finish what they started. Whatever the case, I need to find a way to lose them. I am not about to risk being hauled back into captivity, and if they know I can survive a drowning, they won't hesitate to cut my throat if they get hold of me again. And no amount of changing shape can get me out of *that*.

Or can it?

I give it some thought. I have changed back into my Fae self and my Merrow identity is gone, but can I get it back again? Can I change freely from one identity to the other? I don't know. I won't know until I give it a try. But I am not persuaded that trying now, when the men pursuing me have every reason to try to kill me, is a good idea. Any failure to change would give them all the chances they need to end me.

It is late by now and the docks are mostly deserted save for the occasional drunkard stumbling home from an evening's outing. The gulls are still about in force, and now and then harbor owls swoop by, as silent as the darkness they inhabit. I take it all in, the way I learned to do while studying with Harrow and Ronden, developing my tracking skills and my innate understanding of the way things feel when you are being hunted.

Eyes shifting from one potential hiding place to another, from one possible escape route to the next, I push on. But the boardwalk is now entirely empty, and I am depressingly alone.

Then, everything changes in an instant.

Abruptly, a clutch of figures rush out to confront me—a pack of homeless waifs from the look of them, tattered and worn but hungry for excitement. Teens and younger, I guess. I let them come right up to me, their faces expectant as they wait to see what I might do in the face of their supposed threat.

"Give over your coins," demands the biggest of the bunch, "and no harm will come to you."

The demand is so ridiculous I almost laugh. I give the speaker a doubtful look. "How old are you?"

He snorts, drawing himself up to full height. "Old enough to teach you a lesson or two."

"But not old enough to recognize trouble when you see it?" Already, I see the pair of Trades men picking up their pace, hurrying to reach me. Maybe I can use this mess to get away from them. "Tell you what," I say. "Do you see those men coming toward us? Get in their way. Block their efforts to reach me, and I will give you every coin I've got."

The boy stares. He is perhaps close to my age, but it is hard to tell. He is vaguely irritated, looking first at me and then down the dockside to where the two black-cloaked men are coming toward us.

"Mess them up yourself!" he snaps. Then he turns to his followers and shouts, "Run!"

And they all turn and sprint for cover. Which means nothing has worked out as I wanted it to. What kind of would-be thieves are these kids, anyway?

Still, if I stay where I am, I will have to turn and fight—not a good idea where Faraway Trades is involved, even in circumstances as desperate as these. So I turn and flee after the kids.

I am young and strong and quick, so I overtake a handful of them and pass by, charging into the backstreets beyond the docks. Then, instead of continuing in the same direction, I cut back toward the Black Spot, hoping my pursuers won't think to do the same. The sounds made by the fleeing street kids mask my movements. A few more minutes, and I will be back at the Spot if I can just continue on down the dockside.

But all too quickly they find me again, as if I am a magnet drawing them to me. They break from the shadows to confront me. It is the worst possible result, but there is nothing I can do about it.

I square myself away, taking a quick moment to size up my attackers. They are big men, each more than twice my weight and size. While I can't see obvious weapons, I am certain they will be carrying them. I have the curved blade Portallis gave me and nothing else. In any case, I don't care to engage in a knife fight with two grown men whose fighting skills are likely better than mine. This will be over pretty quickly if I let them get their hands on me.

I wait until they are less than ten feet away from me, then attack. I make for the closest, sidestep as he comes at me, then drop and roll into him, making him trip and fall. A moment later I am back on my feet, using my hands to deliver quick blows to my second attacker, but it isn't enough to stop him. He grabs at my clothing, using his weight to throw me off balance. Down we both go, and even though I hit him with two sharp punches to the throat that leave him gasping for breath, he hangs on to me.

In seconds, he has me in a headlock as he bears me down and flattens me against the wooden dock. I can't allow him to take me prisoner. I can't! I struggle beneath his weight to get free, but he has me pinned. I thrash angrily, trying to reach any vulnerable point: eyes, nose, mouth, below his belt. No good.

"Hold still!" he bellows, obviously enraged. "We've got you and we're keeping you! There's no escape from us this time, little hellion!"

So they know about me and the rack. I am in trouble.

Then a cry rises up from behind us, and the man on top of me hesitates. A second later he lurches sharply backward, tumbles away, and goes still.

A familiar, barrel-like form hovers over me. "Get up now. Quickly, Fae girl. We don't want to wait around for others."

Glad Jack.

I straighten up and catch sight of my attackers. One has a shark hook sticking out of his back, while the other lies unmoving a few feet farther away.

My rescuer reaches down with one huge arm and yanks me to my feet. "For a young girl, you are a load of trouble."

I nod in recognition of the backhanded compliment. "So I have been told."

"You were pretty quick with these two, but they were clearly more than your match, given their weight and size. You're lucky I decided to see how this would turn out."

I brush myself off. "I wouldn't have thought you would bother."

"Surprised myself, I'll admit. But I like you, and I don't like them Faraway Trades skunks. You can smell their stench a mile off."

"How did you get to me so fast?"

"It helped that ye cut back toward me. Besides, I know these docks well. A few shortcuts get me everywhere I want faster'n most. Saw these skunks was gonna follow ye from the Spot, but dinna know how to stop 'em there. So, I tracked 'em down the boardwalk. Sneaky, coming at you like that, weren't they?"

I glance over at his victims. Both dead. "Guess they won't be coming at me again."

"Dead is dead, and for some the better way to be. You know what they were after?"

I shake my head, deciding to keep that to myself. "Not really." I could make some guesses, but now is not the time. "They obviously wanted something."

"Well, away with you," Glad Jack advises, motioning for me to get going.

But I stand where I am, still confused. What is happening here?

Glad Jack frowns and gives my shoulder a push. "You still in there? Some reason you're not listening to what I be saying? You're wasting precious time. Get going to wherever you need to go!"

"I would," I snap, "but I don't know where that is!" I give him a sharp look. "Maybe you can help?"

The big man emits an audible *humph*. "That so? Well, maybe I don't want to."

"But you said you would, didn't you? Back at the Spot. If I ever needed help, you said, come find you."

He grimaces. "So I did. Regretting it right now, though."

And just like that, I decide.

———

GLAD JACK MAKES MY NEWLY CONCEIVED PLAN SOMEWHAT EASIER. He seems eager to help the moment I reveal it—or perhaps just eager to be rid of me—but the end result is the same. I am on my way before I have time to rethink what I am doing. But my instincts whisper that I have made the right decision.

"There she is, all shined up, fueled, and ready to go," Jack announces as we stand on the dockside just after daylight, looking down at his 520 Furrow Slough Flier.

I will admit I am impressed. When he told me that he had a boat that could make the trip I needed, I had my doubts. What was a retired sailor doing with a vessel so sleek and capable that I can almost imagine it flying as well as sailing?

"As a matter of fact, she can feel at times as if she's flying," Glad Jack says when I make this very comment. "For short distances, with sufficient power boosts, you'll think she's lifting off."

She is lean and shiny, with thirty feet of mainsail strung out from mainmast to boom's end. Her belowdecks cabin sleeps two, twin directional engines provide additional stability at sail, and the storage bins are filled with all the provisions one could require. She carries in-hull fuel for the support engines embedded in the hull, extra sails for strong winds, and ballast in rear storage. She is fast enough when challenged, Jack is quick to point out, and she is built for endurance and speed.

"How did you get hold of a craft like this?" I ask in disbelief. "Did you steal it?"

He laughs. "Not hardly. Up your opinion of me, if you please. Remember my profession. A good pirate needs a good boat. I've done a few favors, earned a few coins along the way. I like the sea enough I don' want to leave it entirely. So now I have this pretty little craft." He pauses. "For those times when I want to dip my toes back in the waters a bit more."

I give this treasure another look. "I've never sailed in one of these. Only on larger craft."

"She's pretty easy to handle," he tells me. "Wind, waves, sea monsters—almost nothing can sink 'er. You can seal 'er up tight, if you need. She's equipped for thirty days of hard sailing with no cause to stop for additional supplies. All you'll need is already aboard. Tested this young lady out myself and found 'er a smooth and willing lass."

I grimace at the comparison, but he doesn't notice.

"Aye, she'll have you back in the Fae world in maybe five days."

I shift about to face him squarely. "Why are you doing all this for me? You don't even know me."

Glad Jack shrugs. "Don't I? Well, now. You don't need to know someone to see that helping them is the right thing t'do. I like you, girl. I like your spirit and your courage. I find it refreshing t'know there's still young things like you out there, trying to make their way in the world. Besides, what else I got t'do? I'm an old man. Life is passing me by, and I don't want it doing so too soon and too fast. I want to live a bit yet."

I shake my head in wonder. "I don't want to be a burden. I want to know it's something you feel comfortable doing."

He laughs. "I feel comfortable enough, young lady. Now then, something else ye need t'know. If you run into any of those Goblin slavers that sometimes prowl these waters, they won't be able to lay a finger on you. You'll be twice as fast as almost any of those cumbersome warships they favor. The waters of the Helles and Roughlin Wake will belong to you alone. And you'll have Tryn's skills and experience to guide you."

This is the first I've heard this name spoken. "Who is Tryn?"

"My nephew. You'll be needing a shipmate to help with the sailing, and I can't go with you."

"You can't?"

"How would I do that, seeing as I be Human? My sort isn't allowed to go prowling into the Fae world."

"So Tryn isn't Human?"

"Tryn's a halfling—Water Sprite on the one side, Human on the other. I keep him on because he's my nephew, like I says. Long story, which doesn't need tellin' just now. But he's a dab hand with a boat, and trustworthy to boot. He will be your captain, and you'll be his mate. He will protect you, provide for you, and see you safely to your destination."

If you say so, I think. But I wonder anew what I have gotten myself into. It is bad enough being hunted by those Faraway Trades goons. With two of their own dead at my hands (or so they will assume), they will likely be looking for me a lot harder. Reason enough to flee these shores. But add to that my discovery that I am of Merrow blood, and I know that I have a lot of questions about my life that I must answer. I must learn how I ended up at the Protective Leaf Orphanage to become Ancrow's daughter. I must learn how I got to be what I am.

Time was when I would automatically turn to Brecklin for help, but that time is gone, because Brecklin is gone as well, and I don't know for sure if I will ever see him again. I certainly have no idea when he will resurface, and I can't risk waiting around. Instead, I will try to solve the questions about my past on my own.

Which means I must return to Viridian Deep to find the answers I need. I can visit the Protective Leaf Orphanage and see what I can learn. And though I am still not sure of what my reception might be, I miss my family, and I want to see them again.

I look again at the 520 Furrow Slough Flier bobbing calmly in the waters of the Helles. Morning is under way, and pleasure craft of all shapes and sizes zip through the waters all around me. That Glad Jack will let me use his boat to reach home is a true blessing—a bit of Fae magic, to my way of thinking—so I have to take advantage of the gift.

"All right," I acknowledge and glance again at my companion, who is standing off to one side, beaming with satisfaction. "How do I find Tryn?"

"No need," says a voice from behind me. "I'm right here."

NINE

I TURN TO FIND THE MAN WHO MUST BE TRYN STANDING RIGHT behind me, and stiffen in shock.

Because he is beautiful.

Not just *sort* of beautiful. Not beautiful in one or two identifiable ways. But exotically, breathtakingly, all-encompassingly beautiful.

Okay, maybe this is just a first impression. And I might be over-reacting. But this is what beholding him makes me feel.

He is incredibly dark-skinned, but not in a way with which I am familiar. He is entirely black from his short-cropped hair to his shoeless feet, and his skin glistens like onyx.

I am no stranger to different skin colors. Sylvan Fae are all shades and hues of green; my own skin is somewhere between deep emerald and celadon, and has a tendency to suggest both colors depending on the light. Water Sprites tend to assume various shadings of blue. Humans vary in shades of pink and brown and tan, from light to dark. But I have never seen anyone as black as Tryn.

He is so beautiful that I feel the impact of his presence deep inside. His features are perfectly shaped, his body slim and lithe. Overall, he has an athletic look, without being overly muscular.

In short, he is perfect.

Although, curiously, unlike all the Water Sprites I have ever known, he has no gill slits; his neck is completely smooth.

He smiles, and I flinch as if blinded by the bright flash of his teeth. "Good morning," he says, and holds out one hand.

I blush as I extend my hand to take his. The pressure it provides is warm and reassuring. I want to say something intelligent or meaningful, but my ability to express myself is suddenly on vacation. I settle for a warm smile.

So beautiful.

No. This is ridiculous. What in the world is wrong with me?

"I'm Char," I manage to say.

"Are you ready for your journey?" he asks.

Anywhere, I think.

Glad Jack chuckles. "Told him what ye were about and where ye wanted to go," he advises. I glance over at him. I had almost forgotten he was there. "He knows the 520 backward and forward. Ye'll be in good hands, lass."

I see a flicker of surprise in Tryn's eyes and realize he didn't know I was female. I am still in the clothes Portallis gave me, which I know make me look more man than woman. Impulsively, I pull off my headscarf and let my long, curly, leaf-strewn green hair tumble free. I don't know why I do this save that I want badly for him to admire me as much as I admire him.

He smiles. "My uncle speaks the truth about my skills at seafaring, and I am indeed at your service."

"I can help," I offer. *As if I have to prove myself. Saints of the Fae! Why am I feeling like this?* "I've crewed all sorts of craft, big and small, for over three years. I'm not familiar with the 520 in particular, but I know my way around a vessel."

"All well and good, then. And I can teach you about the 520," he replies. "It helps when there are two of us to manage her."

I try to stop looking at him, though I don't want to. Instead, I force my gaze back at Glad Jack, whose face is beaming with pleasure on noting my very obvious fascination with his nephew.

"I am very grateful to you, Jack," I tell him. "More so than words can express. I owe you a huge debt."

I turn back to Tryn. "And I am grateful to you, too, for agreeing to help me get home."

Jack pats us both on our backs. "Best ye get going now," he says. But suddenly he turns to me, adding, "Be careful out there. There's many a scoundrel and Backwash Sammy hanging about, and all of them would love to have my boat and the use of a young lady like yourself. And remember to run, if there's nothing else that can save you."

I don't quite know what he is talking about, but I nod. "I'll be careful. No need to worry."

"But I do, lass. I do." He pats my back again. "Well and good, then. Day's well started, weather's good, tide's in to carry you out, and time's slipping away. Go now. Listen to Tryn, do as he tells you, and stay safe."

His good wishes are welcome, and for the first time since my return from the deep, I feel an odd sense of control.

Before long, Tryn has taken us out of the harbor and into the bay that leads to the deeper waters of the Helles. He stands confidently at the controls, operating everything with such dexterity and ease that I am immediately reassured. He doesn't say much as the shoreline fades and his uncle disappears, his attention all on his duties as helmsman. I stand at his side, wondering how all this is going to turn out—not so much about whether we will get to our destination as about how much of a fool I will make of myself before we get there.

We draw away slowly at first, and for a long time neither of us says a word. Finally, in desperation, I ask, "So are you from Viridian Deep as well?"

He shakes his head. "I'm from farther south, on a set of islands in the Rough. Fishing country."

I am surprised. Those are harsh waters, and the islands are small and sparsely inhabited. I didn't know there were any Water Sprites there. Why do his people live so far away from everyone?

"You're from the Deep?" he asks.

"I am. I think I was adopted very young, because I don't remember anything from before the adoption."

"What happened to your parents?"

"I don't know." I'm not sure yet how much I want to tell him. "Tell me about yourself, Tryn. How did you come to be with Glad Jack? He says you are a Water Sprite, but you don't really look it."

"I know." He looks away. "I am the halfling child of a Human father and a Fae mother. My mother was a slave. My father found her, fell in love with her, and stole her away from her keepers. He took her to the most isolated place he could find in an effort to keep her safe and made her his partner. He knew the people he stole her from would do anything to get her back—not because she was inherently valuable to them, but simply because she was their property. She rarely spoke of her previous existence; only said that my father was the one great love of her life. I was pretty young when she died, so I don't remember her well."

"I'm sorry. That must have been hard."

He shrugs. "Not so much. I never knew another life but the one I spent living on the islands."

I find myself leaning closer to him, caught up by the smooth sound of his voice. I lean away a bit when I realize this, but not much. "It was just you and your father, then? He didn't try to find your mother's people?"

He smiles a bit ruefully. "I think he'd gotten used to that life by then, and also I don't think he knew exactly where she had come from. Besides, as a Human, he could not have passed through the Fae wards anyway. I also think he was trying to protect me from those that might claim to own me, the child of a slave. So yes, it was just us. He taught me everything I know. He taught me how to live on and around the water. He taught me to fish and sail and survive. We were poor, but it was the life I knew, so I stayed on. I was happy enough."

"How did you find Glad Jack? Or did he come looking for his brother?"

"Jack isn't my uncle by blood, just by agreement. He and my father were friends and partners before my father met my mother, and the two stayed in touch over the years. When my father died, Jack asked if I wanted to come stay with him. He was worried about me living on my own and worried about my slave-birth background. Said he would be my uncle, if I liked, and I would be his nephew. I decided to try it. I'm still trying, I guess. I like Pressia and Jagged Reach well enough, but I'm not sure what I want to do next. City life can be hard to adjust to, with so many people around you all the time. And I have not yet found a crew I am comfortable joining. Jack was a pirate back in the day; he would have helped me become one, too, if I wanted. But I wasn't sure I did."

He looks over, those amazing eyes sharp and penetrating. "But you don't need to know all this. Let me show you something of how to handle this lady so you can stand in for me when needed."

He walks me through the mostly unfamiliar controls of this wondrous boat. I concentrate on everything he shows me, even when distracted by his eyes or smile or voice, as I genuinely want to learn. The little 520 is not close to the size of a ship of the line, or even a small working boat. It is a pleasure craft, with some extra capability that can be used for fishing and exploration. Many of the operational controls relate to the use of lights and pumps and engines, but little physical strength or ability is required once you know which levers to push and which knobs to turn. The sleek 520 practically sails herself once you understand what everything does.

We spend most of that first day in this fashion, and by nightfall I am able to sail the 520 on my own. I might not know everything yet, but I know enough to keep us safely afloat and out of trouble.

Tryn tells me we are five days from where we need to go, so I am happy to know I can be of use. He also tells me he has never been where we're going.

As you might imagine, I stare at him in disbelief. "You've never been there? But you're half Water Sprite! Even if your father never took you, you've never been tempted to try going there on your own?"

"Tempted, maybe, but I wouldn't even know how to begin to find my people."

"So then, how do you intend to get me there? Do you even know how to find it?"

He laughs. "I'm a sailor. I know how to get from one place to another, and I can read the charts that tell me where to go. And you know where we are going, right?"

I nod.

"Then I can use instruments that plot out our path. I've never been there, and you gave me a reason to go, so there's nothing to worry about."

Except that I immediately do. When someone tells me there is no need to worry, I always do.

My initial infatuation with Tryn also loses its edge after we have spent hours working on my sailing lessons. He is meticulous about his work, while I have a tendency to brush past things that don't seem to matter all that much. We go back and forth on how to best employ the ship's capabilities—he governed by experience and an attachment to ritual, and me more influenced by common sense and my instincts. So there is some heated give-and-take, but we do manage not to lose our tempers or engage in harsh words.

We also continue to exchange stories about our lives and worlds. I start out telling him very little, but as the day passes and I grow more comfortable in his presence, I begin to open up more. I tell him I am a Sylvan Fae who ran away a month before I turned fifteen. I have a loving family with whom I am close, but with whom I frequently differed. I tell him that I am the youngest, and I grew tired of everyone always telling me what to do. So I left to find my own way.

"At the age of fourteen?" he asks, surprised. "They let you do this?"

"I didn't ask for permission, or tell them I was going. I haven't even told them where I am. I haven't talked to them since I left. I wanted to be on my own."

"Which you now are?"

"Which I now am. Close to three years ago, I joined a band of pirates led by a man called the Silver Blade, and he has taught me everything I know."

He stares. "You seem very young for the pirate life."

"I've been told as much repeatedly. First by my family, and now by almost everyone else. It gets boring."

We are sailing farther out into the open waters of the Helles by now. The shoreline and the surrounding islands have disappeared behind us. The day is advancing, the sun moving steadily west. Neither of us speaks for a while. I can tell that Tryn is considering my situation and wondering what to say about it.

"So, the Silver Blade took you under his protective wing?" he asks at last.

"If you've heard of him, then you know his reputation. He takes care of his crew and his friends, and woe betide any slaver he encounters."

"I know very little about him—no more than a few rumors." Tryn pauses, as if considering something. "It's said he's a highly skilled bladesman. Is that right?"

"It is. He saved my life the day we met, not long after I had arrived in Jagged Reach, and invited me to join his crew. So I did."

"Few pirates take on a girl as young as you. He must care for you."

"He does. And I care for him."

I regret my choice of words instantly. I don't say I am in love with Brecklin or he with me, but the way I speak the words clearly suggests it.

Tryn, lifting an eyebrow, smiles. "You feel the same way about each other?"

I cringe, then shake my head. "I don't want to talk about it." Then, changing my mind abruptly, I say, "Well, I guess I don't really know."

"But you wish it were true?"

I bridle. "I said I don't want to talk about it."

Those lean, fine features brighten. "Very well. But if he is the right one for you—and you for him—then one day it will happen."

"You know this? From personal experience? Is there someone somewhere that you love?"

He shakes his head. "I'm just telling you what I believe. I've never met anyone to fall in love with. I'm not really close to anyone other than Jack."

"Well, you should have someone. Everyone should. You certainly could, given how . . ." *How beautiful you are*, I almost say. But I pull back, searching for better words. "Given how much you seem to understand about what it means."

He gives me a look, then laughs. "But I don't have your pretty eyes. Or your courage, either. I don't even have a family left to love me. I can have understanding and still not have the experience, Char."

He breaks off abruptly, reaches into the shelving of the helm next to where we stand, and withdraws an odd circular object with lines and numbers cut into its surface.

"Enough talk. Time to resume your lessons. Let's start with the sextant."

As we travel on, keeping our pace steady, I find myself revisiting my impressions of Tryn. I am not as smitten by him as I was at first, my adoration diminished by knowing that he thinks me young and naïve. He probably sees me as an ungrateful young girl who fled her perfectly good home to chase a life of adventure. It is all there in the way he questions me, and even in how he looks at me.

To him, I am a child.

But then, how am I looking at him? What was my first impression? That he was beautiful, and I was immediately smitten. I still find him uncomfortably attractive, although it is already clear that he has no particular interest in me beyond carrying out his duties as my travel guide and caretaker—and I am not even sure about this last. So how adult can I claim to be when what draws me to Tryn first and most strongly is how he looks?

Admittedly, he is holding back a lot of himself, just as I am. But what have I done to encourage him to reveal his secrets? What sort of reassurance have I given him that I am adult enough to be trusted with whatever secrets as he keeps? Instead, I have revealed all too much about my own selfish behavior. I have revealed my infatuation with a pirate captain who may have no real interest in me, and I have demonstrated my tendency to indulge in willful, self-serving acts.

Yet my *inish* responds to him in a positive way, and my instincts tell me he is right for me.

I am disgusted with myself and lapse into a disgruntled silence.

Our journey continues until almost nightfall, and then, after consulting his navigation charts, he turns us northeast. We travel for perhaps another hour until he spies a collection of small, heavily vegetated islands. By then it is nearly fully dark.

"We'll sleep there tonight," he abruptly announces as we anchor the boat just off the shoreline. "How do you feel about beaching it? We can make beds up on the sand and sleep under the stars. We won't get another chance to do so until we reach Viridian Deep."

Admittedly, I am attracted by the idea. The nighttime sky is perfectly clear, a trillion stars spread out across the sky above us, and the air is warm and welcoming. My thoughts of earlier are abandoned, and I nod my agreement eagerly.

We wade ashore carrying food, drink, and blankets, and find a comfortable place to rest on a beach that spreads away in both directions. We are out in the open—the sky and the stars and the ocean revealed in full—and all of it so wonderful to see. I am smiling in spite of myself, and Tryn is back to speaking to me in a friendly, open manner, so I am momentarily at peace.

We prepare and consume food and drink from our ample supplies. We don't talk much, and I keep most of my real secrets unrevealed. I don't say anything about my newly discovered Merrow heritage, nor anything about who my family members in Viridian Deep really are. Nor much of anything about my past. I am more interested in hearing something more about him. But he doesn't want to talk about personal stuff, either, so mostly we just talk about the weather.

The air is warm enough that soon we grow drowsy, and after a final draft of ale we stretch out not too far from each other and drift off to sleep.

IT IS STILL NIGHTTIME WHEN I NEXT WAKE, BROUGHT OUT OF SLEEP by my instincts whispering that something is wrong. I don't even realize why at first, but as I sit up warily, I can feel them continuing to nudge at me.

Look around!

I do so. Tryn lies next to me, sound asleep, his breathing deep and even, his body rolled onto its side. I scan the beach. I see nothing that wasn't there before. I glance at the sky and the stars and discover nothing unusual.

What is going on?

Then I look out over the ocean and realize that the boat is gone.

TEN

AT FIRST, I CANNOT BELIEVE WHAT I AM SEEING. OR NOT SEEing. I must be wrong. A craft like ours doesn't just disappear from a deserted island. But there is no mistaking it. The 520 is gone.

This puts such a serious crimp in my plans to reach Viridian Deep that for a moment I panic. To be stuck out here in the middle of nowhere, marooned on a deserted island, is a problem I do not need.

But I can't afford to lose control, so I rein myself in and ask my *inish* to help me find what I seek.

And this time I see what I am looking for—though I almost miss it because the 520 is so far out in the ocean from where she was anchored that she is little more than a dot. How she got there is a mystery—perhaps a slipped holding knot or a broken anchor chain, or something worse? At least she hasn't disappeared entirely. I feel a rush of gratitude and relief for that.

Then I realize I am going to have to bring her back. I can't just leave her out there, slowly drifting away. Eventually, the tides will take her entirely out of sight, and she will be lost.

In that moment, I don't think. I just act.

Without bothering to reflect on what I am doing, I start to strip off my overclothes. I keep on my underwear, but cast away every-thing else. I have to retrieve the 520. I have to. It has to be me be-cause I have the best chance of reaching her. Tryn might be a good swimmer, but he's not as good as me. Even if he can access his Water Sprite powers—which seems unlikely, given his lack of gills—I am Merrow-born. I have the ability to shut down my lungs and produce my gills—at least in theory. So now is a good time to discover if I can make the transition once more. I've gone both ways—from Fae to Merrow and back. Can I do it at least once more?

Not bothering to wake Tryn, I rush into the ocean. I am in the water so fast that the shock of its chill barely registers. I am swim-ming hard, stroking and kicking, pulling myself through the ocean, glancing up occasionally to be certain I am traveling in the right direction.

For the first few minutes, I seem to be getting nowhere.

But when I submerge, everything changes. My vision blackens, and I feel my lungs shut down. My entire body is changing in a way I recognize. I feel my legs swelling, tearing apart my underclothes, then fusing into my powerful Merrow tail. Gills erupt once more, and I am back to being a creature of the seas. And I am so grateful that my body seems to have learned to adapt without bringing me to the brink of death that I want to shout with joy.

In seconds I am tearing through the ocean waters, a being of im-mense power and ability, swiftly closing the distance between my-self and the 520.

A fresh joy floods through me. I am Merrow once more, Merrow through and through, and rather than feeling strange and unfamil-iar, it feels like coming home.

In short order, I have caught up to the 520. Curious to discover what caused it to drift away, I circle the hull underwater and note that though the anchor line trails the boat, it is attached to nothing at all. I haul it up and examine the end, which has been sliced neatly away.

A chill runs through me. Who or what could have done this?

I bundle up the line and toss it aboard as best I can. Then, instinctually, I flip my tail and propel my body into a flying leap—an actual leap, out of the water!—and am aboard the boat and lying on the smooth decking, gasping for air.

Air that I am immediately able to inhale and exhale as my Merrow form dissolves and my Fae one returns. Gone are the gills and the fins and the scales and the massive tail. I lie half naked and shivering, breathing hard from my efforts, struggling to regain my strength. But within moments, my body re-forms and I am pulling myself to my feet and making my way toward the controls to fire up the engines. I quickly turn the 520 back toward the island where she had been previously anchored.

It takes me only moments to reach my destination, and then I am back in the water with the anchor line in hand and Merrow once more. I swim around the area for a bit until I locate the anchor, which still has a stub of rope attached. I free that, secure the rope back to the anchor, and swim toward the shore.

I am curious to see if Tryn woke from his sleep when I darted off. I beach myself in the shallow waters, and the moment my gills leave the water, I am Fae once more. And again naked from the waist down.

But at least my discarded clothing is still lying where I left it in the sand.

A familiar voice says, "I am trying not to look, but it would make things easier if you put your pants back on."

I am embarrassed, but I find myself smiling as well. I pull on my clothing and walk over to sit beside Tryn. We don't say anything for a moment. It is still darkest night, long before the dawn's coming.

"The anchor line was cut," I say finally.

He nods. "My fault. I should have used the chain instead of the rope. Razorbills and some types of rock crab can climb right up the lines and sever them. No one knows why they do it."

I feel a wave of relief at this mundane explanation. "There wasn't time for me to wake you."

"No apologies, please. You did a good job of it on your own. A much better job than I could have, given your abilities." He pauses for a moment. "I saw you when you came up on shore, you know."

I nod. "I thought you might have. As you have probably guessed, I'm half Merrow."

"Is there anything else you've been keeping to yourself? Maybe it's best if I know now."

"Maybe. Would you be willing to do the same?"

A long pause. "You go first. You might be Fae-born, but you're a halfling, nevertheless. Like me. Isn't that strange? The two of us, thrown together?"

I smile in spite of myself. "In truth, I only just found out about my Merrow side a few months ago. Until then, I thought I was simply a Forest Sylvan."

Then I begin to tell him my story. I have decided that it is best to tell him everything. Well, almost everything, starting with my journey to Jagged Reach. I end with a description of getting captured while trying to save Brecklin and being thrown into the seas chained to an iron rack in a crude attempt at interrogation, and how that led to my transformation and introduction to the Merrow.

"I've heard of the Merrow, but it's always seemed to be more fable than truth. I've never met one."

"Before now," I correct.

"And you never suspected what you were?"

I shake my head. "I guess I never had any reason to. I was never around water all that much. Or at least not deep water, like in the oceans. I think something happened to me when I was close to drowning—an automatic response to the threat I was facing. And that enabled me to make the change."

I pause, leaning closer to him. "And what I just discovered tonight, when I went after the boat, is that now I can change back and forth whenever I want. I transformed into a Merrow once I dove underwater, then turned back into a Fae once I jumped into the boat. And again when I went down to find the anchor, then came back to shore."

"So you can now control the change? Fates of the Fae, what does *that* feel like?"

I don't know how to explain it. "Different from what I would have thought. I am still getting used to the idea. Going out after the boat was the first time I made the change easily, without needing to be on the brink of death. Honestly, I didn't know if I could do it, but something told me that it was possible, so I just decided to try. Anyway, I had to do something, or our boat would have been lost. Then we would have been trapped here. Which reminds me . . . I tied the rope back to the anchor, so won't those creatures just cut it again?"

He walks me through chaining the anchor, while I flip from boat to water, from Fae to Merrow, and back. And each time he watches the changes with an intent fascination. When I am finally back on shore, reclothed and Fae once more, he studies me carefully. "Let me see your hands."

I hold them out to him, and he examines each one carefully. "There," he says, holding up one hand and spreading my fingers. "Webbing." He points. "Here and here."

I smile. "I hadn't noticed."

He releases my hand, looking slightly embarrassed. "I must admit, you fascinate me, Char."

Somehow, I manage to keep my voice steady. "Thank you."

I can't help wondering if his fascination is mostly because I can tap into both sides of my nature in a way I suspect he cannot. I rush on before the moment gets any more awkward than it already is.

"Now let me ask you a question. You don't look like any Water Sprite I have ever known; they are usually blue-skinned, and have both gills and some scales. Can you breathe in the water like other Sprites? How did you find out what you were? Or were you told?"

"I guess I have always known, thanks to my dad." He clasps his arms around his knees, gazing out toward the ocean. "Given where I grew up, I'd never really met any Water Sprites other than my mom, and she died before she could teach me too much. I never really learned to swim well, and I have certainly never had either gills or scales. As for my skin, my dad's was quite a dark brown and hers was a fairly dark blue, so maybe it's that mixture that colored me as I am—almost pure black. Neither of my parents knew quite what to make of me. But it sounds like you know more about Water Sprites than I do. How many have you met?"

I tell him about Zedlin and Florin, and the times I have spent with them, and he seems fascinated, hanging on my every word.

Finally, I lie back, stretch out, and close my eyes. "I'm going to try to sleep until morning," I announce. "That swim wore me out."

Tryn doesn't respond, but I sense him stretching out beside me. Long minutes go by, and still he doesn't say anything. I start to nod off, and see no reason to resist it.

In moments, I am asleep.

I AM AWAKE BEFORE SUNRISE, BUT NOT BY MUCH. TRYN IS ALREADY moving about, restoring our gear to the bins of the 520, checking out the hull, decking, and masts, and testing the controls. The tides are out, so the water is shallow where the boat sits. He is not hurrying in his efforts to complete the repacking, and he does everything in relative silence. I watch him from where I am lying on the sands, wondering once again how I feel about him. On the one hand, he knows what he is doing as a guide and hasn't done anything to make me feel inadequate or troublesome. On the other hand, there is still a reticence to him that makes him feel vaguely standoffish. I can't explain why or in what particular way he makes me feel so, but it is definitely there.

I give myself a few further moments to wake and cast off my blanket, pull on my boots, then climb to my feet to help him. He greets me with a smile and a wave, then carries on. We work side by side until everything is in place, pause to eat a quick breakfast, and then we are off once more.

The seas are quiet this morning, the winds almost nonexistent, and the skies clear of clouds. It is a perfect day, and while Tryn steers our craft, I sit on the bin seats and gaze out at the water, wondering how my journey will end. I am still anxious about seeing my family. I think I have to; I think I owe it to them. I remain concerned about the reception I will receive after I'd abandoned them without a word, but I can't let that stop me. They will likely be furious, and I cannot fault them if they are. For me to disappear as I had and never once attempted to contact them must have caused a serious amount of worry—not to mention pain. To act in this self-serving a manner was wrong, and I know that now.

But I think that the discovery of my dual identity will help ease some of the awkwardness of our reunion—if only because it provides startling new information that I am sure none of us expected.

We sail all that day and the next. We are in deep open waters the entire time, and there are no places to stop. We see a few other vessels at a distance, but Tryn recognizes none of them and we stay clear. Late on the second day, we pass a cluster of small, uninhabited islands. No one occupies most of these bumps and atolls, which have a barren look, but I can't help wondering if it is someplace like this that Tryn's father settled, after he had freed his wife.

He hasn't said anything more about his background since we met, and I don't feel comfortable prying.

But on the third day, when the winds have begun to demand our combined attention, I ask him anyway.

"Your mother," I say. "She was a slave when your father found her?"

He gives me a look. "She was."

"I was just wondering what happened to her. You said she died, but you didn't say how it happened." I see his expression tighten, and I hold up my hands. "You don't have to answer if you don't want to. I would just . . . like to know about her."

"Why?"

A single word, and I am instantly uncomfortable. Why, indeed? "Because I am interested in your story. When we passed those islands yesterday, I kept wondering if it was somewhere like that you grew up. And . . ." I shrug. "I guess I feel like we have something in common. We're both halflings, and we both lost our mothers. Admittedly, mine was my adoptive mother, but I am still coming to terms with what losing Ancrow cost me and how badly abandoned it made me feel. Am I making any sense, or am I just rambling?"

Tryn grins faintly. "I think that's just part of who you are. And it's fine, your question. My mother went swimming and never came back. My father and our neighbors and friends searched for her everywhere, but they never found anything. She just disappeared into the ocean, and they all concluded she must have encountered something that was stronger than she was. Or perhaps she was struck by a boat. My father believed her years of slavery had weakened her enough that rough waters overcame her. I think he might have been right."

"Maybe she was recaptured by her owners and enslaved again."

"I don't think so. We were far enough away from where she had met my father that finding her would have been difficult. Did I tell you about that? She found him washed up on a beach after his ship was wrecked and hid him away, visiting him in secret until he had healed. That was how they fell in love. She hid him from the slavers, and he rewarded her by taking her away from them. Good story, right?"

"But is it a true story?"

"I saw how they behaved toward each other. They were very much in love. Even as small as I was, I remember that."

"I understand," I whisper. The winds are beginning to whip harder at us, and the waves grow higher. "It is probably best to trust your memories, and not try to read something into them that isn't there. That's my problem. I keep trying to make up stories about things I don't understand, and mostly they are wrong."

Tryn laughs softly. "I think you're feeding the wrong demon, Char. You have strong feelings and the sort of determination that backs them up. We could all use more of that. I know I could. I spend too much time doubting myself."

I smile back. "It doesn't seem that way to me. You always seem completely in control. Then again, maybe how we see ourselves is always suspect."

"Learning to trust yourself is the hardest lesson of all—mostly because we almost always tend to doubt ourselves." He claps me on the shoulder. "If it makes you feel any better, I believe in you!"

I don't know why he says this, but it does make me feel better. And I find myself smiling as we fight the winds.

We sail into our fifth day—the day Tryn has promised we will arrive on the shores of Viridian Deep. And indeed, our course soon curves toward the shore, with land once more in sight. I feel both excitement and trepidation about finally coming home, but I force my thoughts elsewhere, studying the waters we are passing through.

I am not sure I have done the right thing by returning, but the joy I feel on being near my homeland once more outweighs all my dark expectations.

"Where to?" Tryn asks me.

I make a sweeping gesture toward the shore. "Anywhere will do. Find a place you like!"

He grins and sets his course, laying the mainsail out so that it catches the shorebound winds and arcs toward a mix of mountains and grasslands, forests and rivers—all of it a part of a life I suddenly decide I very much want back again.

Which is when I catch sight of a much larger ship bearing down on us. Its insignia, boldly displayed on both flag and forward bow, is that of the Faraway Trades Company.

ELEVEN

TRYN SEES THE SHIP WHEN I DO, AND REACHES OVER TO NUDGE my arm. "Trouble."

I recognize the vessel right away—or at least its insignia, because this particular type of craft is new to me. It is not a full-sized warship with rams and weapons everywhere, but smaller, sleeker, and recognizably swifter, built for speed and not for firepower. But still designed for capturing vessels and selling on their crew.

I feel a shivering in my *inish*. The 520 is fast, but the Faraway ship is faster.

I have no idea what it is doing out here, just outside the Fae territorial boundaries. I cannot see who is manning her, but I have to assume her crew comprises Goblins. Ancient wards keep Humans outside our waters, but Goblins are another type of Fae and can enter Viridian Deep anytime they wish. What brings them toward us just now, however, is a mystery.

They approach deliberately, though there is nothing to indicate this is anything more than bad luck. Yet.

Tryn slows the 520 to let them approach unchallenged, his eyes studying the Faraway craft carefully. I say nothing, but I am already making an escape plan just in case matters deteriorate further. Maybe this is not what it seems. Maybe it has nothing to do with us in particular.

But I don't ever believe in trusting solely to luck.

The Ministry ship pulls alongside us, and a pair of Goblins thump out of a hatchway and onto its exposed decking. Because Goblins are so large, they are unsteady aboard their boats and must cling tightly to safety rails and stanchions for support.

"Throw down your weapons!" one of the Goblin pair demands, speaking in the common tongue of Jagged Reach.

"We don't have any weapons," Tryn replies.

"Then prepare to let us board and conduct a search!"

Tryn shakes his head. "Boarding denied. You have no rights in these waters—especially since your insignia identifies you as the ship of a private company. You have no authority to invade Fae vessels, so back away."

His speech is bold and firmly delivered, but he has nothing to back it up and the Goblins actually laugh. "We have weapons enough to sink you where you float. If you refuse boarding, we will do just that."

My attention is drawn to the way Tryn's hands are moving over the 520's controls. He is definitely doing something, but I cannot tell what it is.

"What is it you want from us?" I demand, thinking I might be able to help by distracting the Goblins from whatever Tryn is doing.

The Goblin looks at me. "You would be wise to stay quiet, little twitch. This business is between me and your companion."

I have to mask my astonishment. I had assumed this was about me, but Tryn? What secrets has he still been hiding?

Tryn quickly jumps in, his voice calm, his tone reasonable. "What is it you think we have aboard?"

"Contraband, of course!" The Goblin's voice turns nasty now. "We know that boat, and we'll be searching both of you, as well as your craft."

Tryn shakes his head. "There is nothing aboard but the two of us and our supplies. There is no contraband of any sort."

"We will be the judge of that!"

"Again, you have no authority in these waters, and boarding under pressure is piracy. Now back away and let us be."

The Goblin growls—as only Goblins can. "We'll give you ten seconds more to do what we say, and then we will sink your vessel. Don't think we won't."

His harsh, guttural voice makes the threat plain enough. I look at Tryn. To my shock, he gives me a cheerful wink.

"Edge out a boarding plank, then," he shouts over at the Goblins.

The Goblins whisper to each other. "We don't cross using planks," one replies. "You'll have to let us lash you."

"Use ropes then, and swing over!" Tryn is clearly having nothing to do with being lashed together like a large sea creature. "Unless you think it is too much for you? It does require strength and a bit of agility."

The Goblins exchange a look. Both are clearly insulted by the insinuation. "Hold your boat steady, then!"

"Aye," Tryn agrees. Then he says, so softly that only I can hear, "Grab the panel railing and hold on tight."

What happens next is entirely unexpected. Just as one of the Goblins is swinging aboard, Tryn ignites the accelerators, and the entire boat roars to life with fresh power. In a mixed burst of fire and water, the 520 leaps away with such velocity that the Goblin trying to board loses his balance and grip on the swing line and tumbles into the water. I am now hanging on to the railing of our craft for dear life. The 520 is every bit as fast as Glad Jack had promised, and by the time our pursuers are able to retrieve the unfortunate Goblin, we are almost out of sight.

Then Tryn works the controls with quick, sure movements, and the 520 gains *more* speed. We are literally flying through the wave caps, barely touching the waters of Roughlin Wake. But even that doesn't satisfy Tryn. Within minutes, he engages additional engines that lower the mast and sails and lock everything down, and we take on the shape of a missile. We fly like an arrow, straight and true; I cannot believe we are going so fast. Our speed is astounding, and in spite of the brief, sudden rush of fear I experience as I imagine losing control and flipping upside down, I whoop with undisguised joy.

Then I turn and grin over at Tryn. "You knew she could go this fast, didn't you?"

He shakes his head. "I've never tried it before. But Glad Jack always claimed she was fast. 'Not much out here that can catch her,' he's told me. 'You just give her power and hold on. And be careful not to lose control. Too much power or too little control and she can flip and sink. Don't want that!'"

I understand. "He's used her to run contraband?"

"It's how he's earned his living. 'You can shake the old pirate free of the salt,' the saying goes, 'but you can't shake the salt out of the pirate.' He never could just give up the old life. So he still keeps a hand in when it suits him. Says it keeps him from boredom."

I laugh, and we speed on. I lean back to where the wind can catch me in the face and I take it all in, trying to remember if this is what it felt like when Auris and I were flown into the Skyscrape by the Aerklings a few years back.

I don't think so. I don't think anything living can fly like the 520.

If I have the chance, I decide, I will ask Tryn to take Auris and the others in my family out for a ride and let them experience it for themselves. A small forgive-me treat from their wayward sister.

A big *if*, though, considering I am still not sure what my reception will be. I can't be sure they will even be willing to talk to me.

Really, when it comes to meeting up with them again, I cannot be sure of anything.

———

WE SPEED ALONG FOR ABOUT HALF AN HOUR BEFORE TRYN SLOWS
the boat down again. By then, we are well up the north coast and
closing in on the beginnings of the shorelands that abut the valleys
of Viridian Deep. Even after three years away, I still recognize the
territory immediately, and find myself embracing the tastes, smells,
and look of my homeland. And as Tryn pilots our craft to a smooth
ocean landing, I take note of everything I know.

There, still far ahead, are the massive peaks of the Skyscrape
Mountains with the hidden kingdoms of the Dragons and Aerklings. Closer in, the lesser presence of Spawn Ridge recalls tales of
the Demon Wars from not quite fifty years back. Closer still lies the
panoramic spread of Cressidon Woods, home to and haunt of the
darkest and strangest of all the magical creatures that inhabit
the Fae world. Along the coast, I can spy the morass of Strewlin
Swamp, with its seemingly endless stretches of bogs and wild
grasses. And somewhat farther on than that, the homes of the
Water Sprites await.

I find myself wondering what Tryn—who has never met a Water
Sprite save for his mother—will think of them, once we meet some.
I don't think we will be able to avoid an encounter of some sort.

We continue on our course, our craft moving smoothly and
steadily toward wherever it is that Tryn has decided to land us. I
don't ask, and it doesn't matter. This land is my home, and strangely
welcome—even with the uncertainties that lie ahead nudging the
back of my mind.

We advance at a slow but steady pace toward the shore, still
traveling in deep waters, as the day stretches toward midafternoon.

Neither of us says much of anything. Tryn indicates at one point
that we need to stay under sail power until we can obtain more fuel,
as our reserves are low from our burst of speed. And I try not to
think about what awaits me.

Like Auris before me, I need to go in search of my family—my
birth family, the one I never knew. What will I discover? Maybe
nothing, at this point. Maybe it has been too long.

I am reflecting on all this when Tryn suddenly turns our boat sharply left toward the shore, his brow crinkled.

"Red flags ahead. Something dangerous is out there, and I don't know what it is."

I see now what he's talking about. Buoys sporting bright-red warning flags float in the waters toward which we are sailing. Tryn is trying to skirt their perimeter, but without the engines engaged, we must rely on our sails, the winds, and the ocean currents to steer us right. I cast about for some indication of what the flags are signaling but cannot find anything save the relatively calm surface of the ocean.

"What is it?" I ask, my hands unconsciously gripping the control panel railing for additional support. "Do you see anything?"

Tryn shakes his head. He has steered us out of the red flags and put us back in safe water, but we remain uncertain about what we are being warned against. Still, Tryn puts a finger to his lips as he turns to me. *Quiet now,* he mouths. I don't mistake the worry in his gesture. There is a hint of fear reflected in his expression. I feel a decided nudging from my *inish*. Red flags are a universal sign from Water Sprites that something dangerous is at hand.

I can't see it, but I can feel it. Something is approaching.

I peer down into the darkness of the waters, and suddenly it looks like the entire ocean floor is rising toward the surface. Then I see its movements expanding as pieces of it begin to twist and turn, and the released chunk of seabed assumes a life of its own.

"Tryn . . ." I begin.

But before I can finish, the entire world erupts in a maelstrom of water, rocks, and sea life. Huge waves rise up, and the bulk of something massive collides with the 520. For a fraction of a second, I am certain the world is coming to an end. Then I am tossed from the boat. I see Tryn thrown clear as well, though in a different direction, and our vessel is upended as if it were nothing more than a child's toy.

I finally get a clear glimpse of what has caused all this, and I am instantly terrified.

A monster has woken.

Admittedly, it is hard to miss. It has a massive body with multiple, gigantic, twisting tentacles, and a tail that thrashes against the waters in fury. For just an instant I see its maw opening beneath me—an ocean-filled well of darkness within a hooked beak from which nothing is likely to emerge once swallowed. I can see the ruins of several ships caught in its throat as a tongue lashes out at me and only barely misses.

I don't have to wonder what it is, even though I have never seen one before. I have heard this beast described many times during my years on Jagged Reach, and always in tones of abject horror.

It is a Kraken.

I regain my senses out of desperation and instinct, and twist my body so that it falls beyond the immediate reach of that horrid mouth, entering the waters of Roughlin Wake amid chunks of seabed and floundering fish. I strike the waters and feel myself changing instantly—my clothing ripping away as my powerful tail takes form and my body elongates into its familiar nine-foot length.

I have no idea what has happened to Tryn or the boat. Both have disappeared. I can only hope that Tryn's Water Sprite heritage will somehow save him.

The ocean about me is churned into a frenzy as the Kraken thrashes about, creating currents too powerful for me to withstand, even in my Merrow body. So I let the surges carry me clear, using my tail to guide my passage away. What I would do if attacked directly, I have no idea. I am in shock from what has just happened and in no way ready to protect myself were the Kraken to come for me.

I wonder again about Tryn. I cannot just leave him to his fate. I cannot abandon him.

I swim as far into the maelstrom as I can manage and set up a search pattern through the debris and destruction. The Kraken is still flailing, and I can barely tell if I am up or down, horizontal or vertical, sideways or inside out. I sweep the area, identify everything I can make out, and still I cannot find Tryn.

For a few horrible seconds, I am afraid the creature has swallowed my guide and protector. I swim faster, more furiously. I can't have lost him. It isn't right; it isn't fair. I am furious with myself, with the injustice of it, and with my inability to change what has happened.

Tryn!

But then I realize there is a better way to go about this. Gathering my *inish*, I search for him, and it takes only moments before I see him. He is floating not far below the surface a dozen yards off, his body limp and unmoving. But he is safely away from the Kraken, which is finally sinking back toward the ocean floor, its fury spent. Still, I must swim above it to reach Tryn—an act that has every possibility of attracting the creature's attention once more. But I clamp down on my fears, tighten my resolve, and remind myself of who I am and what I have become. I am Ancrow's child by adoption and a Merrow by birth, and I have the strength to do what is needed.

In what feels like no time at all, I am over the creature and past it and have Tryn safely in hand. He is unconscious and not breathing. But to my delight, I discover that part of his Water Sprite heritage has finally surfaced. On both sides of his neck, small gill slits have opened and are rippling. He is breathing water, just like me!

Quickly I look about for any sign of land—the 520 is lost—but find nothing save a stretch of shoreline that is at least several miles off.

There is nothing for it but to swim if I am to save us both.

I set out with one arm wrapped about Tryn's chest and shoulder hauling him behind me through the water, my other arm stretched out behind me to help with balance and direction, and my endlessly powerful tail working to provide propulsion. I am able to do this, I tell myself, over and over. I am a Merrow; the sea is my domain. I can do what is required.

But after almost an hour, during which I am certain that I am making great progress, my destination seems no closer.

I pause and see Tryn looking at me. I sense he is urging me to slow down, to pace myself better. I wish I could reassure him, tell him I will do whatever is needed. That I will see him safely to land. But it is impossible to speak underwater, and he is still only half conscious anyway.

Nonetheless, I feel his doubts. He is bigger and heavier than I am, and seemingly unable to help me. He knows I must be weakening. I glance at him, and once more—maddening as it is—I am momentarily stricken by the beauty of his face. I admire the glistening ebony tones of his dark wet skin; I wonder at his perfect features and lithe form. I love how he looks, but I love, too, that he seems so much more than that to me—that he seems almost magical in some immeasurable way.

Before I can think better of it, I lean in and kiss his cheek. I don't know what possesses me. It is an impulsive act, but I don't regret it. In fact, it feeds a sudden, desperate need I have to be closer to him. His skin feels soft. He tastes good.

I kiss him again before I resume swimming.

TWELVE

AT SOME POINT DURING MY SEEMINGLY ENDLESS SWIM, WITH Tryn gripped under one arm and my other arm and fish tail working as hard as they can to pull both of us through the waters of Roughlin Wake, I wonder how I am ever going to make shore. We are a long way out, much farther out than I have ever swum, save for the time I visited the underwater grottoes with Winnis and Douse. I have maintained my Merrow form, but already I am beginning to tire.

I lose track of time quickly. Where I am no longer seems to matter. How I move through the water becomes an unending repetition. What I am trying to do narrows down to a single goal: reach the faraway shore with Tryn still in my arms. I am largely unaware of everything else—only marginally conscious and swimming out of habit by the end. Or at least I have to assume something of this nature is what happens, because when I finally wash up on shore and return to my Fae form, my unconscious charge gripped close against my body, I just lie there trying to think through what it is that just happened.

For a moment, I cannot make myself move. I feel such relief and gratitude at being safe again that I am persuaded it is all right to allow myself to rest. The swim was long and hard, but evidently I was able to do it. I glance over to where Tryn's dark face rests against my shoulder.

Once again, I am relieved to see that his gill slits have tightened down and nearly disappeared. His lungs are working again. Like mine, his body seems to be able to transform automatically in response to his surroundings. Though he seems to be still unconscious, I am able to detect his breathing both from the feel of his breath against my skin and the movement of his chest against my arm where it grips him.

Eventually, I gather myself and scoot away, then rise to my feet and pull him ashore. Then I sit there beside him, thinking of how I had kissed him for no better reason than that the urge was there and I gave in to it. Yes, it was for reassurance when I was struggling so hard, but it was mostly because I was eager to know how it would feel. I wanted that kiss, so I took it. I'd kissed boys and men before, but it had never felt particularly special.

But Tryn?

I guess I am not sure. Kissing him was different, but I am having trouble defining how. There was definitely something special there, but exactly what that specialness was escapes me. I think back to the moment when I first saw him, how struck I was by his beauty. But that feeling ebbed somewhat as he became more than just a face—as he became both guide and shipmate, more of a companion. Yet there in the water, I experienced a deep attraction that demanded a response. So I kissed him. Twice.

Fates of Fae, I think. *What is wrong with me?*

Next to me, Tryn gasps sharply and rolls over. He lies on his stomach, as if embracing the solid earth, then looks up at me.

"How are you feeling?" I ask, my hand reaching for his shoulder and giving it a squeeze. "You've been through a lot."

"So have you. That's why I'm still alive."

"We lost the 520."

"We couldn't help it. That was a big fish."

"It was a Kraken."

"Ah." He seems bemused. "So I guess my father was right all along."

I stare at him. *Right about what?* But it does not feel like the correct time to ask.

"How do you feel now?" I ask instead.

He rolls over on his back and looks at me. "Fine. Bit of a headache. I think I got a boat to the head in all that chaos. You?"

I shrug. "Kind of tired."

"You kissed me."

Drat! I force a smile. "You wish. You must have been hallucinating."

He gives me a long stare. "I don't remember hallucinating. But I do remember the kiss."

I shrug. "I was bumping up against your face a lot. Maybe it just seemed like a kiss."

"Maybe," he agrees. "But you saved my life. I would have drowned, if not for you."

I find myself grinning. "No, you wouldn't have. Your gills came out; did you know that? I swam you all the way back underwater."

He looks amazed, putting a hand to his now gill-less neck. "They did?"

I nod. "They vanished again when I got you back on land, but you're a Water Sprite for sure."

He laughs delightedly. "And you're pretty strong for someone your size. You should start wearing pants, though."

Oh!

Sure enough, I do seem to keep forgetting about this sideline to my transformation. I cringe, then take my shirt and pull it down over my hips as far as I can.

"This is the second time I've caught you with your pants down." He laughs. "It's getting to be a habit."

"Couldn't be helped if I was going to get us both back to shore."

"I'm not complaining. Not at all." His eyes survey me boldly.

"Hey, stop staring!"

His grin broadens, but he looks away. "It's pretty hard not to look at you, you know."

Now I blush, and I am furious with myself. But at least he can't see it, turned away as he is.

"In fact," he adds, still without looking at me, "I am amazed by you. How did you manage to carry me all the way to shore? You are so small."

"In my Fae form, yes. But as a Merrow, I am much larger and stronger. Lucky for you."

"I appreciate that more than I can say. You have my deepest respect and gratitude, Char."

I blush anew, and nod. "Though I wish I hadn't gotten you into this mess."

He keeps his eyes averted, even now. "None of this is your fault. I offered to take you to Viridian Deep, and I don't regret it, even with the 520 at the bottom of the ocean. Just having a chance to meet you and know something about you is worth everything that's happened."

I doubt it, I think, but give him a smile anyway. "So what did you mean about the Krakens, and your father being right?"

He shrugs. "When I was young, after my mother died, I wanted to go swimming around the reefs, but my father wouldn't let me. He told me there were Krakens out there, hunting for boys my size. My mother hadn't managed to teach me much about my Water Sprite side before she died, so I figured he was just protecting me. I was certain he knew I could not transform, so he had made up the Kraken story as an excuse to keep me safe and on land. I did what he told me and stayed out of the water, and I never really did learn how to swim. But now it seems that, maybe, he was telling the truth all along."

He sits up, strips off his tunic, and hands it to me without looking. "Here, use this to cover yourself. Best I can do for now."

I take the tunic, which fortunately is long enough to cover me like a dress.

"That will do," he says, his lean, dark body as beautiful as his face as he looks at me openly now. I look back at him just as boldly, entranced by the glow of his ebony chest and limbs. Right away, I feel an urge to start kissing him again. Whatever it is about him that attracts me, it hasn't lost its luster.

"We have to find help," he tells me. "Do you know where we are?"

"I do. We're not more than a day's march from Water Sprite country. Are you okay to walk?"

"I think I can manage," he says. "So will I really get to meet other Water Sprites?"

He looks ridiculously eager at the prospect, and I laugh. "I'll make sure of it."

"But what about you? I'm not the one who swam two people to shore."

"I'm fine. If you're ready to go, so am I."

He grins. "I have the feeling that you are almost always ready. For anything."

I roll my eyes. "Stop saying things like that. I am just a little more determined than some others I could mention."

His grin widens. "You better not be talking about me."

I grin back at him and start walking.

WE TRAVEL ALL DAY, MOSTLY STICKING CLOSE TO THE SHORELINE. Our most difficult obstacle is Spawn Ridge—a huge and sprawling collection of cliffs that span the shoreline below Water Sprite country.

If I didn't know better, I would suggest swimming around it, but I was told by Florin early on that the waters below Spawn Ridge were far too dangerous for even the best swimmer. Riptides, rogue currents, predators, and jagged rocks fill those waters, so walking is all that is left.

It is a treacherous route. Our path alternates between rocky high ground and shoreline coves, and our passage is constantly damp, slippery, and water-soaked. We struggle often to avoid dangerous drops and slides, landfalls and precipices, as we pick our way forward. It is slow, demanding work, and it is nightfall by the time we are north of the ridge and back on even ground. By my estimation, it should be midday or so tomorrow before we reach our destination.

By sundown, we are thoroughly exhausted from our efforts, and sleep comes quickly. We manage to stay awake long enough to eat some berries and nuts we scavenge, but there is little else other than springwater to provide us with sustenance.

We are up early the next morning, the bright sun and our hungry stomachs waking us. The day is once again unclouded and warm as we set out. The path is easy, but our overall lack of energy and sustenance wears us down more quickly. We walk as steadily as we can, but we both feel the need to stop and rest more often than we would like.

"I don't know how much longer I can go on," I admit at one point when we are resting in a rare patch of shade.

Tryn shakes his head. "Complaining doesn't help."

"It helps *me*!" I snap.

He gives me a look. "You sound like a child—and I know you are anything but. Do you have any idea how tough you are?"

"I'm not all that tough."

"Nonsense. You are tough clear through. You are so tough you make me feel completely inadequate. I don't know how you do it."

I am glad he sees me this way, but I am not sure I want him to feel that way about me.

"Honestly," I admit, "I don't think of myself as being very good at much of anything. In my family, I was the one who was always doing the wrong thing, making the wrong choices, finding ways to get myself in trouble. I suppose I'm still like that a lot of the time. But I also like to think I am a kind and caring person."

He shrugs. "I didn't say you weren't, Char. I just told you how I see you. It's supposed to be a compliment."

"Then thank you," I say. "But you might change your mind once you get to know me better."

He stares, trying to figure me out. "I might. There's still some time left for that, isn't there?"

I don't know. I suppose there is. When we get to the homeland of the Water Sprites, what happens then? I have to go to the Sylvan lands and the orphanage and speak to anyone who might have been there when I arrived and might remember something about me. Will Tryn want to accompany me? Do I even want him there when I discover the truth about myself? Or will it be better if he remains behind with his people—whom he has never met—and leaves me to make my discoveries alone?

"I suppose," I say. Then I rise and start off again. "We'd better keep moving."

So we do, and the day moves past noon and into afternoon and still we are trudging along with no sign of anyone or anything ahead of us. I grow steadily more dispirited, wondering if we will ever reach any sort of community. I know rationally that the villages of the Water Sprites are out there, as I have visited them on numerous occasions to see Florin. It was Auris's connection to Zedlin that led me to his sister, and it was always the most important of the relationships I formed outside the family. Florin and I were very much the same—wild, independent, self-confident, and always on the lookout for some new way to test ourselves. We were never afraid—or perhaps *seldom* is a better word to use—so we dared each other at every turn and stood up for each other when needed.

She was the one who saw me safely to Jagged Reach once I determined to leave home. She was the one who cautioned me—so unlike her normally—of the dangers, of the nature of the men and women I was likely to meet, of the risks I would be taking and the traps into which I might fall. She offered to stay with me, but I knew I needed to do this on my own. So she had left me, and I have spent the last three years discovering more of life than I did during the first fifteen. Not all of it was good; some of it was debasing and demeaning. But nothing was so terrible or so traumatic that I couldn't recover from it, and I managed to make my way.

I wonder about her now—this closest of friends whom I have not seen since she left me behind and went home again. I thought she might come south to see me at some point, but she never did. I even thought her brother might come, but Zedlin stayed away as well.

I miss them terribly, but even so, I do not regret what I have done. I do not think for an instant I should have done something else.

I am content with who and what I am, and what I have experienced in life.

With Tryn a step ahead, always in the lead, I walk on to whatever waits.

THIRTEEN

By the time we encounter the first of the Water Sprites, the day has gone and night has arrived. Tryn and I are both struggling by now, and my awareness of the world has diminished to almost nothing.

We are in a heavily forested region that abuts the shores of Roughlin Wake, making our way along what appears to be a well-traveled pass, when we come upon a group of children playing hide-and-seek. One is creeping through the trees in search of the others when he comes upon us. He is clearly a Sprite, with traces of webbing between his fingers, tangles of hair, and scales down his arms and legs. Tryn has none of these attributes so far, but—much like Auris—I imagine he soon will, should he choose to stay here.

The boy stares at us for a moment, then vanishes as if he were nothing more than a momentary vision. Tryn and I stare after him and then at each other. We can't believe how fast he is.

We start calling, and a bunch of the game players appear to greet us—apparently relying on sheer numbers to protect them. When I mention Zedlin and Florin, cautious welcomes morph into a pro-longed explanation of their origins, their names, their village location, and their agreement to guide us in. We set off in a group, and before long are settled in a lean-to with fires burning and meals cooking and adults gathered to hear our tale.

I don't say much. I am exactly what I appear to be: a Forest Sylvan. For Tryn, things are a little more difficult. As my companion, he is granted admission. But no one, it is openly agreed, has ever seen anything like him—even though he has explained that he is, in part, a Water Sprite like themselves, but part Human as well, which gives him his immensely dark skin. As the discussion goes on, I concentrate on my meal and slowly feel my strength and concentration return, though I am still exhausted.

Conversation rises and falls and eventually comes to an end as we thank our Water Sprite friends and retire to our lean-to. We have been given blankets and fresh clothes for the morrow, but we simply toss the latter aside, lie down, and fall asleep so quickly I barely remember the lying-down part. I don't know about Tryn, but I sleep so hard that it is nearly noon before I wake again. I look around for my companion, but he is gone.

Yet someone even more important is there instead.

"Welcome home, wild girl."

Florin is sitting off to one side, cross-legged on a pad. She is wearing typical Water Sprite garb—a shift that barely covers a minimal portion of her cerulean skin, bangles and beads that drip off her in bright arrays of sun-colored light, and hand-stitched leather sandals. She looks much the same as when I left her, three years back—with two big exceptions.

First, her once bright eyes that used to be dancing with mischief now feel heavy and sad. In fact, her whole demeanor is oddly subdued. And second . . .

"You've shaved your head," I observe, forcing myself from beneath my blanket into a sitting position. I rub the sleep from my eyes and look closely at her. "Why did you do that?"

She shrugs. "Various reasons. I regret it a little, but it's done now."

Her hair used to be a thick mass of spiky black tresses that always looked enticingly damp even when they weren't. She had loved that hair.

"I'm afraid I've made a few other bad choices since we were last together. But then, you've probably done a little of that, too, down there in the Edge, with all those wild men. I bet you regret a few things you've done by now."

She says it in an almost pleading way, almost as if she hopes I have somehow outdone her.

"I've missed you," I tell her, trying to change the tone of the conversation. I rise and embrace her. "It's so good to see you again, Florin! I kept waiting for you to come back down south and visit me. I always thought you would, but you didn't."

Her smile is thin, subdued. "I had other things to do."

What has happened to my bright, brash friend in the years since I have been away?

I remember when we were younger and found such joy with each other. Then, we were inseparable, friends to the end. For most of my teenage years, I was closer to Florin than to my own family. To everyone else in the whole entire world. And it seemed like that would never change.

But it has, and we are different now. Perhaps it is simply the passage of time or our long physical separation, but there is a distance between us now. We are still friends. We still share memories of the years we spent with each other, two young girls against the world. But we are neither of us the same as we were.

"So, what have you done with yourself since living down south?" she wants to know, with an echo of her old spark. "Have you found someone to partner with? Maybe that amazingly beautiful black man you walked in with, whom you claim is some variety of Water Sprite? Is he your lover?"

Bold—and not a question I would have asked her. "No," I answer, "just a companion." I force a smile. I find myself oddly reluctant to share these sorts of intimacies with her. "I met someone else I care about, but I am not so sure he cared as much about me."

Her laugh is tinged with bitterness. "Oh, I know that feeling. I've had it myself." She runs her hands over her smooth-shaven head as if to find the tresses of her thick, lustrous hair grown back. "Tell me more about what's been happening to you. How have you managed to survive in such wild country?"

I do as she asks, but abruptly decide to tell her nothing of my discoveries about my Merrow half—at least not for now. I will keep that to myself.

"I joined up with a band of pirates after I caught the eye of their young captain. He took a liking to me, and trained me to take a place among his crew."

"So you've become a pirate? That seems about right. Is this pirate you've fallen in with the man you wanted?"

"He is. His mates call him the Silver Blade."

Her eyes widen. "Do they now? Well, well, I can't say you don't aim high! Who hasn't heard of the Silver Blade? They say he's the quickest and fastest of all the swordsmen that inhabit the lowland countries. A real fighter." She pauses. "So, you never became lovers?"

She is pressing me in a way I don't appreciate, but I simply shake my head. "We are just friends and comrades, nothing more. At least from his side of things. What of yourself?"

The tiny spark our conversation has kindled dies out again, and the subdued sadness returns. "The less said about that, the better."

What has happened to her in the time since I went away? "How do you spend your time now?" I ask, trying to find a way to dig into her past.

Another shrug. "Doing this and that. Looking for a new adventure." She suddenly flashes with excitement again. "Maybe you and I can find it together! Like we used to do. Like in the old days!"

But the old days are gone, and I am not going back. I already know that much about myself. I have a new life to find out about, and old secrets to uncover that I hope will reveal much about my past. Whatever else is going to happen, that is going to happen first.

"I have somewhere I have to go, and I have to go there alone," I tell her, watching the excitement ebb from her features. "I am only here for a short time, and then I have to leave."

"Where are you going?"

"Back to Viridian Deep. You know I was adopted. Well, I need to find out how that happened and what became of my birth parents. I need to know more about my early life."

She looks dismayed. "But what difference can that make now? You have a new life. You need to spend time enjoying it and let the old one go."

She should understand; she and her brother are orphans as well. Does she not want to know about her past? But then again, she and her brother were not adopted and raised in a family, as I was. They simply ran wild with other orphans as a kind of collective. So maybe that is part of the difference. Well, that and the fact that she does not have a secret half life she wants to know more about.

"Maybe I can wait until you come back," she suggests. "You are coming back, aren't you?"

I decide to be straightforward. "I don't know yet. I really can't be certain what I am going to do. It depends on what I discover after I return home again."

"I suppose it might." Her smile is forced. I have essentially turned her away, and she knows it. She rises and stands, looking down at me. "You better rest some more. You look pretty beat up. We can talk again later."

She departs without looking back, and I find myself unexpectedly saddened.

I SIT ALONE FOR A WHILE AFTER FLORIN LEAVES, BUT BEFORE LONG, I am visited by a series of young Water Sprites who come bearing food and drink, and the offer of a bath—which I readily accept.

Afterward, I dress in the fresh clothing I was given last night. My own garments are all but shredded from our journey, and I am grateful for the new ones.

Around midafternoon, Florin's older brother Zedlin appears. He is his usual warm and cheerful self. He tells me he now works with navigational equipment for the submersibles, still piloting when the chance comes, still mostly a creature of the waters.

"You talked with Flo, I gather," he says, after a bit. He has grown more mellow, more mature, with time. When I first met him, he was a brash young boy, completely full of himself, but that phase has fortunately passed.

"We visited," I offer, not knowing exactly how much I should say.

He shakes his head. "She isn't the same girl you remember, is she? She's had a rough run of it lately."

"But she's still Florin inside, isn't she?"

"Not entirely—but it is her story to tell, not mine. I will only say that if you have the chance to speak to her further, I wish you would. She could use a caring friend."

I wonder if that's true, but I nod my agreement.

"Still, I have to leave soon," I tell him. "I need to go back home. I have to find out some things about myself."

Zedlin nods. "Auris said you had run off. She came looking for you here, maybe three years ago. I suspected that you and Florin had left together, and I asked Florin about it when she returned, but she just shrugged me off, insisting she didn't know anything. I never believed her, of course, but I could never get her to reveal anything about your location. She was already beginning to break away from us, just as you did from your family. How long have you been gone now?"

"Three years." I see the look on his face. "Too long. I probably need a way to fix that. If anyone will let me."

He grins. "I think Auris probably will—but you'll hear a few hard words, first. She really loves you, and she was devastated when you left as you did." He pauses. "Why don't you let me see you back home? I would feel better if I knew you got there safely."

I survey him, trying not to grin. If only he knew what I'd been through. But I have resolved to keep it all to myself for now. Even so, company on my journey home would be welcome. Tryn has already told me he intends to stay here and discover more about his people, and that I should go on alone. He understands me better than Florin does. He realizes I have a need to go back on my own, and I understand that perhaps he also has a similar need. I think he also wants to learn more of himself by exploring his past and his identity.

"Your company would be welcome," I tell Zedlin. "Can we leave tomorrow? Now that I've made up my mind to return, I don't want to give myself a chance to change it."

He smiles, then asks me if I would like to take a walk, stretch my legs, have a look around.

The remainder of the day passes pleasantly enough. Zedlin joins me for dinner, and Tryn is there, too. He greets me with a hug and a brief kiss on the cheek, then murmurs on releasing me, "Turnabout is fair play," giving me a private wink. During our dinner, I am certain he is going to say something about our journey that will reveal my Merrow heritage, but he does not. Instead, he tells me eagerly of what he has discovered of the Sprites, and their theories about why he never possessed gills or scales and does have ears as more and more Sprites gradually gather around us. He talks about staying on for a while and learning to swim better and feel more at home in the ocean waters. Since so much of his past has been lost, I think he wants to try to recover whatever he can through time spent with the friends he is making here.

He does, however, describe the 520 to those who have gathered and laments its loss, and our company assures him they will help him replace his craft and lend to him whatever else he requires.

They also assure him that facing and fleeing a Kraken is something to be proud of. There is nothing worse than an encounter with a Kraken.

I go to bed that night well fed and ready to sleep. I will leave at sunrise with Zedlin.

Florin does not reappear.

I WAKE RESTED AND READY TO JOURNEY, AND YET INCREASINGLY ANX-ious about my family and how they will receive me. They may welcome me home gratefully or they may chastise me. I feel like I have matured sufficiently to stand up to what is, in truth, probably a well-deserved criticism. But I am still not sure if I intend to stay with them or to return to Pressia and my pirate life. Or even to rejoin the Merrow. Too many paths lie open to me right now.

The day is bright and clear, the skies a depthless blue, as I walk through the camp to where I have agreed to meet Zedlin: a tree-shaded spot by the Spindly River. I sit on a public bench where I can look out over the swiftly flowing waters that wash down out of the highlands, breathe the morning air, and think once again about how much I have missed this land.

And then . . .

"Good morning."

Florin walks up from behind me, places her hands on my shoulders, and begins a slow, strong massage. "Did you really think you had seen the last of me?"

I close my eyes and luxuriate in the comfort of her fingers. "I wondered."

"Are we still friends?"

"Of course. We were always friends. We always will be."

"Friends try to help other friends when they are in trouble." She pauses. "Are we still that kind of friends?"

"Mostly," I hedge. "Do you have something specific in mind?"

"Very specific—but let me ask you something first. Was I helpful to you when I took you to Jagged Reach three years ago and never told anyone where you were? Even your sister, when she came looking for you?"

"What sort of trouble are you in?"

She continues rubbing my shoulders for a while longer without speaking, and then comes around the bench to sit down beside me. "I am not having a great life right now," she says.

I hear the crack in her voice as she speaks these words, and I feel my heart breaking for her. "How bad is it?"

She sighs. "Bad enough that I can barely stand the thought of telling you. Bad enough that, as long as I stay here, I'll never stop thinking about it. There are too many reminders. I'm hoping that an adventure with you might help get me out of my head and back into living my life again."

She is barely holding herself together, and I reach over to take her hands in mine. "What is it you have in mind?"

She wraps her arms around me and embraces me with such passion that I am suddenly very afraid of what I am going to hear. Florin remains my closest friend, and I cannot stand knowing that she is in such pain. Clearly, something terrible has happened to her.

"I need you to do something for me," she whispers. "I need you to let me go with you into the Deep. I need to go somewhere or do something or become someone else. I need to start my life over." She exhales sharply. "But I don't want to talk about it just now. Later, I will. But not now. Please agree to take me with you. No questions, no objections, no arguments. Just . . . say yes."

"But Zedlin . . ."

"Has already agreed to let me go in his place. I know the way as well as he does, and can keep you as safe as he could. Will you let me come? Please."

I can tell how desperately she wants me to agree. Her words, her tone of voice, her grip about my shoulders, the dampness of her tears on my neck—they all affirm the depth of her need. The way she speaks of it makes it clear that she will not say more at present.

I have a choice to make, but it is easily made. I love this girl. She remains my closest friend—maybe my last friend from the old days.

I disengage from her and stand. A travel pack is strapped to her back. She confronts me, her eyes and face smeared with tears but her determination reflected in her expression.

"Well, then, let's start walking," I say. "Everything else can wait."

Florin's smile is filled with relief and gratitude as we set out for Viridian Deep.

FOURTEEN

WE WALK ALL DAY THROUGH A PATCHWORK OF BOTH TERRAIN and memories. How many times have I come this way over the years to see Florin and the Water Sprites? I was here so often, I cannot begin to remember all of it. I was so young when I first started coming, but always old enough to feel it was something I could manage. By my early teenage years, I came alone, well enough versed in the ways of these lands to know the dangers. Besides, I was sufficiently reckless that very little troubled me in my youth.

I relive those days once more as I walk with Florin out of Water Sprite country and into the highlands that form the northwestern boundaries of the Sylvan homeland. I have not been here for three years, yet it is immediately familiar to me.

We encounter no other people and few creatures. There are no threats on this journey, no dangers. There are only the two of us together once more, finally comfortable enough again in our companionship that we require nothing else.

I do think constantly about what Florin might be hiding, but I know my friend well enough to know that what she has to say must wait until she is ready to speak of it.

As no one in Viridian Deep knows we are coming, we are able to take our time, letting our feet guide us as they will. The morning passes in silence to the afternoon, then Florin begins to talk. At first, we focus on our past, reminiscing about happier times, better times. Rehashing it all makes me realize how many childish, foolish, crazy undertakings we engaged in, and I find myself flinching a bit, finally understanding my siblings' concerns. We dared each other to swim across lakes filled with unknown predators. We raced up cliffs to see who could reach a destination first. We once tried facing down a snow bear—which neither of us, I might add, could manage; good thing we were both quick of foot and able to climb to safety. We even spied out a band of Goblins and dared to steal a pair of their long knives—though we did that at night, under cover of darkness.

We were constantly stealing things, just to see if we could do it, each of us daring the other to undertake something more and more impossible. We mostly gave back whatever we stole—the Goblin knives being an exception. Our adventures took us well outside our respective boundaries, and while we never actually got caught, our minders—Auris, in particular—almost always seemed to know where we had been. But Auris doted on me in those days, and always forgave me my transgressions. With no parents, Florin managed to get away with almost everything.

There are a lot of stories, and as we recall them, I see hints of the old Florin beginning to emerge.

The afternoon lengthens, and I soon realize it is growing oppressively dark. A massive cloud bank has rolled in, and try as I might to find a way past it, I can tell that we are in for a drenching. The best we can do is find shelter somewhere—which in mountainous, forested country is not all that easy.

"We need to take cover," Florin shouts to me as I trudge along, leaning into an increasingly powerful wind.

I nod in agreement, but I don't see anything but trees and more trees ahead of us. We soldier on, fighting back against the approach of the storm, already feeling the first thick droplets of rain striking our faces. We gain another two hundred yards and the beginning of a very heavy rainfall when she indicates something ahead. It seems to be little more than a dip in the ground, but when we have worked our way close enough, I can tell it is a large ravine that drops into a river already filled with surging waters.

There are better routes to take into Viridian Deep, and I suddenly wonder why our wanderings have brought us this way. But perhaps it is only our old impulses at work, to always take the riskiest path.

I reach over and grab her arm. "We're *not* going to cross that in this storm! Let's find whatever cover there is and wait it out."

I am shouting, and even so I can barely hear myself over the rush of the winds and the drumming of the rain. The storm is worsening, and we are both soaked and shivering. We need to take cover somewhere. I scan the ridgeline behind us and find a series of clefts that might shelter us, if something else isn't already hiding there. I point it out, my voice no longer audible through the roar of the deluge, and Florin nods in agreement.

We climb the hillside and begin searching. Many of the available spaces are too small or too shallow, and we pass one where a nest of wolves regards us with baleful red eyes and back away at once. We hunch over against the wind and try to ignore our drenched clothing. I am so miserable I consider just sitting down where I am and waiting things out.

But eventually we find what we are looking for. A cleft in the rocks provides entry into a short, narrow alcove that is still mostly dry and protected against the inclement weather. We make our way inside to the deepest point and sit side by side with our backs to a rock wall so that we can look directly out of our refuge and into the weather. What we see is not very reassuring, but at least we are out of the worst of it.

As we sit there in our private bubble in the storm, Florin says, "I am grateful you let me come with you, Char."

I sense from her words that she is finally ready to tell me what she has been hiding. I reach over and put a hand on her shoulder. "It wasn't a hard decision. I don't like seeing you in pain, so if there is anything I can do to ease it for you, I am happy to do it."

She brushes the rain from her shaved head, then draws her knees up to her chest and embraces them. "Honestly, I don't think anything but time is going to ease this one. It's hard to think about. Harder still to live with."

I give her shoulder a reassuring squeeze. "You don't have to talk about it if you're not ready to."

"No, I need to tell you. And I have to do it before I lose my courage once again. Will you hear me out fully before you say anything?"

"Yes. I'll keep quiet."

She takes and releases a deep breath. "After I left you in Jagged Reach, I came home again, but I didn't have anything to do with myself. I was lonely, and I was bored. I thought about joining you, but that seemed unfair. You already had enough to worry about without adding me to the list."

She hugs her knees. "Instead, I met Okrin—a boy older than I was, but not by much. He was a Water Sprite as well. I started spending time with him—a lot of time. I liked him. He was funny and he was genuinely attracted to me. People warned me about him, said he was reckless, ungrounded. But then, so was I. And he was fun. We took a lot of hikes, fished together, camped together, talked about everything . . . It was almost like being with you again, except he was a boy, so it was different, too."

She lowers her head into her knees and her voice drops to a whisper. "He never made me any promises of partnership, but still I let him make love to me. Many times. More so when I felt him start to drift away."

I say nothing. I promised I wouldn't.

She looks up at me sharply. "Of course I got pregnant. At first, I was excited. I thought maybe this could bind us back together, that we could be a family for real. Because the more I thought about it, the more that was something I wanted. Stability, belonging." She gives a harsh laugh. "Who would have thought it could happen, right? Me, settled with a family? A mother? Crazy."

Her voice is full of bitterness and pain, and my heart aches for her. I sense we are coming to the crux of her story.

"When I told him he was going to be a father, he smiled and said that was what he had always hoped for. But then he disappeared completely. He was just gone, and no one knew where. He was an orphan like I was, so there was nothing to hold him here but me. And, apparently, I wasn't enough. I told Zedlin what I had done, and he said he understood and would be there for me. And he was. But there was a bit of *I told you so* in there as well. He had been one of those warning me against trusting Okrin."

There are tears in her eyes by now. I nod reassuringly.

"I didn't know what to do. All my dreams for a family had gone up in smoke, but I was still pregnant. I was still going to be a mother, and I wasn't ready to do that alone. Some of the girls I knew tried to help me, but they knew less than I did. Zedlin kept asking me what I planned to do after the baby was born, and I didn't know. It just all suddenly felt so wrong. So instead of dealing with the reality of my pregnancy, I kept looking for Okrin, as if he could solve it all. But I never found him."

I lean over and hug her—just to give her a small moment of reassurance—and then lean back again, not wanting to do more until I am sure she is finished.

She is not. She has more to tell me. "I carried the baby to term, though most of the time I kept wishing that something would go wrong, that something would prevent me from having to deal with the consequences of my mistake. And then . . ."

A huge gulp and a heave of her shoulders. "Right before my daughter was born, I changed my mind again. I could feel her moving inside me, and I fell in love with her. I *was* ready to change, to grow up, to be her mother. But . . . it was a hard delivery, and she died at birth. And I can't help thinking it was all my fault, that this was somehow the Fates' judgment on me: that she was better off dead than having me for a mother."

THIS TIME, WHEN I TAKE HER IN MY ARMS, I DO NOT LET HER GO. SHE is shaking hard and crying freely. I hold her against me so that she will not feel quite so alone and run my hand over her back to soothe her. I cannot imagine the guilt she must feel, thinking her bad behavior cost her child its life.

For a young woman of perhaps eighteen to have endured this experience must have been heart wrenching. And even though her daughter's death was in no way her fault—I know that as clearly as I have ever known anything—what matters now is how she is handling it. How she has handled it since it happened, in fact. Florin is clearly still mired in guilt and grief, but at the same time trying to move on with her life. Albeit rather poorly, I am guessing.

"That must have been so hard for you," I whisper, thinking I should say something. "I know I said I would stay quiet, but you need to know how I feel. I love you and I support you, Florin. Is there something I can do?"

She shakes her head. "No. Not anymore. Just having one friend to stand by me means a lot. Most avoided me completely after I lost the baby, probably thinking my reckless behavior caused her death. As if it didn't mean I was suffering for it. I *was* suffering. But maybe they were right. Maybe I'm really not cut out for motherhood. Maybe I'm at my best out here in the world, having adventures with you."

She forces a smile, and I know the topic is closed. Instead, we just sit there, listening to the heavy slap of raindrops as the storm continues. Eventually, the heavy weather lessens, and the rainfall becomes little more than a slow drip from the trees that stand outside our crevice. Florin sleeps, though I remain wakeful. I cannot stop thinking about what has occurred, and how terrible it must feel.

The night passes slowly, but eventually the storm ends and calm sets in. I have drifted off several times myself as Florin rests, but never for long. I cannot sleep with what I am feeling, knowing how badly my old friend is hurting. It seems she has lost everything, including her way. I want to help her, but I don't know where to begin.

Then, while daylight is still just a glimmer on the distant horizon, Florin stirs awake. For a long time, she doesn't say anything. She doesn't move. I only know she is awake because her breathing slows and steadies.

Then suddenly she whispers to me, "Sometimes, I want her back, Char. I want her back so badly. Sometimes, I can hardly stand it. But maybe she is better off without me?"

What can I say? "None of this was your fault, Florin . . ."

She grimaces. "If I could just make myself believe that . . . even just a little bit."

"You can," I tell her. "Because it's true."

"It still feels like a judgment. And I can't seem to find any way forward again."

"Patience, brave girl. You will find a way."

Then we sit holding each other until the sun rises and the new day begins.

EVENTUALLY, WE RISE AND RESUME OUR JOURNEY. THE WORLD IS still sodden; rainwater drips from trees and streams run down the slopes to either side of our shelter. I can already hear the water that has collected at the bottom of the ravine churning and frothing in a wild deluge. We step out of our nighttime shelter and feel droplets of water rain on our heads from overhead branches in a chilly, steady rhythm. The air has gone still, and the temperature has dropped. The skies are still cloudy but no longer threaten rain. I can tell that the day will warm as it lengthens and walking will be much easier.

Ahead, the ravine comes back into view as we descend the slopes of the hills into which we retreated last night.

"Look, Char!" Florin calls out.

She points down to our left, where a heavy tree brought down by the storm has fallen across the ravine, forming a bridge to the other side. "We can cross there!" she shouts gleefully.

I am not sure about this, but I see no other way over the gap, so when she starts toward it, I follow. The damp ground is slick beneath our feet, and we take our time descending. I do not trust my footing, and I use everything within reach to steady myself.

My *inish* kicks in as we descend to the ravine, my instincts telling me at once that this is a mistake. But Florin is determined, and her confidence persuades me that I should put my doubts aside. It is also the first time I have seen her so excited about something since I left, so perhaps that is what sways me more.

"I will go first," she declares boldly.

She steps onto the tree trunk and secures herself, boots planted, hands gripping branches so that she can make her way. I follow, staying close.

The bark is inordinately slippery, but we stay low to the trunk, picking our way across with care. I glance down at the river below us—a maelstrom of surging water filled with roiling debris and tumbling rocks.

"Careful!" I shout ahead to Florin.

She glances back, grinning confidently. "Don't worry about me. I can do this blindfolded!"

We are halfway across, and the moisture on the tree trunk is actually dripping off in rivulets, working its way through the heavy bark.

Then, just like that, Florin's feet slip out from under her. She slides all the way down the side of the trunk, thrashing. Her hands fight to hold fast, but one slips free and then the other, and she is falling.

I scream out her name in shock, but she is tumbling away into the rapids below. I don't stop to think. I don't hesitate. I go over the side after her, feetfirst, arms spread wide to control my fall. I see her plunge into the river and disappear. I follow her in so quickly I expect to be able to grab hold of her at once, but I can't find her. I look for her as I twist about, but the waters are so riddled with mud and debris that I can't see anything. I surface, then go back down. Any moment now, I tell myself, I will transform into my Merrow self and be able to withstand the river's swift, scrambled flow.

But to my shock, I don't change.

I surface once more, the river sweeping me downstream at a steady pace, its currents first thrusting me forward and then tugging me down. I search frantically for Florin, but there is no sign. I turn in every direction, scanning the waters, but Florin is nowhere to be seen. I thrash my way to shore and crawl up frantically onto grassy banks. I have lost my pack and all my supplies, but I don't care. I struggle to my feet and start jogging down the bank edge, searching the river as I go, begging silently for a glimpse of her, for just one quick sign. I run, and I run some more.

I keep looking for hours and hours. Until it is darkening again. It doesn't help. I don't find a sign of her.

Florin is gone.

FIFTEEN

For a long time after it is too dark to bother looking anymore, I sit and cry. I cry for Florin and for everything else that I have somehow lost. I cannot believe what has happened.

Worst of all, I blame myself. My *inish* warned me. My instincts told me that crossing the ravine by using that fallen tree as a bridge was a mistake. But because she was happy, I didn't stop her. I didn't even try. Instead, I went with her.

And why did my Merrow side fail to materialize when I went into the water? I had been counting on it, and yet it never showed. So how could that be? I think on it for a time, then wonder if maybe it has something to do with the differences between ocean and river waters. Is it possible that if you are an ocean creature, adapted to the salt water, you do not respond in the same way to fresh river water? After all, are there not fish of all sorts that can only survive in the one but not the other? At some point, I will have to find out.

I don't cry myself to sleep, but I do cry myself into exhaustion. I was never the weeping type, not in all these years, so why am I suddenly so tearful now?

When I do manage sleep, it is fortunately deep and dreamless.

When I wake the following morning, I am lying on my side, curled into a ball as someone shakes my shoulder. I have been found by a grizzled bear of a man who is possibly hairier than bears themselves. He is a Fae Forest Ranger in search of stray livestock that might have escaped the deluge, and he has found me instead.

"Greetings, miss," he says to me.

I sit up to face him. I am aware that my face is a mess and my clothes are ruined, but I don't care.

"Good morning," I manage.

"You got caught in that storm?"

I nod. "With a good friend. She fell off a tree spanning the gorge, disappeared into the waters, and never came up. I searched for her all day yesterday and couldn't find her anywhere. I think she . . ."

"Is your friend's name Florin?" he asks.

I stare at him in shock. "Yes! How did you know?"

He grins. "I found her earlier this morning, washed up on a bank of the river, unconscious, but alive. I have her tucked away not far from here. She's weak and very tired, but insisted that I find you. If you are up to making the trip, I'll take you to her."

I break down in spite of my determination not to and bury my face in my hands. "She's alive? Oh, thanks to the Shades!"

"Here now, easy does it. You just let it all out. I lost a friend myself to these waters years back. Never did find him. Wicked bad stuff, those waters, when there's a storm. They'll drag you down no matter how strong you are. Had better luck with your friend. She's a strong young girl."

"Yes, she is."

A long silence follows. "Rustab's my name. Yours?"

"Char. I'm from Viridian Deep. Or, at least, my family is."

He nods. "Good people, those. Don't get down there much anymore. Can I make you some coffee?"

He makes a fire of mostly dry twigs he somehow scavenges, adding wood burners and scrap from a pouch. He lights it up with flint and stone and has a small pot boiling within minutes. He sits by me afterward and waits for the coffee to brew.

"You get lost or injured out here in a storm like the one last night, you're likely done. You're lucky yourself to be alive. Here, this coffee will set you right. We'll add a touch of spirits to it to give you energy."

He fills two cups and adds a generous dollop of something amber from a pouch. He hands me one and takes the other. We both drink. It feels like my insides are on fire, but it wakes me up. I can hardly believe that Florin is still alive, that she managed to survive and is waiting for me. That we will see each other again.

Rustab gestures at me with his cup. "Strong stuff, I know. But good for you." He gives me a wink.

When I have finished, Rustab collects and repackages the pot and cups and stands up. "Well, then, time to find your friend."

We set out at once, working our way through the debris and muck of the storm, the trail made difficult by fallen trees and broken limbs. But we soldier on.

Before long, we reach a grove of fir and find Florin wrapped in a blanket and sleeping. I cannot help myself. I rush to her and wake her and take her in my arms and cry as if I might never stop. We hold each other and cry together, so happy that the disaster we had both envisioned has not come to pass.

"Do you have a place to go?" the woodsman asks after we have finally settled down enough.

"We do," I tell him. "We are returning to my family in Viridian Deep. It's not too far from here."

He reaches down and shoulders his pack. "Then you ought to get under way. Day's nice enough now, and you should be there by nightfall. I have to be going, too. Got work to do in these hills that will take me most of a week."

He turns away with a wave of his hand and disappears into the trees.

Before long, Florin and I are on our feet and moving ahead. We have lost everything but the clothes we wear and our long knives, but with any luck we will not require more before reaching Viridian Deep.

Florin, in particular, is a sight, her clothing barely hanging on her slender form, all tattered and ragged. She is very quiet as we walk, barely saying anything. It is as if she has lost herself as a result of what happened, and I think I must give her the space she needs to find her way back.

The closer we get to Viridian Deep, the more determined I am to see my family first. Whatever it takes to gain their forgiveness and reunite with those I love is worth any amount of pain and discomfort.

We walk through the balance of the day, my thoughts shifting from Florin to the discovery of my Merrow identity to my feelings about Brecklin and Tryn and finally to what I remember of my siblings. My thoughts come and go randomly, and I do nothing to try to bring them under control. At one point, I think again about my failure to transform when leaping into the surging river. Why did I not change? I have always changed whenever my gills hit water. Is it really possible the transformation only works in salty ocean water? I store the information away for further consideration.

We reach the outskirts of Viridian Deep by midafternoon and start down into the valley. By nightfall, we are at the edges of the city, and I am beginning to anticipate what will happen when I arrive back home.

As we pass other members of the Fae community, most heading toward home on their way from work, I catch glimpses of recognition and more than a few surprised looks. But no one speaks to me. I do not think they are angry or disappointed; I think they are just surprised to see me again. I nod at a few, receiving smiles and waves in return. It is a strange feeling to be coming home like this after three years away. In one respect, nothing seems to have changed. The buildings, walkways, and tree lanes are all familiar.

Nevertheless, I worry that it might be too late. I worry I might have been gone too long to be able to reclaim this place that was once my home. Is this my home anymore or am I an exile? It feels like something of both, and I am having difficulty deciding how much of either is accurate and how much simply a false impression.

"You look worried," Florin says to me—the first words she has spoken in hours.

I nod. "I'm not sure what to expect."

She puts an arm about my shoulders and gives me a hug. "You are a good person and the best of friends. Your family still loves you and will welcome you. I know them. I am sure of it."

I pause to hug her back.

We climb into the tree lanes that lead to the homes now occupied by Auris and Harrow, and Ronden and Ramey. Do they all still occupy the same residences? I cannot be sure. I will have to knock on their doors and see who answers. But I cannot shake the feeling of strangeness that blankets me as I try to find a way to fit into the Deep again.

Beleaguered by doubts, riddled with misgivings, I press on. I have made my decision to return and there is nothing for it but to keep going.

Do the others in my family know anything about my past, about my time in the orphanage before Ancrow came for me? She kept so much from all of her children over the years. Now that she is dead, is there anyone else who might be able to tell me something about myself? I have to hope so. I have nowhere else to turn for answers but here and the orphanage.

I slow down as we reach the home that was once Ancrow's and was for a time Ramey's and mine. It is a large, magnificent building, and for a moment I only stand facing it, unable to do more. The windows are dark, and it has a look of emptiness about it.

Then I glance down the way to find the one where Auris and Harrow were living at the time I fled the Deep. There is a light in the window, and lights to either side of the doorway. Someone definitely lives here. But will it still be my brother and sister?

I feel suddenly ashamed and frightened, and now I really do want to leave. I cannot face up to what my flight from the Deep might have cost them. When I left, Auris and Harrow's first child— a little boy named Parse—was three years old. Do they have other children now? Auris always wanted more.

I muster my courage and lead Florin up to the door and knock firmly.

For a moment, there is no response. Then my sister's voice answers from within. "A moment, please."

I stand waiting, besieged by doubts. I try to stiffen my spine, to ward my fading courage, to remind myself how close Auris and I always were, to assure myself all will be well.

The door opens, and there my sister stands. Auris holds a baby in her arms, wrapped in a familiar blanket—one that I remember used to cradle Parse. This new child cannot be more than a few months old—a tiny thing with amazing blue eyes that burn deep and sure as they fix on me. Then the tiny fingers of one small hand, colored a soft jade, lift from the blanket and wiggle at me. I reach out to her without thinking, and her hand catches hold of mine.

"You are a little darling," I whisper to her.

Florin, standing behind me, says nothing—and I suddenly realize how this must be affecting her, being faced with the one thing she did not realize she wanted until it was too late.

Then Parse is there, too, peering solemnly over at me. His skin is a deep emerald, and his eyes are the same penetrating jade as his sister's. He stares fixedly at me as I meet his gaze and does not look away. He has grown so much taller than when I last saw him, gone from toddler to child. He must be almost seven now.

Love you, Char.

The words are his, but also unspoken. Still, I know it is his voice; the sound of it echoes in my mind. It is just like him: quiet and oddly mature, yet also young. I am stunned into silence. This boy hasn't seen me in three years, yet he recognizes me and has now spoken to me in my mind? How, by all that's true and sure, is this possible?

Auris smiles as she sees the look on my face. She nods at her baby. "This is one you haven't met yet. This is your niece, Safra. I got her from the Protective Leaf Orphanage. I wanted another child—Harrow and I both did—but after years of trying, we realized we couldn't have any more after Parse. So we adopted this one."

Auris has not noticed my confusion. It makes me wonder if she even knows what I am confused about—if she realizes what little Parse just did, speaking to me only in my mind.

"I'm so glad you've come back, Char," Auris tells me. "And pleased to see that you have brought Florin with you! Please, come inside."

I step through the doorway, still wondering about Parse. Why is he speaking by thoughts alone? Or is he?

Most six-year-olds erupt into floods of words at some new event, but Parse is oddly silent. Does he speak this way—through thoughts, rather than words—to his mother and others, or is it just for me?

Auris takes Safra over to her cradle and lowers her into place, adjusting her carefully within a nest of blankets. Parse retreats to a small table filled with board games and resumes one he must have been playing before I appeared. He has still not said a word aloud— and no longer in my head, either.

My sister turns then and hugs me close, and I cling to her fiercely. "I knew you would come back. I always knew! I understand why you left. I was upset about it, but I also understood. You were so unhappy for a time. I hope you are happier now. Are you, sweetheart?"

She says nothing of my bedraggled condition or my three-year absence. I manage another nod. "I am. I'm sorry I left, but I felt like I was suffocating here. I needed to be somewhere else for a while. Did you really miss me?"

"Did I miss you? Only all the time, every day! But we all need to find a way to grow up, and for each of us it is a different journey. Remember, I was locked away in a Goblin prison for five years. I could only hope that wherever you were, and whatever had happened to you, it couldn't be worse than that."

"It wasn't. And I do want to tell you about it. I want to tell everyone in the family. Some of it is important for all of you to know."

"Then you must tell us everything." She pauses as Florin, standing beside me, clears her throat.

"Would you excuse me if I said I needed to sleep? We've been walking all day, and I had a bad fall. Char can tell you about it. But I'm exhausted."

And probably needs a moment away from Auris and Safra, to get her emotions in order. But Auris doesn't argue. She takes Florin's hand and leads her down the hallway to the bedroom we will have to share—there are only two—and settles Florin in before returning to me.

"Do you know that I missed you so badly at first that I thought about going to the Seers and asking them to seek you out? But I didn't do that. It felt like it would be an intrusion that you would not appreciate. You were my strong little sister, and nothing could ever touch you. So I chose to let things be. I waited, trusting that you would come home when you were ready."

I am astonished. I could never summon such patience. I could never make myself wait for her like she has waited for me. But Auris is different from the rest of us. She has endured and suffered and survived so much. She is a legend among the Forest Sylvan people, and there is not a Fae anywhere who does not know her story.

"I'm no longer a Watcher," Auris is saying, her back to me as she studies her daughter. "In the end, what I mostly want is this— a mother's life with children and friends and small difficulties that trouble no one but me. And Harrow, when he is not away on Watcher duty."

She looks at me. "Maybe you've found the place you belong, too. I know you were looking for it. Come, sit down with me. Harrow is away for another day, and I am alone with the children. Did you find what you were searching for?"

What do I say to that? I did, and I didn't. I found something of what I was looking for, but not all. What I really found out was that I have never been who I thought I was. Like Auris herself, I have thought of myself as one thing, then discovered I am another. I want to tell her all this, but I cannot think how to do it.

"Can you tell me about my sisters and Harrow first? How are they? I have a lot to say, but I think I should tell you all at once. So, for now, maybe . . ."

She is nodding in agreement, and I stop talking.

"Harrow is well, and we are still very happy together. He leads his Watcher's life some of the time, and he trains new recruits on the skills and the lore at other times. Ronden still works with him. Ramey? Well, Ramey has changed the most. She and Atholis are partnered now, and he has become interested in integrating magic into mechanics. He now builds machines that think, and engines that create—just like the Humans do with computers, but on a different level. Ramey is helping him. As you know, she was always very smart and very much a student, so they are a good match. They have been living and working together for two years now."

I consider the idea of Ramey partnered and shake my head in amazement.

Auris pauses. "She took your disappearance very hard. I will tell you that up front, because she was angry for a long time. More so than the rest of us." She smiles. "But for me, at least, that is in the past. I think it might finally be for her, too."

I am sorry about Ramey. We were so close growing up. Before Florin, we were our own best friends and companions, and seldom without each other. Leaving her behind was the hardest thing I have ever done, but at the time I was at odds even with her. I loved her, but I could not take her with me on my journey without taking too much of the past with me. And even then, there was Atholis.

Auris stands and reaches down for my hands. "Enough of that

for now. Look at you. You have obviously had a tough journey. Let's get you something to eat, then draw you a bath so you can clean yourself up. Then you can get your own good night's sleep. I'll feed Florin when she wakes."

She leads me into the kitchen, sits me down, then prepares me a dinner of bread and cold meat sandwiches, accompanied by fruit and milk. It is a wondrous feast, after two days of deprivation. I do not try to hide my obvious hunger or carry on a conversation. I just eat, and Auris seems happy enough to let me be.

Afterward, she takes me into her own bathroom, draws hot water, and leaves me alone to soak and wash. I sink down into the warm bathwater with great relief and let the wear and tear of my travels and a bit of my inner sadness drift away. Soon enough, however, my thoughts drift to Auris's firstborn and the way he is able to communicate with his mind alone. What other child can do that? Since Auris possesses vast Fae magic, it is not out of the question to think that her child could possess some, too.

But does Auris realize that her son has this strange ability? I still don't know.

During my bath, I change my mind about waiting to tell my story to everyone in the family at the same time. The others will not be able to listen to it until at least tomorrow, but Auris is here now. And really, I think I would prefer to speak to her first. She is not the oldest of my siblings, but she is the one I feel closest to. Telling her everything now might help prepare me for telling the others later, so I make up my mind to do so.

When I leave the tub and drain the water, I find that fresh clothing has been set out for me in the adjoining bedroom. I am grateful. I was so worried about how Auris would respond to me, and I had no reason to be. She has always been kind and gracious—even back when she was under constant attack from Ancrow and had only Harrow and my sisters and myself to stand by her.

I walk out to join Auris in the living room, where she rocks baby Safra in her arms. If her plan is to encourage sleep, she is failing.

Safra wriggles and squirms and makes all sorts of baby noises. I laugh in spite of myself and go over to look down into that little face. She smiles up at me.

Then I glance over at Parse, still seated at his game table.

Love you, Char.

There it is again, that communication through thought. I look at Auris to see how she is responding, but she is engaged in whispering to Safra and appears not to have heard her son. Though, honestly, I think she hasn't. I think Parse speaks only to me.

As if on cue, Auris rises and hands me the baby. "I want to go put on a nightdress. Would you hold this wee one for a bit?"

I take the baby and cradle her in my arms. She wriggles in her blanket and stares up at me, but she does not speak in my mind. I guess only Parse does that. Safra just lies there, little arms and legs flexing. I hold out my finger so Safra can grab it, which she instantly does.

"All right, you little rapscallion," I whisper down to her once Auris has left the room. "Can you talk to me, too?"

She can't. She's a baby.

Parse. I know the voice right away. I look over at him. He looks right back, undeterred.

I want to ask you something.

"Ask me, then," I tell him.

You have Fae blood. But you are Merrow, too.

How does he know this? I take a chance. "Are you also of Merrow blood?"

No. But I was born with inish *skills.*

It seems those skills allow him to sense magic in others and sometimes determine its nature.

"Do you talk to your mother like this?

Only to you.

"Why only me?"

Only you know Merrow speech. So only you can hear me when I speak it.

I suppose that explains it—in part. But before I can ask more, he continues.

You seek your past.

"How do you know this?"

I sense things.

"About me?"

Orphan child, who are you?

I don't know, of course. I thought I did before I was thrown into the seas to die, but I realize now that there must be much more.

"I don't know who I am. That is what I am trying to discover. Who would know more about me?"

A longer pause than before. When he speaks again, I can barely hear him. *The Seers will know.*

Then his bright eyes blink, and he turns away.

SIXTEEN

 URIS RETURNS TO THE LIVING ROOM IN HER NIGHTDRESS and robe, bends to kiss her daughter on the cheek, then joins me on the couch. By then, I've had time to think about what has transpired between Parse and myself. I do not pretend to understand it. I do not even know how it could have come about, this six-year-old child choosing to communicate with me—and only me—by thoughts alone. He apparently doesn't do it with his mother. Or perhaps with anyone else in his family.

Just me.

Because I alone can speak Merrow—although, it seems, so can he. But how? Or why? I glance over at him once more, but he is busy with his games and doesn't look my way. I wonder if he can explain anything of what is happening with his abilities—if he knows how unusual this is. I wonder if anyone else knows about it.

"Can we talk now about what has happened to you since you left us?" Auris asks, her voice so kind and reassuring I am tempted to throw myself at her feet and reveal everything.

But I simply smile and nod my agreement. "I think we need to."

I am still one of the family, but I am not the girl that left them three years earlier. I am stronger and wiser. I have become—at least in my own mind—an equal in every way that matters. And I need to make it clear that, while I love and care for them more than ever, I am no longer in need of anything other than their love and respect.

I have discovered my Merrow self. In the process of doing so, I have developed the use of my *inish*. I am nowhere near as strong or competent in its use as Auris is, but one day I might become so. In any event, I am strong enough to stand by myself.

But I do want to talk about it. I need to know more. I have to find out if any of them have knowledge about me that might help unravel this mystery.

I smile at my sister. "Where to begin?"

Even though I shouldn't, I glance once more at Parse. This time, he is looking back at me intently.

"Does Parse ever speak?" I ask. I can't stand it any longer. I have to ask. "I mean, out loud?"

Now Auris smiles. "He does—though he doesn't talk very much. Mostly just to me or his father. He likes to ask questions. He's very interested in learning about things. But he's also very self-contained, content with being alone. If he speaks to you, consider yourself special." She leans toward me. "Come now, tell me something of yourself."

I decide to let my confusion over Parse rest for now and tell her everything.

When I am finished, she leans over and kisses me on the cheek. "It's been very difficult for you. You need to tell the others. The rest of the family needs to know. We're a family riddled with secrets, thanks to Ancrow. I sometimes think that all of us know things the others don't, and that might be so with your Merrow heritage."

I think about this. It is possible this is another secret that Ancrow has taken with her to the grave, but perhaps she has divulged it to one of us at some point. Parse suggested I visit the Seers, but he did not mention my other family members, so I am still in the dark.

Auris takes my hands in hers. "This must have been so hard for you, discovering what you really are. You must have been terrified. But you were brave enough to make a new life among the Merrow. That's quite an accomplishment. I never believed that the Merrow were real. I always thought they were a myth. Yet so much of what I thought from the old days is wrong."

"I thought they were a myth, too," I confess. "But visiting the orphanage where Ancrow found me is the only way I know how to find out the truth about myself, and just now this is what matters. Everything I thought I knew about myself is just a small piece of a larger truth, so I can't leave it at that. I want to know more."

I glance away from her and back to where Parse is sitting silently at his table. He is looking down at his work again and paying me no attention, yet I feel him listening. I know he hears everything. I wonder again if I should say something to Auris, but I stay silent.

"I know what that's like," Auris says. "And sadly, I don't know anything about your adoption. Ancrow never talked about your childhood or the orphanage, and none of the others ever said anything about it, either. We should ask the others, though. Ask them what, if anything, they know."

"I was planning on it."

She thinks about it a moment. "But I think I have a better idea. We could talk to the Seers first—just as I did about my past when I first came to Viridian Deep. We might get better answers that way."

Again, I look over at Parse. Again, he is looking back at me. But his expression reveals nothing.

Auris leans forward to embrace me. With her face close against mine, she says, "I love you, Char. I've missed you so much! We must make sure we don't let three years elapse again."

I nod silently and hug her back. "I promise."

She moves away. "Now go join Florin and get some sleep. You must be exhausted. Tomorrow, we will visit the Seers and listen to what they have to say. We will discover the truth about your parentage, whatever it is. We will face it together."

I am so grateful she isn't angry with me. I am so relieved we are still sisters. I close my eyes for a moment to stop the tears.

It doesn't work, but it doesn't matter. The anger and resentment I feared I would find were simply in my head. What I have found instead is the love I remember from before. The tears I am crying now are tears of joy.

I sleep that night in Parse's room with Florin while Parse sleeps with Auris and Safra. I am exhausted and fall quickly asleep, but sometime later, deeper into the darkness, I wake to find the boy standing next to my bed. He is watching me in silence when my instincts trigger and I wake. He stares at me for a long moment, then wordlessly climbs into my bed and snuggles up against me. I am amazed that this shy child has chosen me. I put an arm around him and hold him close, savoring the warmth of his body until I fall back asleep.

WHEN I WAKE THE FOLLOWING MORNING, PARSE IS GONE AND FLORIN is still asleep. I lie back in bed quietly for a time, thinking about the day ahead. When I rise and go out into the main living room, mother and children are already awake. I greet them with a smile. We begin our breakfast, and Florin joins us before we are finished.

After we eat and dress for the day, a young woman who helps Auris comes by to watch the children while Auris and I go to the Seers. Florin offers to come with us, but I tell her I need to do this alone. Whatever I discover I want to face by myself first, and if I am to share it, I want the choice to be mine. I follow my older sister with some trepidation, because I am nowhere nearly as close to the sisters as Auris is. But I understand what it is they do and a little of how they do it.

Their magic is legendary in the Fae world, particularly among the Forest Sylvan people. They have been alive for a long time, although no one seems to actually know how long. Maven, Benith, and Dreena are all elderly ladies by now—although it seems that they have always been—able to see secrets and truths that are hidden from us.

"We will ask them to take a look into your childhood," Auris tells me. "To look into the past you no longer remember, just to see if there is something that lingers."

I know what they can do. I have seen them do it once or twice in the past. They will sedate me and tease out what is hidden in my mind. I am not afraid of this, although I am wary. They have never done it to me personally, so I have no clear idea of what to expect.

"It is simple enough," Auris tells me. "You will be asleep through much of it and may not remember everything you recalled when you wake, but the sisters will see it and tell you of it when they are done."

"I am not afraid," I say quietly—although I am wondering if that is true.

We walk along the tree lanes, then down to the city streets and along their twisting, winding lengths to the northern outskirts. Our journey through the city is a familiar one; the buildings, shops, work centers, markets, and businesses are all mostly the same. A few new ones have appeared since I left, and some others departed, but almost everything we pass is well known and oddly welcome. Even the Fae who greet Auris and occasionally me make me feel warm inside—as if this is still a place where I could belong again should I choose to do so.

I ponder the possibility as we walk. I imagine myself living here once again, a member of the community into which I was born. It does not feel as odd as I thought it would.

We pass the entrance to Promise Falls and the gardens that ward it, then turn north to reach the Seers' strange, oddly configured house.

A walkway that twists and turns like a serpent through wide-bowed conifers and sprawling, flowered trellises lies ahead. The house awaits at the top of the path: a three-story conglomeration of rooms that are stacked like blocks, one atop the other. It has a whimsical, fairy-tale look, like a child's toy, brightly painted in bold colors and decorated with charming porches, balconies, and walkways all about. It makes me smile every time I see it.

I make no move to advance. Instead, I simply stand there for a long moment, regarding it.

"Listen to me, Char," my sister says. "The Seers are their own mistresses and will do things as they see fit, but they will never hurt any of us. They will only be trying to help. Still, some of what they uncover may be difficult to accept. You will do best, I have discovered, not to resist or struggle. Just accept what you find, think about what it means, and do what you must to come to terms with it. You can share with me what you choose. All I wish is that you can find and accept the answers to your questions."

"As you yourself have done on more than one occasion," I remind her. "I understand. I was there with you more than once. I know not to resist or reject what I am shown, just try to learn whatever I can."

She ruffles my tangled hair as she used to, and for a moment I am a little girl again. "Let's go do it, then."

But I pause, thinking. My instincts tell me this is something I should do alone—which is what I already said to Florin. I am cautious but not frightened, and I feel the need to reassert my supposed independence.

"I want to do this by myself," I say.

She stares at me, uncertain.

"I am old enough," I persist. "Look at everything I have done since I left. I can do this, too."

She nods and steps back. "Will I see you back at the house later? Will you be staying for at least another night? I want a chance to say goodbye to you this time."

I smile. "I am done with running away. I will see you later tonight, I promise."

She leans forward to give me a brief hug, then turns away. Auris is smart enough to understand. And it seems she always was.

I wait until she is out of sight, then I start up the walkway toward the Seers' home. Right away, my instincts tell me I am on the right path. The surroundings welcome me, bright and open and marked by scads of flowering plants. Their colors are vibrant and artfully arranged so as to capture the magic that all flowers are capable of bestowing upon their admirers. The walkway is graveled and smooth, and the trees offer a canopy that shields it from the sun and withdraws to allow the light to penetrate. Ahead, the house has a magical feel, and the birds seem eager to partake of its wonders. Wings flutter and calls sound at every turn, and I find myself smiling at the delight of it.

Ahead, a solitary figure stands on a balcony, ancient gray head tipped down to view me better.

"Why, look! If it isn't sweet Charlayne. Welcome back!"

Maven. I wave up to her, flattered that she remembers me. Also, she is one of the few who ever uses my full name, and it always makes me feel special. She watches a moment longer, and then retreats into her house. I continue on, and in seconds I am at the doorstep. The three sisters are standing there with open arms, ready and eager to embrace me.

"Such a surprise!" gentle Benith declares as she takes me in her arms and steps back. "So grand to see you again."

"And high time, I might add," declares no-nonsense Dreena in her no-nonsense voice. "Traipsing off without a word to anyone! I have half a mind to whip your wayward backside for such insolence."

But she only hugs me and pats my back.

Maven regards me as she would a fine piece of art, measuring me. "You seem well, yet I sense that perhaps you are not. Something troubles you, child?"

"I do have something to ask about, but can we have some of your wonderful tea first?" I ask.

I am a grog-and-ale sort of girl by now, but I know the rules here.

Always partake of tea, whether you like it or not. Always pay honor to your hostesses.

We enter the sitting room and take our seats while Benith departs to prepare the tea. I make it a point to ask after all of them specifically, noting and commenting where appropriate, always paying deference. They smile and nod, and Dreena makes a point of declaring that she is pleased to see I have not forgotten my manners. If only she knew. But she doesn't, and I intend to leave it that way. Though I do have some secrets to reveal, nevertheless.

Which I begin to do once Benith sets out the tea and some delicious cookies. I skim over the events of the past few years until I reach the part about discovering my Merrow heritage. The sisters smile but do not seem surprised; did they sense this already? I cover my brief time among the Merrow, my return to land, and eventually my journey back to Viridian Deep in the company of the Water Sprite halfling, Tryn.

Here I do hesitate once or twice, not wanting to give too much away about my feelings. But these are seers of the first order, and not much escapes them.

"This lad means something to you," Maven observes archly.

"More than one something, if I read her right," Dreena adds.

I dutifully blush and admit as much, but assure them that I am alone and have no immediate intentions of changing that.

"There is something more lingering in the background," Benith declares when I go still. "A sadness, a loss. Not yours, but someone near to you. Something bad has happened. Is that why you have come to us?"

"Aside from the desperate need to be certain we are all safe and well, of course," Deena adds.

I smile in spite of myself. "Of course," I agree. "I am here to inquire about my heritage—to see if there is anything you can tell me that will explain more about my Merrow blood. But yes, there is something more. I was accompanied here by my closest friend, Florin, who has fallen on hard times. The man she loved abandoned her when she became pregnant, and then she lost her child at birth. And she still blames herself for it."

"Oh, that is indeed a harsh experience!" Maven immediately agrees. "Losing her lover and her child both? Very sad."

"A difficult experience to endure," Dreena agrees.

"Worse than difficult," I murmur. "Impossible. She doesn't know what to do with herself, now that she's alone again. I wish I could help her to find her way."

"Difficult, but not impossible," Benith says in her mild voice. "Recovery is always possible, if you are patient. Florin sounds like a strong, brave girl. She will weather this. It is always a matter of strength of will and persistence."

"But let us return to your own struggles for a moment," Maven intervenes. "One set of troubles at a time. Would you like to see what we can do to enlighten you about your Merrow heritage?"

I smile. I am more than ready.

SEVENTEEN

THE PROCESS IS FAMILIAR TO ME BECAUSE I HAVE WATCHED IT performed on Harrow. I sit on the couch while the Seers gather around me. Benith prepares a special cup of tea, and it makes me sleepy almost immediately. Then all three sisters begin singing together in soft, soothing voices, urging me to let go and sleep. I do not resist the lure. I relax myself in their care and let go of my instinctive desire to maintain control.

It is a deep and peaceful rest that awaits me when I finally sink into its embrace. I am not even aware when it happens. One moment I am aware of the sisters and their ministrations, and the next I am somewhere else entirely.

I am airborne, freed of the tethers that bind me to my life. The freedom I feel is exhilarating. I sense the world reshaping itself about me, time and place changing.

"STAND STILL, PLEASE," MY MOTHER IS TELLING ME. "A MOMENT or two more, and I will have your dress all ready."

I am a small child, just four years old, and I have no idea where I am or why. I only know it is my mother who speaks to me, and I know she is preparing me for something. She is a tall, slender woman, and her rare smile wins one from me in return. But she is clearly not a Forest Sylvan, as I am. Her skin is a pale coral, and her hair a darker shade of the same, falling in luxurious waves like the sea. Her legs are now covered by her long skirt, but I know that the skin there is whorled with pretty patterns like waves and scales.

She straightens the collar of my dress and fastens my buttons. I do not know why she is dressing me so carefully, but I can sense that it is impor-tant by the way she speaks.

"Can you remember anything I told you about the lady you are going to meet?"

No. But I nod anyway. "She is my friend."

"Do you remember why I said she was your friend?"

"She is going to take care of me."

"Yes, she is."

"Am I going to live with her?"

"Yes, but not for long. Just for a week or so, while I am gone. But she will take care of you as I would. She will be your second mother."

"Can't I come with you?"

"No, that won't be possible."

I wonder why. I think I know a little of what she would say if I asked. She needs to go back to the water. She is always talking about the water. I have caught her on many occasions, crying in the bath. She is unhappy a lot, because she is away from the water. I used to hear her arguing about it with my father, before he died.

"You told me I'd be enough," he'd say. "That you'd give up the ocean for me and not mind it, because you had me."

"I was wrong," she'd sob. "It's like a fire in my blood, the need to return. But I can't. I can't!"

"Because of me?"

"Yes. Because you stole my tail."

"And you hate me for it?"

Silence. Sometimes he would hit her then; sometimes he would just drink until he passed out. And she would cry and cry and cry.

Once, he said: "And what of Charlayne? Do you hate her, too, for looking so much like me?"

I didn't hear her answer, but it has always bothered me, like a splinter under the skin. Before he fell from a tree lane and died, too drunk to find his way home, we could have been twins, with our green skin and hair.

I know she loves me—she tells me so often—but like my father before me, I am beginning to sense that I am not enough in myself to quell her unhappiness. But since my father died, there has been almost a manic energy to her, as if she is planning something. Which seems to come to fruition today.

"You will listen to Miss Josseline, and you will do whatever she asks you to do. You will be a very good girl for her, just like you always are with me."

"Will you be coming back soon?"

"Yes, just as soon as I have been back to the water. I need to go, to see if I can live there again. To force the change. You understand this, don't you?"

I do—and I don't. Mother loves the water. She talks about it all the time. I think she wants to live in the water, but she can't manage it now, because my daddy stole her tail. I wonder if I will have a tail someday, too. I wonder if I will want to live in the water. I wonder what she means by "the change."

"Will I have a tail like you one day?"

I say it quietly, because she has asked me not to speak of it aloud or in front of other people. There is something about the words that frightens her. I do not want to hurt or frighten her, so mostly I do as she asks and keep quiet. But her departure is scaring me, and the words burst out.

"I hope so, sweetie," she tells me. "It is my fondest wish that I can find my tail, and you can discover yours. Then we can be together forever. But don't tell any of this to Miss Josseline. She wouldn't understand. She will think me mad, have me put away, then you will never see me again."

I promise not to talk, since I don't want that to happen. Just thinking about it is very scary. She's all I have, now that my father is gone. I promise myself I will keep all of it secret.

I HAVE NO MEMORIES OF MISS JOSSELINE, OR OF HOW LONG MY mother was gone. Is this how I ended up in the orphanage? Did Miss Josseline send me there when my mother failed to return?

Yet I now know more than I did. I know that my mother loved me but was deeply unhappy—and that her unhappiness may have helped drive my father to his death. From her appearance, I can guess she was one of the Merrow—likely one of the rare Merrow-shifters that Portallis talked about. But it seems that she had somehow lost her ability to change back—or hadn't had the chance to try. And that the water called to her incessantly.

Under the Seers' guidance, I remember these moments for the first time since I buried them deep inside. I must have been so careful of my secret as a child that eventually I forgot all about it.

My thoughts drift, and . . .

I AM STANDING ON A GRASSY VERGE THAT OVERLOOKS A NARROW beach and an ocean that seems to stretch away forever. My mother stands beside me, my hand in hers. She has returned for me as promised, and tells me that today is the day we will be together forever.

But she does not seem any happier than the day that she left me, and there is a manic energy to her, and a wild light in her eyes, that scares me.

"Did you find your tail, Mommy?" I ask her.

I see tears gather in her eyes, but she blinks them swiftly away. "I did not, sweetie. But I know I will today, if we do it together. When I see you find yours, I know I will remember. All you need to do is listen to what I say, and trust what I tell you. You are Merrow, the same as I am. You and I belong in the ocean, and that is where we will go. Together."

I am nervous as she leads me onto the beach and into the water, un-

sure what is coming. We wear light clothing and carry nothing with us. She explains that she wants me to submerge myself in the ocean waters and revert to my natural self—my Merrow self—which she knows is somewhere inside me. Seeing me change, she is sure, will trigger her own transformation. Then we can swim away together.

I am deeply worried. I have never felt the ocean call me, as she has, and I am so much my father's child. Maybe there is none of her in me. I do not have any idea how to breathe in the water; I don't think I can. I have argued repeatedly that we should just steal a boat and escape that way, but my mother is insistent. My tail is inside me, she says. I just need to find it.

I'm not sure I believe her, and the ocean water frightens me.

She walks me down to the water's edge, talking softly to me, trying to reassure me. We enter the water until we are up to our knees and then our hips.

"Just put your face in the water and breathe," she tells me. "Don't try to rush anything. Just relax."

But how can I relax when my entire body is telling me not to do this, infusing me with an anguished, terrifying certainty that I am going to drown? Suddenly, I can't make myself move. My mother tells me to put my head in the water and try to breathe. She tells me to trust her. But I don't. I don't trust anything about what is happening.

She takes me by the shoulders and pushes my head beneath the water. I panic instantly, take a breath without thinking, and begin to choke. But when I lurch free of her grip, she just grabs me and dunks me again. And the more desperate she grows, the longer she holds me under the waves, the more scared I become.

"Please, baby," she says, tears streaming down her face. "Please, just let go."

But I am four, and scared, and I don't understand.

Why is my mother trying to drown me?

I think of what my father said, and wonder if she hates me, too, for being so much like him.

I am almost glad when a passing stranger wrests me from her grip and pushes her away.

She is left, sobbing on her knees, in the surf, and I end up in an orphanage, as Miss Josseline has no desire to keep me permanently.

I never see my mother again.

It comes back to me, all of it. The fear, the struggle, the sense of impossibility. Looking back now, I understand what my four-year-old self did not, that she was trying to force a change that initially comes only on the cusp of death. And being born able to make the shift easily, she likely didn't even realize what it would take to initiate a change in me. But how did she lose her ability to change? Is it something that naturally vanishes with time, or was it something my father did?

I have no answers to these questions, but I understand her better now. She was trying to force the change in both of us—using me as the catalyst—so she could return to the place she knew she belonged.

I don't know where we would have ended up had we not been interrupted by the well-meaning but misguided kindness of a stranger. Maybe I was still too young to make the change, or maybe I could have done it, had I only trusted her more. And could my change really have triggered her own? There is no way to tell.

All I know is that, for years, I did not understand. I did not know why my mother was caught trying to drown me.

But word got around the orphanage and was used against me for the time I was kept there: the girl so unwanted that even her mother tried to drown her . . .

Time shifts, and I am back in the orphanage. I am older *now, but not by much—perhaps five years of age. I have just finished celebrating my birthday, except it wasn't much of a celebration. It was mostly a chance for the other girls to make fun of me, as always.*

"You know your mother hated you, don't you?" Lisbet asks me very

pointedly. She jabs me in my chest with her finger. "She tried to drown you!"

"That's not true!" I say angrily. "It's all a lie. You're telling a lie!"

But it wasn't, was it?

"Oh, it's true. Everybody knows it. Nobody wants you. No one at all."

Lisbet is older, and she has the backing of several more girls who grab hold of me and pin me against a wall. The first girl walks right up to me and spits on me. "Garbage girl! You don't belong here."

I refuse to cry. I just stand there and take her abuse and wish her dead. She has disliked me from day one. She knocks my food off the table. She messes up my bed. She snickers and laughs about me constantly. She is always calling me names.

She jabs me with her finger once more. "Your mother is dead, you know. I heard them talking about it in the front office. After she couldn't kill you, she killed herself. They said she was found floating in with the tide, all cut to ribbons. She threw herself in front of a fishing boat."

I don't believe her. I know she lies—just like she always lies. But I am afraid anyway. "Leave me alone!"

She laughs. "I'll do what I want. I can do anything I want. I don't have to be nice to you. I don't have to pay any attention to you at all. You want to try to change that? Let's see you stop this!"

She walks over to the table where my few presents sit and knocks them all to the floor. Someone gave me a pretty dish, and she smashes it with her foot against the stone floor. I was given a scarf, and she tears it to pieces.

I break free of the hands that hold me and slam into her. She is bigger and stronger, but I am enraged. I savage her with fists and nails, kicking and punching and screaming. I knock her to the floor and begin pummeling her so hard it is all she can do just to cover up.

But an attendant has heard the noise and rushes over to pull me off. "Here, here! None of that! You're a young lady, not a ruffian. All of you, settle down. Right now!"

"She hit me!" Lisbet screams and tries to come at me again, but the attendant shoves her back. Her face is bloodied, her clothes are rumpled, and her face is a mask of fury. "She is dangerous and should be locked away by herself!"

The attendant calls for help, and two more of her associates appear. They herd all of us to our separate rooms and order us to remain there until we are told we can come out again. Much grumbling and whining ensues, but everyone does what they are told, because we all know what will happen if we don't. We still have the marks on our backs to remind us of the consequences of civil disobedience while in the home.

"She ruined my party," I tell the woman who escorts me to my room. "She smashed my glass dish and tore up my new scarf. She hates me, and I don't know why. It isn't fair!"

"Lots of things in life aren't fair," the woman tells me. "And you have to find ways to live with people who don't like you."

She dabs my face with a cold cloth to clean off the blood. "I am sorry about your gifts, but you have to find a way to get along with the other girls."

"I try."

"Trying isn't enough. All of you live here together. You have to learn to get along."

I nod, but she doesn't understand. No one is trying to hurt her.

"Do you know if my mother is all right?" I ask suddenly. "One of the girls said she was dead."

The attendant shakes her head. "Your mother is fine, as far as we know. I will have a talk with Lisbet about this. She runs her mouth for no good reason."

"She said my mother was killed by a fishing boat."

A sharp look on the other's face. "I will talk to her, I promise, and it will be a stern one. She loves to lie, that girl."

But I can see from her expression that perhaps it isn't a lie.

That perhaps it is the truth.

———

YEARS LATER, I FIND MYSELF WONDERING STILL. HAD LISBET BEEN right? Had my mother's despair finally driven her to take her life? Was her body found, run over by a fishing boat?

This is an answer I still need to seek.

But now that the Seers have unlocked what I hid away for all those years, I can remember my mother's face and smooth, easy speech. I can recall her rare smile. She was a troubled woman, but one who still loved me, who tried to bring me with her to a life she loved. But that is all that remains of her.

I fall back into my memories.

I TURN SIX WHILE I AM STILL IN THE ORPHANAGE. FOR A TIME, I dream of my mother returning, and then of someone else deciding to take a chance on me, but nothing happens and slowly my expectations for a different life drift away. Before long, almost all the girls I start out with find homes with new parents—including evil Lisbet. I am certain that I am destined to be unwanted for the rest of my life—the child whose own mother wanted her dead. I wonder if eventually I will become a member of the staff—another attendant in a constantly shifting swarm of faces that never stays the same for very long. I hate the idea, but nothing else seems possible.

Then one day I am summoned to the headmistress's office for a meeting. I am not told who it will be with or what it is about. I am brought to the administrative wing, deposited in an adjoining office by myself, and left alone to wait. I grow restless. More than once, I think to leave. What is the point of enduring this worrisome isolation when there are better things to do?

But eventually the door opens, and an older woman walks in. She is tall and spare and regal, with long emerald hair sweeping down over her shoulders, smooth greenish skin, and eyes like ice in winter. I feel the power emanating from her instantly. Whoever she is, she isn't like anyone I have ever encountered.

I am sitting when the woman enters, but as she approaches, I rise to face her. I am still very young, but already I know the value of standing firm and looking strong in the face of such presence.

"Char," the woman says to me and holds out her hand to take my own in a firm grip. "I am Ancrow, an elder in the Sylvan High Council. I am also mother to a son and two daughters. My partner is dead, and I have not taken another, but I am keen on having more children. Would you like to be one of them?"

She pauses for my answer, but I just stare back at her for a moment, and then I ask, "Is my real mother dead?"

A long, slow stare convinces me I have stepped too far over the line. "She is. She was in the water when a boat ran over her. She was very brave, and I imagine you miss her very much. But now you are all alone and you have nowhere to go. Unless you go with me."

"Why would you want me?"

She smiles. "A fair question. Now let me ask you one in return. Do you think living almost anywhere else could be worse than living here?"

I remain expressionless. "No."

"Then give me your hands, please."

I hold out my hands, and she takes them in her own. She grips them firmly, and an unusual warmth seeps into me, like I am somehow being invaded. It is not unpleasant or threatening, but it is intrusive. Still, I do not try to pull away or shirk her touch. Something tells me to stand firm and let her do what she wants.

A few long minutes pass, and then she releases me. "You miss your mother deeply; you have no family left that you know of and no friends. You have been subjugated and tormented by the other girls. You wish you were anywhere else, but you have no expectations of that happening. Am I right?"

I nod.

"What if I could change that? What if your new life with me would allow you to start over? You would have a mother and siblings. You would have friends. You would have a home. You could grow up like other girls

and expect to be treated well while you did. If I could give you that, would you like to come live with me?"

I don't have to think about it. I know the answer immediately. "I would."

She drops to one knee so that we are eye-to-eye. "Your potential for inish is immense. Do you know that word? Inish? I will teach you all about it. You are smart and you are tenacious, and I will encourage that. I will never let you down, I will never abandon you, and I will never strike you or mistreat you. I will honor you as I expect you to honor me, in turn."

Her smile is dazzling. "Come."

She rises and leads me from the room.

I never look back.

IF THINGS HAD ENDED THERE, IT WOULD HAVE BEEN FINE. I WOULD have been happy enough, content to live with my new mother and my sister Ronden and my brother Harrow. And in a matter of months, my other sister, Ramey, would come to live with us, and she and I would form a special bond as the closest in age. Four years after that, Auris would arrive, and all our lives would change dramatically.

But something else happened first. The memory of it comes back to me in a flash of insight. As I was soon to learn—and then to be reminded of, over and over again—Ancrow was intent on always being in control. And traumatized children were not part of her plan.

So, when we arrived back at her home that day, hauling what few possessions I could legitimately call mine, I was taken to my room and left to settle in. But within an hour, Ancrow returned carrying a pot of tea and glasses. I did not pay attention to it at the time, and it is only now that I remember it all again. I do not recall her ever taking anything from the pot for herself, only pouring out its contents liberally for me.

After she has drugged me, and I am semiconscious and malleable in her hands, she tells me what I must do.

I must forget my mother.

I must forget my bad memories of the orphanage and its inmates and attendees.

I must forget everything about my former life and remember only the life I am living now.

It requires so little for me to banish the unhappy memories that I have so often longed to set aside. I swiftly purge them from my mind.

Now, realizing what has been done to me, I am brought to tears. I know Ancrow well enough to understand her intentions. She wanted me for herself. She wanted me to belong to her alone. She wanted my life with her to mean everything and all else to fade into obscurity.

Which it has.

Until now.

EIGHTEEN

I WAKE SLOWLY FROM MY INDUCED SLUMBER, AND I AM CRYING when I open my eyes. The Seers are there, enfolding me in their aged arms, stroking my leafy hair, whispering words of sympathy and encouragement. I sink into their collective embrace, grateful for their presence even as I feel embarrassed by what I realize they have learned about me.

"I didn't know," I sob. "I didn't know!"

Dreena, always so tough and forthright, draws from somewhere deep within her kindest self. "Memories are tricky things. Some you just outgrow or willfully banish. Others you lose with maturity. But here, someone with considerable power forced you to forget. Do not blame yourself, child. You did the best you could."

I know this, yet I am still dismayed. My own adoptive mother took advantage of me, and I never realized it. Even after learning how she did the same thing to Auris to hide the truth from her about her life, I didn't think it also might have been done to me. And I did nothing to protect myself when it happened. In my desperation to find a home, I allowed my past to be erased. I lost all my memories of my real mother. I forgot what the orphanage was like and how I was treated. I forgot almost everything I had gone through before finding my new family. Everything that had made me *me* in those early years was gone. Until now.

How much had she lied about? Had she lied about my mother being dead, just to get me to go with her? Or was that the truth? It was hard to know, with Ancrow.

My tears dry, and as the sorrow fades, my anger flourishes. I suddenly hate Ancrow with such a passion that I can barely keep from screaming. She took my childhood from me and made me what she wished. How different would I have been if she had left me alone? I will never know. Though I do suddenly wonder if all my impulsive behavior over the years, always leaping so thoughtlessly into the center of things, forever charging ahead when a calmer, wiser person might have waited, is a direct result of all the unremembered trauma and fear of abandonment.

I detach myself from the sisters' comforting arms. I need to be alone for a while, to process all this. I must find a way to live with what I now know about a woman I once loved as a mother. I must do as Auris once did. I must come to peace with what Ancrow did to me.

And I must visit the orphanage, to find out what they know about Lisbet and Ancrow's story.

"Char!" Maven snaps abruptly, regaining my attention. "Sit back down. We are not yet finished."

"What else is left to talk about?" I declare, standing firm. "How much more grief and recrimination am I expected to endure?"

"As much as is required of you!" Dreena declares. "Are you so weakened by what you have learned that you think you cannot bear to address it fully? Tell me, how will you proceed after leaving here?"

"And where will you go next?" Maven presses.

The questions make me bristle, but they have the desired effect. "The orphanage, first, to see if anything Lisbet and Ancrow told me was the truth. After that, I don't know. I am too angry and upset to think clearly right now. But you are right. I need to think things through. I need to find a path to somewhere that makes sense."

"Then you must find the way," Dreena declares. "But you are right: You must learn the truth about your mother's supposed death first."

"And what of the fate of your young friend, Florin?" Maven asks in a surprisingly soft voice. "Did you not say you were worried about her?"

"Did you not express an interest in helping her find her way?" Dreena adds impatiently.

Florin. I had forgotten.

Still, I welcome any reason to move the conversation away from myself. I return to the couch. "I do want to help her. But I don't know how. Have you any thoughts?"

"Ah, child." Gentle Benith sighs. "Think about the nature of your grief and Florin's. Are they not very much the same? Both of you have lost something dear to you. Perhaps, together, you will find a path forward that will ease your respective pains. Perhaps you can help each other."

"I don't know what I can say to her that will help either one of us," I admit.

"You don't have to know. Just talk to her. Find common ground. Things that matter will reveal themselves if you are open and honest. Go to her and see what you can discover."

I think on it. There is truth in what she says, about how something that matters will find a way to the forefront of any discussion between friends.

"I will do what I can," I promise.

"Though I sense this might mean you will have to leave Viridian Deep once more," Benith advises, her concern evident. "That was not your intention, was it?"

I don't know, but I think maybe it wasn't. I think maybe coming home again felt like the right thing to do once I got here. I know the possibility of staying has been tugging at me, but maybe all that will have to change. Maybe my future lies somewhere else.

I smile. "My family will understand if I have to go. Auris, Harrow, Ronden, and Ramey—all of them would do the same if they were in my position. You might be right in thinking the answers to my life—and maybe Florin's, too—may lie elsewhere. But once that's done, I promise I will return."

I am not at all sure about this, but I say the words anyway—much as I did with Winnis and with Portallis. Perhaps I make the promise because I need to convince myself of its importance. Perhaps I say it because it feels like what I should say. In any case, this time, I know it is the right thing to do for both Florin and myself, and I cannot accept knowing that I have done less.

I rise again to leave, but this time the Seers rise with me, offering hugs and kisses and best wishes. Whatever happens now, I know I will carry their support with me.

"Listen to me, young Charlayne," Maven whispers as she guides me through the doorway and out onto the walk. "I feel as my sister does. I sense trouble coming for you, though I cannot sense the direction from which it comes. So watch out for yourself. Keep your guard up and your wits about you. Stay alert. Stay ready."

She is gone almost before I realize it, disappearing back into her home.

But her words linger.

I BACKTRACK DOWN THE PEBBLED WALKWAY TO THE MAIN ROAD, AND from there to the Protective Leaf Orphanage. To my surprise, the new headmistress is one of the attendants I remember from my time there. She welcomes me warmly, says how glad she is to see me well and thriving.

After we chat for a bit, I tell her what I have come for, and ask if Lisbet's story was the truth or a lie.

"As near as I know, it was a lie. We never had any word of your mother's death," she says, "and Lisbet was a notorious fibber. But I suppose you could ask her directly, if that would help."

She tells me Lisbet still lives in Viridian Deep with her adoptive family, and tells me how to find her.

"You know, when Ancrow came to adopt you," she adds, "she asked specifically if either of your parents was still alive. We told her that your father was dead, but that your mother had vanished and we did not know where she was. But we also told her of Lisbet's story, and how we never could quite manage to convince you that it *was* a lie."

Which explains how Ancrow got the story, so I suppose that the only thing left is to confirm it with Lisbet.

I FIND MYSELF ALMOST MORE NERVOUS TO SEE MY CHILDHOOD TOR-mentor than I was to visit the Seers, but when I knock upon her family's door, it is far from the reunion I expected.

A girl about my own age opens the door, and we stand there staring at each other for a few moments. I think I can see traces of the old Lisbet in her face, but then her eyes widen, and she speaks first.

"Char?" she says.

I nod, and she astonishes me by bursting into tears and flinging her arms around my neck. "Char, I am so, so sorry for how I treated you all those years ago. My parents had both died in an accident and I was so angry with the world, and so hurt, that I kept taking it out on other people—especially you, who still had one parent alive. It was . . . it was just my way of taking control of my life, of making everything feel a little less unfair. It wasn't until my new parents adopted me and made me trust in love again that I truly understood how wretched and mean I had been to you. Years later, I saw you and tried to apologize, but you just looked through me as if you didn't know me, and . . ."

A fresh sob breaks out, and I find myself hugging her back. I suppose it is the nature of hurt children never to consider the trauma of others. I had been so wrapped up in my own misery that I had never seen Lisbet's.

I break our embrace and back up a bit, looking into her tearful face instead. "Honestly, Lisbet, I *didn't* know you. I regret to say that my adoption did not seem to be as loving as yours—at least on my mother's side. It seems Ancrow stole all my childhood memories away, to make me more perfectly hers. It was only today, when I went to the Seers, that it all came back. So I wouldn't have had the slightest idea what you were talking about then."

Lisbet's tearstained face looks stricken. "I am sorry, Char . . ." she begins, but I stop her with a smile.

"Ancrow's actions are not your doing, Lisbet, and I got four amazing siblings out of it, so I have no complaints. And rest assured that, had I retained my memories then, I would have gladly accepted your apology. I gladly accept it now."

We hug again, and she laughs. "But I was *such* a witch to you, Char. Do you know what I still feel worst about? The fact that I lied to you, on your *birthday*, about your mother being dead. I got in *such* trouble for that, but it really was a lie. Did you ever find her again?"

"It is what I am trying to do now," I tell her, and she wishes me luck.

"If you ever want to get a meal or . . . just talk," she says.

"I'd love that," I assure her. "I may be going away for a while, but when I get back, I will come see you."

After a bit more reminiscing and another round of hugs, we part, and I feel like another weight has been lifted from my shoulders.

I HEAD BACK TOWARD AURIS'S HOME. I HAVE A LOT TO THINK ABOUT, so I walk slowly. It is already well into midafternoon from the position of the sun and the slope of the shadows. I think about the orphanage, and about Lisbet and her pain. I think about Florin and the loss of her child, and I wonder how willing she will be to revisit the subject. And what about me? How willing am I to talk to Florin about all this? After all, I am only just remembering these memories for the first time since Ancrow banished them, and am still dealing with the impact they generate. An impact painful enough that I have trouble even considering speaking about it. Even to my once closest friend.

I get as far as the flower-strewn entrance to Promise Falls and its attendant Gardens of Life before slowing. On a whim, I wander down the trellised paths and deep into the gardens, where a semi-circle of widely spaced wooden benches provides a place for visitors to sit and look down on the falls as they tumble down in a wild cascade.

I find an isolated bench at one end of the third row and rest there in silence for a time, thinking through everything I remember about my mother, and everything I now know about myself in the time before Ancrow. My whole life feels oddly in limbo. I exist in a place somewhere between my past and an unknown future. I wonder which of my two lives will gain dominance, and if I will ever find a place where I fully belong. And I wonder if Florin will ever find the same place for herself.

I think anew about my time as a Merrow, of how it felt to live within the ocean, surrounded by water. I recall how strange it was at first, and then how quickly I adapted. In many ways, I loved living in the depths with Winnis and Douse, swimming effortlessly and weightlessly through the water. I loved that feeling. I loved that time. I wonder again if perhaps that is where I belong.

But then what of Auris and Harrow and Ronden and Ramey? What of this magical place that always soothes the restlessness inside me?

Eventually, the darkness deepens sufficiently that I find myself all but alone in the gardens, staring up at a sky in which stars are winking into view. Moonlight bathes the whole of the Deep as I rise and leave, still caught up in my thoughts, still wondering what I have committed myself to doing. I have not yet seen anyone in my family but Auris, and I know I must do so. I have not even gone to make my peace with Ramey, and I must especially do that.

Perhaps now is as good a time as any.

Yet still I wander alone for a time. I cannot make myself face Florin just yet, and I don't even want to talk about this revelation with Auris. I have had enough for one day. Tomorrow will be soon enough.

I wander until it is very late. Late enough that night-lights are burning everywhere and most of the residents are fast asleep. I am still thinking about my life and its mysteries, reconsidering the discoveries of the day, wondering how I am going to decide my next move. The sisters seemed convinced Florin and I would find that direction together, yet I wonder.

I turn home, back to Auris's cottage, back to Florin and the children, knowing I have many important tasks ahead. A long day of quiet thought in the Promise Falls gardens has calmed me, but now I am worrying once more. Time is slipping away. Tracking down the rest of the story about my parents will likely take time and effort, and before I can even think of that, I have to meet with the rest of my own family and straighten things out.

When I reach Auris's home, I find the lights all extinguished save one that brightens the entrance. And seeing that all the members of the household have gone to bed, I slip off to join them.

WHEN I OPEN MY EYES ONCE MORE, IT IS MORNING, AND RAMEY IS there, sitting across from me. She is dressed in typical Fae clothing and wears her hair up, pulled back and banded. Her dark eyes fasten on me as if she has never seen anything quite so amazing, but she says nothing.

"Hello, Ramey," I say.

Her face squinches. "Please tell me you did not come all the way back here simply to turn around and leave again. Because that would be more than I could tolerate."

So, I think. *All is not forgiven*. I shake my head. "But I do have to leave again. I just wanted to see all of you first."

She rises and walks over to stand beside me, folding her arms across her chest. "Do you have any idea what you've done? Do you have a single clue about how much trouble you've caused?"

"I didn't mean to."

"Yes, you did. You could have told me what you were doing, or where you were going. You could have given us some sort of notice of your departure. You could have been grown up enough to deal with your issues instead of running away from them. But, no, you had to sneak off in the dead of night without a word to anyone, leaving us to wonder if you were dead or alive. For three years!"

The way she says it makes her feelings quite clear. In her opinion, I have betrayed her and the family. I have been selfish and cruel. I have been entirely self-centered, and unconcerned about everyone but me. And it is difficult to deny any of it.

I take a deep breath to steady myself.

"I know what I have done, and I am sorry for everything. I'm sorry I left without notice and never bothered to send a message later. At the time, it seemed like the best approach. Because I had to go, Ramey. I had to get away from everyone's expectations in order to discover who I really was. And I have done that."

Ramey shakes her head in disapproval, and the anger in her eyes ignites. "I am your big sister. I'm the one closest to you, and I always have been. We shared everything. We never hid anything from each other. Until now. Until this." She pauses, her voice catching. "I loved you so much, Char. I always stood by you. I always watched out for you. But you just cast me aside like I didn't matter. And I cannot tell you how much it hurts, to know I can no longer depend on you."

"I'm sorry, Ramey. A thousand times sorry. I want you to love me again, just as you once did. I want you to let me love you in the same way. I promise, I will find a way to prove to you that I deserve your forgiveness. Auris has forgiven me, so maybe you can find a way to do so, too? Even if it takes time? Even if I have to work hard at it?"

She shakes her head. "I cannot even talk to you about it."

Now I am crying, too. "Then let me talk to *you* instead. Let me tell you something about what has happened to me."

She does not respond, so I forge ahead with my story. I tell her everything about my time away, much as I did for Auris, leaving nothing out. At first, her face is stony and unrevealing. But as I get deeper into my story and start telling her of my time within the waters of the Helles as a Merrow, I can see her wonderment at my words. There is a sudden look of understanding and surprise that wasn't there before.

"You knew nothing of this?" she demands at one point. "Nothing at all? You didn't even suspect that you might be different?"

"If I had known—or even suspected—I would have told you first. But Ancrow took all that from me. She stole my past—just as she stole Auris's. The gap created by that theft hurts me more than I can tell you. I realize now how it left a hole that, all my life, I have been trying to fill. I was so unhappy, Ramey. I knew there was something missing, even if I did not know what or how. After a while, that emptiness was all I could think about—and there was nothing anyone could do about it. Not even you."

I go on with my tale, closing with a brief recitation of the events surrounding my meeting with Glad Jack and Tryn, which led me back home. I leave nothing out save only the parts about Florin and her child.

When I finish, Ramey looks at me the way you might a warthog or a slimy toad, and shakes her head. "Nothing has changed—nor will it ever where you are concerned. You have always been one step away from your next problem. You were born looking for trouble, and you seem to have no problem finding it."

"I do not go looking for trouble, and nothing that has happened to me is my fault! I did not ask to be born a Merrow. I did not ask to be kidnapped by Goblins. I did not ask to be hunted by Humans. All I am trying to do is to find out about my past and make some sense of it."

"Which is why you made such a quick connection with pirates. Which is why you managed to find the Merrow and your identity and still not know anything much about either. Which is why you forsook your piratical caregiver—the so-called Silver Blade, heathen of the south seas, a man you said you loved—for a new adventure and a different man. Which is why you got attacked by a Kraken. Are you listening to yourself? Are you at all aware of how ridiculous it all sounds?"

She throws up her hands in a dramatic gesture. "Well, all the best to you. I hope you find your way. Come back again sometime and share some more wild stories. I'm always here, eagerly waiting to listen to your next impossible tale, waiting to learn what happens next!"

She gives me that riveting look of displeasure that only she can manage, then storms out of the room and slams the door behind her. I watch her departure in shock, wondering if things will ever be right between us again.

NINETEEN

I REMAIN IN MY ROOM FOR THE REST OF THE DAY, SLEEPING ON AND off, drinking a variety of fluids that Auris brings me, and thinking about my mess of a life. Florin is away exploring Promise Falls and the Gardens of Life with Parse as her guide. I am surprised at first, given the boy's quiet reserve, but Auris reassures me he has taken to Florin. I am told they plan to take lunch together and will not return until dinner.

When evening arrives, the entire family gathers to share dinner and conversation, for Harrow has now returned. I once again relay my story and beg their forgiveness for having run away three years back. Harrow is as quick to forgive me as Auris, but Ronden and Ramey remain a different story. Ronden always did think I was spoiled and overpraised at an early age, and that I'd never applied myself as I should. While I speak, I see her shaking her head more than once, and her comments repeatedly suggest that she feels it is time I grow up. Ramey has already made her opinion very clear and says nothing. She will barely even look at me, and she leaves early without saying good night. I doubt there is much chance of her forgiveness, at least for the moment.

When the others have departed, Florin takes it upon herself to read stories to Parse until he falls asleep, while Auris feeds Safra and puts her to bed. Then I sit alone with Auris and speak to her about what I learned from the Seers, and what they have suggested I do next. We are not alone more than half an hour before Parse returns, sits down at his small table, and returns to his building project. It is Florin who has fallen asleep. I try to catch Parse's eye, but he is too engaged in his work.

"I know I said I was back to stay, but now I am not certain," I tell Auris, keeping my voice down. I glance now and then at Parse, worried that he might be listening, but he never looks up. "As the Seers advise, I have to speak with Florin. I don't know how that will help, but the Seers seem to think it will."

"Do you have something specific in mind?"

That's typical of Auris—always have a plan. "I don't. Not exactly. And I might not recognize it until I find it."

"Do you want me or one of the other members of the family to come with you? For company and maybe assistance?"

I shake my head. "This is my quest, and I need to do it alone. Or with Florin at most."

"You seem to have matured quite a bit, Char. And I suspect you will be fine so long as you can remember to think things through before acting." She pauses. "I thought you might want to ask Ramey to accompany you."

"Not this time. Ramey will barely speak to me. She is still furious at me for leaving without telling her. She thinks I should have confided in her, and she is probably right. But I chose badly, and for the moment she is not interested in forgiving me for my mistake."

"That won't last. Ramey isn't the sort to hold grudges." Auris hesitates and then says, "Whatever happens, remember that your family is here. Remember you are important to us, and we love you."

We talk awhile longer, and then Auris rises to check on Safra. I sit alone with Parse as he remains at his worktable, putting together some sort of contraption he is building out of sticks, paper, glue, and bits of stone. I have no idea what it is. He is intent on finishing his work, and he barely glances at me until I rise from where I am sitting. Worn out by the events of the day, I decide it is time to go to bed.

Parse gets up immediately and comes over to hug me. I wrap my arms around him. "Brave boy," I whisper. "I will miss you."

I will miss you, too.

"Take good care of your mother and sister."

He nods, then says in his voiceless whisper, *Be careful. I see shadows. They surround you. Don't trust them. Don't let them come too close.*

Then his arms tighten around me, and he whispers, *Where are you going?*

"I don't know yet," I confess. "I have to decide."

He stares into my eyes. *There is a Water Sprite who has memories of your mother. Florin knows who it is. Go to him. Listen to his memories. Find out the truth.*

Then he pauses, his eyes locked on mine. *Go save those who were stolen. They are waiting for you.*

Abruptly, he breaks away from me and goes into his bedroom, closing the door behind him.

Save those who were stolen? Who is he talking about? I wonder at the meaning and clear urgency of his words, but I am not getting any more answers tonight.

I SLEEP BETTER THAN I HAD THOUGHT I WOULD, MANAGING TO PUSH aside all the troubles and difficulties I am facing and simply giving in to my weariness. The next morning, I dress and go into the dining area to eat the cereal and fruit Auris has left for me. She has gone out with the children and I am alone in the house with Florin. As I eat, I think of what I must do. Parse has given me a place to start. How he knows what he does eludes me, but somehow he does. It is time for me to act on it.

I go back to our bedroom and wake Florin. She is rumpled and vaguely irritated. She mutters into her pillow. "Don't want breakfast. Just want to sleep. Go away."

I rough her up sufficiently that she finally sits up. "I need to go on a journey. I thought you might want to come with me."

She surveys me, then holds up one finger—an unspoken request that I wait a minute. Then she rises and goes into the bathroom, leaving me alone. She washes, dresses, then packs a bag right in front of me—wordless the entire time. Afterward, she goes into the kitchen to eat, and once she's finished with all that she says, "Okay. Where are we going?"

She says it with such enthusiasm that I laugh.

"Don't laugh at me. Bad enough that I have to spend months with some sort of weird mushroom head without you chuckling away the whole time."

Florin has begun growing back her striking black hair, which was always her best feature—so spiky yet shiny. But growth is slow yet, and the fuzzy carpet that coats her head is oddly reminiscent of forest undergrowth. Still, with girls like us who have always kidded each other relentlessly, everything is fair game.

We are out the door and starting down the winding length of the tree lane when Auris appears, carrying Safra in her arms and leading Parse by his hand. She sees Florin beside me, takes a good look at the packs we are carrying, and nods in approval. We embrace wordlessly. There is no need for further talk, and she does not offer it. Instead, she reaches into her cloak and pulls out a knife tucked snugly into a sheath.

"Take this," she whispers in my ear. "The blade is of the most excellent work and will never break. It was given to me by Harrow, and now I am giving it to you. It will be protection for you on your journey."

She kisses my cheek and mouths the words, *Be careful.*

Then, with a smile and a brief nod for Florin, she passes me by as silently as she approached and goes back inside her house. *Back to join her life-mate*, I think in envy. Back with her two wonderful children. Back to the world and the happiness she has made for herself.

I tuck the sheathed knife within my cloak and pat it comfortingly. I will treasure it.

In moments, Florin and I are on our way. The sun is more than an hour risen, a blaze of white light in a cloudless eastern sky. I turn toward it—toward the Roughlin and the villages of the Water Sprites. I know by now that my journey begins there.

Florin follows me wordlessly for a time, and then asks, "So, where *are* we going?"

I tell her everything—almost. I reveal what little I know about my real parents and my mother's disappearance. I tell her how the Seers uncovered bits and pieces of my early life by retrieving my lost memories, and of Ancrow's efforts to banish those completely. And about how I have decided it will be good for us to share one more adventure. I do not tell her what Parse told me or how he seems able to divine the future. That can wait. *Start slow*, I think. Reveal things in order and as needed. Florin is still coming to terms with her own life difficulties. There is no need to address these yet.

"Wow," she exclaims. "An adventure! Just like the old days. So what are we trying to find out about your mother, Char? And does any of it matter now?"

"I don't know," I reply, thinking it through. "I want to find out what happened to her. Where she is, if she is still alive. It's important to me. The past forms a foundation for the present; everything that happens builds on itself. Like the way Parse builds whatever it is he is working on right now, one piece at a time. I can better understand the present if I can come to terms with the past. Besides, I now know my mother did not die as I believed, so where did she go? And why did she never come back for me?"

Then I remind her how both of us must find ways to come to terms with our pasts if we want to continue to expand and grow as adults.

"I'm not even that old yet, and I know this to be so. I am able to accept the truth about myself much better now that I know more about the forces that have molded me. Ancrow would have hidden my past from me forever, but she was wrong to do that. I am happier knowing the truth. And now I want all of it. I want to know everything about myself that there is to know. Don't you want the same for yourself?"

The question results in a long pause as Florin considers. "I don't know. Much of what has happened to me is so unpleasant that knowing it at all is difficult to bear. I can hardly stand knowing I have lost my baby . . ."

She trails off and goes quiet. I leave it at that for now.

We are deep into the forests in what seems like no time at all, close to the walls of the valley where we will climb to leave Viridian Deep and continue on into Water Sprite country. It is midday, and the sun is overhead.

Impulsively, I turn to Florin and take her in my arms. "If I could do so, I would change everything back for you. I would make your life happier. I don't know if I can do that, but I can still be your friend and try to help make things better. I need that from you, too. That's why I asked you to come with me. I think we need each other."

She hugs me back. "We share similar lives, don't we?" she whispers. "Both of us have lost something precious. You've lost your parents and I've lost my child. But you have found something that matters to you. You have found another side to yourself, another life, while I am still locked into the one I was left with when my lover abandoned me and my child died. I am so unhappy, Char."

I break the embrace and hold her out at arm's length. "Then we will have to find a way to change all that. We will have to make you happy again, find you your place in life. Won't we?"

She laughs. "You were always the positive one, always the girl for whom anything was possible."

"And you were always the girl who insisted there was nothing we couldn't do. Which of us was the craziest?"

Florin makes a face. "Obviously, it was you. Look at what you are—some sort of Mermaid! Hey, you have to show me how it works. You have to get into the water and change yourself into a Merrow! First chance you get, you have to! Promise me."

Now I laugh, too. "I promise."

For those few seconds, she is herself again—the girl I was so close to, my best friend forever, my other self. I am so happy to see her like this. I will find a way to make it last. I will do that for her.

Somehow, I will find a way.

OUR JOURNEY THAT DAY AND THE NEXT IS SWIFT AND SURE. I AM feeling much better about everything—reassured about the possibilities of what we can do and anxious to get on with doing it. We talk at length as we travel about everything we intend, yet still I keep what Parse told me to myself, not yet ready to enter into that discussion. We rediscover our old ease with each other. There is much laughing and teasing. And for the moment, nothing else matters.

Not that I have forgotten what brings me this way. The words and advice of the Seers, combined with Parse's cryptic warnings, have set me on my path. But where once I would have chafed at the effort to exercise patience, I now do it with ease. *Everything will come in time*, I tell myself. And I do believe it.

Our first evening on the road, in the cool of the forest twilight and beneath the rise of a full moon, I finally decide to tell Florin what Parse told me—though I will not tell her about Parse himself. That seems both complicated and an invasion of my nephew's privacy.

"I have something important to talk to you about," I tell her as we sit gazing at the moon. "It might sound strange, but I have been told that, to learn more about my mother, I must travel first to Water Sprite country. There is someone there who has memories of them. And apparently, you know who that is?"

She gives me a look, rubbing the fuzzy top of her by-now only partly shaved head. "Do you have a name?"

"No. I was just told you would know it."

"That's a bit vague, Char. Why would *I* know it?"

I shrug. "I'm as baffled as you. But they said you would know who it is, and I should listen to his memories and then do what I feel is right. I know: This makes no sense to me, either. But my instincts tell me it is true."

"Well, then, what are we trying to find out from this person? What is it exactly that this person knows?"

I sigh deeply. "I told you. Just memories about my mother. I don't know what those memories are, or anything else." I decide not to say anything whatsoever about being asked to save those who were stolen. I think that might be a bridge too far. "One thing, though. I felt like I was being cautioned about this person, that it was someone who might not be so friendly."

"Ohhhhh, Shades!" Florin draws the words out in what amounts to a long-hanging hint of recognition. "Maybe I *do* know. But if I am thinking of the right man, he is not going to be of much help. He never is. The man I am thinking of is mean-hearted clear through."

All of this sounds bad to me, but I still don't know who she is talking about. But if he is a Water Sprite, I should know him.

"Who is he?" I ask.

"A dealer in souls. A trader of lives. Auris could tell you. She knew him well enough. Better than she would have liked."

Right away, I know who Florin is talking about.

And my heart sinks.

WE SET OUT EARLY THE FOLLOWING MORNING, INTENT ON REACHING Water Sprite territory before sunset. It is still a ways to go, but we know our limits, and the path we follow this day is not daunting. The weather is fine, and our journey is relatively simple and unchallenging. We are avoiding the ravine and the roughness of the land we passed through on our way to Viridian Deep, even though it lengthens our path.

But after only two hours of walking, I am already beginning to tire, thinking over what I know about the man we are seeking. Of all the choices available, this one is the worst.

It takes us the rest of the day to complete our journey, and we are both a bit worn down by the time we reach our destination. We work our way through the village to Zedlin's house.

Zedlin has never taken a partner, which I find odd for someone with such a cheerful personality. He is a good, hardworking man with real skills and experience, yet work seems to be all that matters to him. But perhaps the cause for that walks at my side. If Florin has ever had a regular home, it is with Zedlin, and perhaps caring for his wayward sister is all he feels capable of now. Or maybe he worries that, by taking a partner, he would be abandoning his duties to her.

More reason, I decide, for me to help Florin find her place in the world.

When we reach Zedlin's door, Florin and I both call out to him through the entry. In the Water Sprite world, doors are seldom closed—or often even present—but visitors are supposed to announce themselves nevertheless.

When Zedlin appears, he breaks into a laugh. "Looks like trouble to me!" he teases. "What happened? I didn't expect to see you both back here so soon."

We exchange hugs, enter his home, and take seats in two of the chairs before his stone fireplace. His cottage is small and efficient, built for endurance and minimal upkeep. Because of our proximity to the Roughlin, evenings are cooler here than in the Deep, so several chunks of wood burn low and warm in the fireplace.

I've known Zedlin since he was still a boy, about five years older than me. He was also an orphan, with Florin as his only family, and his friends mostly orphans like himself. Harrow helped him find a path into his adulthood, though he abandoned the Watcher's path he had once aspired to for the underwater navigational skills that now earn him a living. I met him soon after Auris and Harrow partnered—now more than nine years back—and we became friends, though we were never as close as Florin and I became.

Still, I have always liked and respected him, and he has done me many favors in the years when I was wandering between my home in Viridian Deep and his oceanside community.

I wait patiently as he fetches food and drink, and then we all sit down to eat. Zedlin begins questioning us almost immediately.

"You've had an opportunity to speak with each other? To catch up on everything that's happened since you separated? You told Char everything there is to tell, didn't you, Florin?"

I see Florin flinch at the unvoiced suggestion that she might have chosen to hide something and quickly step in.

"I think we have covered everything, yes, both good and bad."

"Good. I'm sorry to be so abrupt, and I don't mean to be accusatory. I am glad she has a friend. She has not had an easy time of it lately. So what do the two of you plan to do now?"

"We are on a quest for information, and might require your help. Are you willing to aid us?"

"Of course! I will help in any way I can. What is it you need?"

"Nothing pleasant," Florin announces, scowling. "We need to speak to Trinch."

"Trinch?" Zedlin looks appalled. "What business could you possibly have with him?"

"He has information I need," I tell him. "I doubt he'd be willing to speak to me, but you know the man. You have worked for him a time or two. Can you arrange a meeting?"

"No!" he says at once. "Please, find another way. Don't walk that path. Just don't. You know what he is."

I know. But knowing isn't enough to make me change my mind.

TWENTY

THE FOLLOWING MORNING, AFTER SPENDING THE NIGHT AT ZED-lin's cottage, Florin and I break our fast with him in relative silence, then we all leave the house and walk through the village toward Trinch's place.

It took some doing for Zedlin to agree to this, but I eventually prevailed.

Everyone in the Water Sprite homeland knows Trinch, but you would be lucky to find even a couple who have anything good to say about him. He is best known as a facilitator—someone who does the unpleasant jobs that no one else wants to do. Name something you couldn't bear the thought of doing, and odds are good that he has done it. He is the one who took Auris from Ancrow because Ancrow didn't want her, and I am still devastated that this is the way my sister had to start her life. And now it seems he had his hands all over my life as well—though in what way, I have yet to discover.

Trinch lives in the same ramshackle house he has occupied for as long as anyone can remember. It is set well apart from the main

village and encircled with a combination of barbed wire and electri-
fied fencing that makes clear no one is welcome. But Zedlin has
been coming here since he was a boy, serving the old man doing
chores and favors for coins. They were never friends, but Zedlin was
honest and capable enough that Trinch came to trust him and paid
him what he promised.

"Even so," Zedlin warns me, "you will be at risk. He will do you
no physical harm, but he will consider you fair game for every other
form of mistreatment. I am fairly sure he is not entirely sane, so
don't make the mistake of accepting anything he says at face value—
or assuming it is true or accurate. The man is devious. Watch your
back, tuck away your heart, and stay true to yourself. And bring
plenty of coins."

Zedlin knows of a secret way into the sealed compound, so he
opens it up for Florin and me and walks us through the ruined yard
and up to the dilapidated porch. It seems impossible to me that the
house still stands, given its ragged and weather-worn appearance. It
is also dark and silent. Its windows are closed, sealed with wooden
shutters and tightly drawn shades. Junk lies all about the yard, much
of it unrecognizable. In places, the ground is swampy and fetid.

"Do not speak about or reveal your feelings," he continues. "Stay
neutral and disengaged. He will take your measure right away and
be searching for your weaknesses. So do not give him even a hint of
what they are."

I don't think I need the reminder, but I nod in agreement. Zedlin is concerned for my safety and well-being, and such worries are
not to be discounted.

As Florin and I watch, he climbs the rickety porch steps and
moves to the closed doorway. Two sharp knocks, a long pause, and
then two more harder knocks follow. Nothing happens. We both
stand where we are, until finally, after several long minutes, the
door cracks open and an inaudible voice emits a dissatisfied growl.
Zedlin answers. I can hear their muffled voices speaking softly, but I

cannot make out the words. I am already anticipating what lies ahead. I have never met this man; I've never even seen him. All I know is what Auris once told me, and I hope that is enough.

The door closes again, and Zedlin turns around and comes down off the porch to where Florin and I are waiting.

"He will speak with you—alone and inside his home. I warned you he might insist on that, and he has. I will wait out here. If there is any sort of trouble, just yell, and I will come right away. Just re-member what I said about what to expect and how to behave."

We both nod, then walk up the creaking steps and approach the door, which opens just as we reach it. It opens so quickly that I am caught off guard. A cackle of laughter greets me, and a ragged arm holds the door open, but its owner remains in darkness. "Come in, young ones, come in."

I don't hesitate. I walk right past him into an interior that is so gloomy, the twin candles burning in the background reveal almost nothing. I turn to face Trinch and find him standing right in front of me, his squinted, harsh features entirely too eager. Even in the poor light and deep shadows, I can see he is an ancient creature, scrawny to the point of emaciation. A mop of gray hair is thin and receding fast, his beard is a choppy mess, and his face is a gnarled mask of healed-over wounds and pockmarks.

"Speak your business," he snaps. "No, wait, not yet!" He glances over at Florin, then back at me. "Give me your names. We should share a bit of information before we talk of other things."

"My name is Char. My mother was Ancrow. My friend is Florin; she is Zedlin's younger sister."

"Ahhh," he intones, staring at Florin with a nasty smile. "I know you. The little hussy. The baby's all gone now though, isn't it? A mistake rectified by nature. Must have been hard. Or maybe you were grateful to have the brat gone." He shrugs. "You look strong enough to bear a few more, though."

Somehow, Florin manages to keep her expression blank. I would have gone for his throat.

He looks now at me. "And you? Ancrow's whelp, are you? Hog-wash and goat spit. Ancrow was no relation of yours. She took you from an orphanage and made you her own little pet. No one knows your real mother. Or maybe I am mistaken? Maybe someone does? You've come to find out, haven't you? Who do you really belong to? Who is your real mother? That's what you want to know, isn't it?"

Zedlin, apparently, was forced to reveal the reason I was here in order to get me an audience. Trinch catches my look, his eyes narrowing. "Wait, now. I see a glimmer in your eyes that speaks of the truth. You already *know* something about her, don't you? How much?"

I decide not to lie. "She was a Merrow."

"A split-tongued lie, you little whelp! Merrow don't exist!"

This catches me by surprise. Perhaps he isn't as much in command of things as he would like to think.

"I thought that, too, but I was wrong. My mother was a Merrow. After she vanished, I was raised by Ancrow."

"Ancrow? Huh, no one misses *her*! Gone now, which makes things better for us all. Gone the way we all go, the filthy witch. But she was dangerous, I'll allow that. People died around her—lots of them. So, what do you want to know? Why have you come to see me?"

He is standing too close. His breath stinks, and his body with it. If I looked more carefully, I would probably see that he has small things crawling on him. I am repulsed, but I stand my ground.

"I need help finding out about my mother. She was one of the Merrow, as I've said. I remember something of her from when I was very young, but someone told me you can tell me more."

"Well, someone told you wrong. I don't take names and I don't remember faces. People come and people go. I can't be bothered to keep track of who they all are. What would she have wanted from me anyway?"

"That is what I am trying to find out. My mother was caught trying to bring out my Merrow side, but folks thought she was trying to drown me . . ."

Trinch cocks his head and smiles, revealing his crooked teeth. "Maybe she *was* trying to drown you. Maybe she knew what a troublesome brat you would become."

". . . so I was taken away from her and placed in an orphanage, and I never saw her after that. But I do know she was looking for her tail, which she claimed my father had stolen," I continue, doing my best to ignore his taunt. "Did she maybe come to you for aid? This would have been about thirteen years back."

Trinch rubs his chin as he looks away and thinks for a minute. "Huh. Maybe I do remember one thing that might be of interest. But thinking is so hard for me when it yields so little. But if you had a coin or two to spare . . ."

The ingratiating way he asks it is repulsive. But following Zedlin's advice I brought coins, and I produce one now, holding it out to him. He snatches it away, bites it to determine its quality, and spits. "Worn, but true. Well, then. Let me see." He scrunches up his face. "A woman who thought herself a fish . . . That stirs a memory. Ah, yes, now it comes clear to me. She said she'd lost her tail and so was walking about like you and me, but she was trying to get back to her people. Although my memory is so poor these days, I might be mistaken."

He wants more money. I have the coins, but before I can reach for them, Florin acts. She is on him so quickly that he has no chance of defending himself. She is lithe and strong, and she bears him down and pins him to the wooden cabin floor with such force that the combined weight of them falling cracks open a handful of the ancient boards. She is on top of him before he can recover, pressing her knife up against his throat.

"We asked nicely. We gave you coins. Now tell her what you know. Otherwise, I will kill you on the spot and find the answers from someone else!"

He sneers. "There *is* no one else to ask. Kill me and your answers die with me."

Her eyes are cold. "Maybe. But you'll still be dead. And at least my friend will have her coins back, once I take them off your lifeless body. Now tell her something of worth—and don't try to sell us anything less, old man! I have no reason to let you live, and I doubt that anyone in this village does, either. Your death will cost me nothing."

He laughs in her face. "At least I will have lived a life that meant something. I wouldn't have wasted it pointlessly, like you have." His sudden grin is horrid. "At least I wouldn't have lost a *child*!"

For a moment, I am certain Florin will kill him on the spot. The bitterness in her expression is terrifying. "Florin," I say softly. "No."

She ignores me. Her decision seems to have been made. She has had enough of this wretch. But then she simply spits on Trinch's withered face and gives him a long, almost tender cut across his throat—not deep enough to kill but a clear sign of her intent. This is no bluff, and we all know it. "Mind your tongue, old fool. At least I won't die hated and forgotten! Now tell us what you know."

"Let me up!"

"I don't think so. Speak the truth first, and then we'll see."

Her face is fierce, her eyes cold. I have never seen her like this. For a moment, I am certain she has turned into someone entirely different from the girl I knew. Her life and experiences have toughened her to a point where anything is possible.

Trinch must see it, too. "This woman came to me, about thirteen years back, like you said. She was seeking a way home again. She was from a colony somewhere south of here. She was Merrow, she said, but her tail had been stolen, and she thought her people could help her get it back. I thought her deranged. Merrow don't exist, and how does one lose a tail anyway? What does that even mean? I had no help for her, and she had no coins, so I sent her away."

"Did she tell you where she was from?" I ask quickly. "Where, to the south?"

He shakes his head angrily. "I've told you what I know. I couldn't help her, and I can't help you. Get out of my house!"

I flush sharply, genuinely infuriated now. "You agreed to tell us everything, yet you've told us almost nothing! Don't play games with us, Trinch."

Florin presses her knife deeper into the cut and I actually see fear in his eyes—though he tries to bluff. "Well, that's as it may be. You choose your own poison. I am prepared to choose mine. And my motto is: Never give anything away for free."

I want to punch him in his horrid face, but I tamp down on any hint of those feelings and nod. "We will give you your life if you tell me something of real value. If you are truthful, I will ask Florin to let you keep breathing. Otherwise, I will leave it up to her."

He spits at me. "The woman—your mother—didn't have a name for her colony, or at least not one I recognized. So I sent her to someone who might know. I don't have any idea what happened to her after that." He pauses. "I suppose you expect me to give you his name and place of business, don't you?"

Florin presses her knife a little deeper into his neck, and he gives me both. There is blood flowing freely down his neck now. I would feel slightly sick at her ruthlessness if her target wasn't so horrid.

I nod to Florin, and she climbs off him. "Stay on the floor," she warns. "I'll help you find a way to stay there if I see you move."

We go out the door without another word, back into fresh air and sunshine. If I never enter this house again, it will still be too soon.

But at least I have a path forward.

TWENTY-ONE

"I'M COMING WITH YOU," ZEDLIN ANNOUNCES AS SOON AS I HAVE finished telling him everything that Trinch revealed. We are standing in his home facing each other, having just returned from our confrontation with Trinch. "And don't bother telling me all the reasons I can't. I know that look, Char. It won't work. I'm coming. I don't want you facing a known associate of Trinch's on your own!"

It isn't as if he knows anything more about the man than me. Like me, he only has a name: Crinksee. And a location in Far Reach City—by reputation, a lawless place. So his instincts tell him we need protection—mostly, I think, because he sees Florin and me as helpless girls who require someone stronger to accompany them on what he views as a dangerous expedition. And he may not be wrong. We could probably use some extra help. Florin only mastered Trinch because of his age. A younger, stronger man, and we both might be in trouble.

But part of this quest is about proving to Florin that she can take charge of her own life, and having Zedlin along—the overprotective big brother—will negate that.

Though given how she treated Trinch, I wonder how ready she

really is for a life without supervision. She was so proud when we left, boasting how she had gotten us the information and saved us the coin, but I am not so certain. I saw his eyes when we left. We have made a powerful enemy.

Still . . .

"Florin and I need to do this alone," I tell him. "We are perfectly capable, and neither of us wants responsibility for something happening to you or anyone else."

Zedlin is surprisingly calm as he says, "It isn't safe for two young girls. Even you two. You've had some experience, but where you are going you will need a good deal more than that." He shakes his head in despair. "You have to have someone else with you."

What we really need is someone who won't spend all of his time second-guessing everything we decide to do. That puts Zedlin out of the picture. Even if he leaves me alone, he won't be able to stop offering Florin unwanted advice at every turn.

"Let me think about it," I suggest, trying to buy some time.

Then I turn and leave Florin and her brother before either one can say anything more, moving out of the cottage and into the surrounding trees. Zedlin is right, of course. This will likely be dangerous, and I have no logical argument for asking him to stay behind or trying to limit his involvement—other than the invasiveness his presence will present. And if I tell him that, he will promise not to be, and will mean it, and will do it anyway. It is just who he is.

So I wander down to a favorite spot on the river and sit looking out as the waters flow past, listening to the birdsong, smelling the wildflowers, and weighing my choices. Until I am suddenly presented with a new choice entirely.

"Char!" A familiar voice hails me, and Tryn appears, taking a seat beside me. I try not to look into his face, into those amazing eyes, but I can't seem to help myself. "I saw you and your friend going into that house with Zedlin," he says. "I didn't catch up to you quite in time, then heard you arguing and decided not to interrupt."

"You heard what we said?"

"Well enough. So I decided to wait until I could speak with you alone. Are you all right?"

"Not so much." I tell him about how Florin and I plan to go to Far Reach to find a man named Crinksee, who might be able to tell me more about my mother's fate. And how Zedlin thinks it is too dangerous for us to go alone.

He thinks about this for a moment when I have finished, then smiles and says, "What if I go with you and Florin instead?"

I feel my heart lurch. It's ridiculous on every level but a visceral one, but I revel in it anyway. "Why would you do that? It makes even less sense for you to go than for Zedlin. This isn't your problem. This is something I need to do for personal reasons."

He looks at me intently. "Maybe I want to do it for personal reasons, too."

Now I am confused. *Is he saying what I think he is?*

He hesitates as he sees the look on my face but then continues. "In the days you've been gone, I've been busy learning about my heritage and life as a Water Sprite. My father never told me much about it, and my mother died too soon. I've learned how to swim and breathe the water. Look at my gills!"

He points at both sides of his neck. Sure enough, gills are now visible on both sides, the lines clearly marked. "At first, they would vanish every time I left the water, but not anymore. Thanks to my time here, I've changed, grown into something different. Not exactly like you, but somewhat closer. I am ready and able to help you, Char."

"But . . ."

"Consider it a moment," he urges. "You're off to Far Reach, right? Well, I know the waters you plan to sail better than Zedlin. Better even than Glad Jack, probably. I've been to the city, and I know the dangers it entails. I can help you. Give me a chance to try."

I love both the words and the implication they carry, but some part of me doesn't understand why he would suggest this. Give him a chance? To risk himself for me? Why would he want to do that?

But the practical side of me slides into place. It doesn't matter. I could use the help. His offer is the best I can hope for, and it solves my problem of not wanting Zedlin along.

"If you really think this is something you want to do . . ."

"It is."

". . . then I guess it would be all right if you . . ."

"Then it's settled. I want to be with you on this journey, Char. I want to help you."

". . . really think it is a good . . ."

"It is exactly what I want."

". . . idea . . ."

I hold up my hand to stop us both from saying anything more. I am aware that I am blushing furiously, and equally aware of why. It is all wrong—and at the same time, entirely right. I admit that I am smitten by this man. I still care for Brecklin, but he seems almost a thing of the past. Besides, what I feel about Tryn is much stronger than what I ever felt about the Blade. I think less and less of the Silver Blade by the day, and my sensible side tells me there is a good reason for this. My attentions by now are all focused on Tryn. I do care about him.

I reach impulsively for Tryn's hand and take hold. "All right. But we need Florin to agree, too."

His own hand squeezes mine back.

FLORIN AGREES IMMEDIATELY. SHE IS AS DRAWN TO TRYN AS I AM, I sense, and loves the idea of having him come with us. I should be worried about this but then decide I am being selfish.

So now there is only the matter of breaking it to Zedlin. But Tryn, of course, handles it masterfully. He proves to be an excellent strategist, neatly and logically countering each of Zedlin's arguments. And once Zedlin is convinced that Tryn is the right person to accompany us, the matter is quickly settled.

We will set out on the morrow and use the remainder of the day to fit out a vessel and pack our supplies.

We are luckier than I would have thought possible. The Water Sprites have been unable to retrieve Tryn's sunken vessel, so they have provided a substitute. It does not have the full abilities of the 520, but it is adequate for our needs. Tryn is a wizard with any boat and quickly learns to sail it. Tryn and I spend the day outfitting and testing the equipment while Florin cleans the cabins and packs our supplies, and by the morrow we will be ready to go.

That night, once dinner is completed and all that remains is sleep, I walk down to the river with Tryn at my side, and allow him to kiss me long and hard. I kiss him back, of course, and I would likely have allowed much more, but he pulls back and suggests that maybe this might not be the right time. I am surprised and disappointed, but I am also grateful. He is enough of a friend and protector to know that sometimes less is more.

WE LEAVE AT DAWN, SETTING SAIL IN A SOUTHEASTERLY DIRECTION, right into the sunrise and the start of a new day, the taste and smell of the sea wind a welcome home. I want to dive overboard and swim in its waters, and the urge is almost too strong to resist. One day soon, I will respond to the pull of my Merrow blood. One day soon, I will embrace this new and exciting part of my life. Especially with Florin urging me on.

Not long after we leave the Water Sprite shores and sail beyond the artificially constructed islands that serve as their defensive outposts, Tryn catches the wind and lets out the sails. The feeling is exhilarating, riding in swoops and surges upon the waves. I am buoyant and flushed with joy.

Impulsively, I kiss Tryn again, anxious for the touch of his lips, treasuring the feelings it elicits inside me. I do it right in front of Florin, who makes faces and rolls her eyes. But mostly I concentrate on the work I have been given, charting our course, measuring our fuel consumption, and estimating the distance it will allow us to cover. I find the approximate location of Far Reach, the last city in the Fae territories, where Trinch told me we could find Crinksee—the man who acts as his agent, and who may have more information about my mother. He supposedly maintains an office in the back end of a tavern called Sweet Sinner, where he carries out his despicable business. I am mistrustful of everything Trinch has told me, but it is all I have to work with. I hope that Crinksee will know something about my mother's fate or even possibly where she can be found. No guarantees of anything, of course. But if I am successful, I might be one step closer to finding out the truth.

Our journey takes us three days. On the fourth, we arrive at Far Reach. The day winds have died down, and it is nearing sunset when Tryn docks our vessel in port and pays the usual fees. We take time to lock her down, secure her engines and fuel, and engage protectors that will warn of anyone trying to board. If anyone attempts entry, it will trigger an unmistakable alarm.

Hooded and cloaked, the three of us walk from our docking slip into the town proper, seeking the Sweet Sinner. I think it might be a bit hard to locate in a town that, as rumor has it, quickly proves itself to be a den of iniquity almost equal to Jagged Reach. True, this is Fae country, but this town is full of Fae living on the edge of more hardships and troubles than I have ever encountered.

Tryn, on the other hand, seems perfectly at ease. He leads the way as if he knows it, and I recall him saying that he has been here before. There is so much I still don't know about him, including what it was like for him to meet other Water Sprites. He has yet to talk at any length about his experience back in Viridian Deep.

After we reach the center of the city, we find the tavern easily enough. It is large, raucous, and filled to overflowing with gamblers, whores, and drinkers and carousers of all sorts. An empty table reveals itself in a far corner, and we take it. I tell Florin and Tryn to wait while I question one of the serving girls about Crinksee. Tryn is reluctant to let me go alone, but I make it clear he does not have a choice. This is up to me.

I find two serving women talking to each other as they wait for their trays to be filled and try to catch their attention.

Finally one of them, an older, tough-faced woman, looks at me. "What is it you want?"

"I need to speak with a man called Crinksee. I was told he has an office here."

They stare at me and then at each other. The tough-faced woman simply picks up her tray and walks off without a word. The other one, giving me a nervous look, moves close.

"Who are you?"

"Just a girl looking for some help."

"You don't look like you need the kind of help he offers. My advice? Get yourself out of here."

She is tall and strong, and she looks capable of taking on any man. If she is wary of Crinksee, then what am I in for?

"I can't," I say. "It's about my mother."

The serving woman gives me a doubtful look. "On your head be it, then. But know this. The man's in the pocket of the slavers, and he's only got one use for people like you and your mother. But if you must, he's back there." She points to a solitary door. "Watch yourself. He's a mean one—full of cruelty and not afraid to show it."

I thank her and walk back to Florin and Tryn. The noise in the tavern is growing louder and more raucous, and everything in me suggests I should get out of here. But I refuse to listen. My mind is settled on this.

I point to the rear door. "I'm going in there for a talk. Wait here for me."

"I don't like this," Tryn says, starting to rise. "I'm going with you."

I push him back down. "No, you aren't. You're waiting here.

Crinksee is far less likely to answer if we all come at him together. If I don't return in the next twenty minutes, come and get me. Can you do that?"

He grins. "Which part?"

"Just sit here and behave," I tell him. I give Florin a look of warning as well. "Just sit tight and wait for me."

I walk across the room, through knots of jostling, laughing, hard-drinking men—and more than a few garish-looking women— to the door the serving girl has indicated. I pause when I reach it, then I knock once and enter.

Three men are gathered around a table playing cards. All are weathered and craggy, and each one looks worse than the others. They pause in their game to look up at me, and what I see in their eyes does not suggest this is a good place to be. "What do you want?" one snaps.

"Information," I admit. "Are you Crinksee?"

"Who's Crinksee?"

"One of you," I snap, already wanting to be somewhere else. "A man named Trinch sent me."

I can see a measure of curiosity reveal itself in the expression of the man doing the talking. "Did he, now? Trinch, you say?" He makes a spitting sound. "That old reprobate wouldn't tell anyone anything ever."

"He would for enough gold. And like I told you, I need some information."

The man shakes his head. "Best I can do is sell it to you, and you don't look like you can afford much."

"I can pay."

Knowing Trinch's methods, I again came prepared. I pull out one of the gold coins I brought with me. "Can I tell you what I need?"

"You can tell me anything you like. Then you can get out of here and return to your mama and daddy."

"My father is dead," I say crisply. "But I *am* looking for my mother. She's all the family I have left, and I don't know where she is. Or even if she is still alive. But you do. Trinch said he passed her along to you, when she came to him looking for help. You may remember her—she claimed to be Merrow, even though she was walking about on land. And she was searching for passage back to her people."

Telling him this is a gamble. And for a moment, I don't know if it's gotten me anything or not.

Crinksee shrugs. "Lots of women come in here looking for one thing or another, claiming one thing and another. How am I supposed to remember?"

"Odd. I would have thought you'd remember a Merrow claiming to be searching for her stolen tail. It is a rather . . . unusual story." I pause, then shove the gold back in my pocket, as if I have decided I won't need it after all. "Are you Crinksee or not? Maybe my information is all wrong, and I'm just wasting my time."

I turn, and a scraping of chair legs against the wooden floor suggests all three are rising. "Hold on, little witch," the one who's been speaking calls out. "I'm the man you've been looking for. But maybe you'll be sorry you did. Maybe you should have asked around a bit more."

I turn and glare at him. "And maybe you should have tried harder to help me. Then at least you would be richer."

"Maybe being richer doesn't interest me." He glances at his two friends. "But maybe you do. Seize her!"

Crinksee's companions rush me, grasping my arms and holding me fast. I struggle to free myself, but their grips are so strong I can't break loose. I quit struggling and stand still as Crinksee walks up to me.

"Who are you? And what are you doing here? Trinch rarely sends anyone my way for information, least of all some girl."

"Apparently, he's willing to sell you out for three gold coins," I lie, and stare at him defiantly. He delivers a hard slap to the side of my head, the blow violent enough to bring tears to my eyes. But I shake them off and face him anew. "You'll be sorry you did that."

"Oh, I will, will I? You'll be a lot sorrier!" he says, and he hits me again.

This time the blow causes me to slump into the arms of my captors in spite of my defiant words, and I have trouble straightening up again.

"Take her out of here," Crinksee orders. "She's too much trouble for the slave camps. Just drop her in the usual place for excess baggage. Make sure I don't see her again. I don't need her sort of trouble."

Without a word, his two companions drag me out through a back door that opens into an alleyway and haul me off into the night. It is dark and misty, and the blows to my head have dizzied me. I can barely make sense of what is happening, but I know enough to realize the danger I am in. I should have brought Tryn along. I should have brought both Tryn and Florin. But I made the mistake of thinking Crinksee was a man who would be swayed by mere gold—and now it is too late.

They haul me down toward the docks—toward what ultimate destination they have in mind, I am not sure, but I can guess. I do nothing to let the men who hold me know that I have the ability to defend myself. They are all so anxious to get rid of me that neither of them thought to check for weapons—though they do manage to relieve me of my gold quickly enough. But they miss finding the knife Auris gave me, which is tucked away within my tunic.

If I can just reach it . . .

Then I smell the ocean and hear the lapping of the waves and the thudding of my captors' booted feet on the planks of the pier and I know I can escape.

I fling myself into the first man, dragging the second with me. The shock and surprise of my body slamming against his are sufficient to cause him to loosen his grip, and I manage to jerk free. I snatch out my knife and plunge it into the first man's waist. He howls in dismay as the blade enters his body, and I roll free, still holding fast to my knife. Instantly, I am back up on my feet and racing for the ocean.

I go into the water headfirst and plunge into the murky depths.

I do not resurface.

TWENTY-TWO

ONCE BENEATH THE SURFACE OF THE ROUGHLIN, I HOLD MY knife blade between my teeth as I quickly strip off my pants; I do not want them torn apart by the forced emergence of my tail. Already, I can feel my body responding to the ocean waters, seeking to change from Fae to Merrow, but this time I exert my will, holding it off until I am ready. Once my pants are off and clutched firmly in one hand, with my knife in the other, I let it go, the transformation familiar and immediate. My skin is altering its look; my gills and finger and shoulder webbings reappear. My legs below my waist are fusing and forming the powerful tail that marks my identity, reshaping and elongating until once again I am close to nine feet in length. Because the transformation is so familiar, I revel in how *alive* it makes me feel. I am wholly beneath the surface of the ocean, breathing in through my gills, knowing that the water will always be my friend.

When my change is finished, I swim toward the surface of the Roughlin—still clutching my pants and knife—to find the pair of would-be killers I have left behind. Part of me wonders if I could launch myself at them like an attacking shark, catapulting from the waters and onto the dock, reveling in the look of horror I am sure to find upon their faces.

But no, that is foolish. There are two of them, and only one of me—and each of them with legs and me with none. I cannot change back instantly, so no point putting myself at a disadvantage. Better if I take my time and figure this out properly.

I swim away from the dock from which I jumped, travel down the length of the pier to where I can quietly climb back up and transform into my Fae self, then re-don my clothing before deciding what I should do about the two men who attacked me. There isn't much to consider. I loathe these people—Trinch, Crinksee, and all the rest of them—and their basic disregard for humanity. How they can justify what they do is impossible to imagine. But they are bigger and better armed than me, and as long as they are still looking for me to resurface, I have gained some time. Their efforts to find me might buy me the time I need to have another talk with their leader. The sooner I get back to Crinksee and get the information I need about my mother, the sooner I can get out of here.

So, after slicing off a quantity of rope from one of the boats tied up nearby—in case I need some extra help with Crinksee—back to the Sweet Sinner I creep, wondering how much time has passed. Too much, I think. I've exceeded my twenty-minute limit, and Tryn and Florin will likely have come after me. I have to hope they haven't done something foolish like confronting the lowlife on their own in an effort to save me. Crinksee wouldn't hesitate to rid himself of them as quickly as he was willing to rid himself of me. He doesn't seem at all the sort of man who would worry about dispatching two more bothersome intruders.

I walk back in the front door of the tavern and stand in the entry for a few moments, looking around the room. My hopes sink. Florin and Tryn are gone. Which must mean they have ventured into Crinksee's den.

I stride across the tavern as if I own it. Then, when I reach

Crinksee's office door, I take a deep breath and open the door as softly as I can manage. Crinksee sits alone at his worktable, studying charts of some sort or other, and for the first time I feel a kick of fear. What has become of Florin and Tryn? I had been depending on their backup this time around, but I see that I am on my own.

I ghost up behind Crinksee, hoping to take him unawares, but somehow he senses me before I make my move. An astonished look appears on his hard features when he sees me, then the look changes abruptly to one of anger and he lunges for me. For a big, heavy man, he is quick. But I am quicker. I dodge aside, trip him up, and he hits his head on the corner of his table going down. I am on top of him before he can squirm away. He is still conscious but momentarily stunned enough from the blow that I am able to use my purloined rope to tie both his arms and legs together before his vision clears. He glares up at me with hatred in his eyes, but I ignore him. I straddle his trussed body and lay my knife against his throat.

"Why shouldn't I just kill you?" I hiss.

I press the blade tightly against his skin as he thrashes beneath me and let him cut himself just enough that he feels it—much as Florin had with Trinch. He goes still, and I let him bleed as I hold him fast, my eyes locked on his. "Where is my mother?" I whisper. "Or should I just be rid of you?"

His jowly face tightens in rage. "I'll tell you what I know, little girl, if you untie me and leave when I finish talking!"

"Depends on what you tell me. Speak up. And no lies. Lie to me, and I'll cut deeper."

"I don't need lies to deal with the likes of you." He sneers. "You're no killer."

"You think not?" I press the knife a bit deeper. "Now tell me about my mother!"

Crinksee scowls. "She was here maybe ten years ago. I can't remember for certain. But she had this crazy story about wanting to get back to her home, where she believed she could find her fish tail. She was all tears and crying and begging me to help her. I thought she was deranged. Plus, she didn't have anything to pay me with, so I sent her away."

I nod as if I understand, then I push the knife blade down against his throat a little harder and open the wound a little deeper. I smile at him. "I told you not to lie, didn't I? I told you I would know if you did."

"I didn't lie!"

He almost manages to scream the words, but I press the blade down a little farther and put my hand over his mouth. "One more time, and then we're all done—you, especially."

"Shades, hellion!" There is evidence of fear in the way he protests that wasn't there before. His eyes are wide, and his throat is covered in blood. "Stop cutting me!"

"You don't lie, I don't cut. Understand?"

With my knife digging into his throat, he barely manages a nod. "She came like I told you. And I didn't believe her, like I told you. But she said she wouldn't leave until I helped her, so I gave her a drink to make her sleep and shipped her off. I never heard from her again."

This time I think he speaks the truth. "Shipped her to where?"

"Where I send all of my problems—to Swansong Colony. It's farther down the coast at the edge of the Human side of the Southern Isles. You can access it from either world, theirs or ours—Human or Fae. Not much down there of Fae wards. Not much of anything but the slave colony and its keepers. She's still there, far as I know." He laughs. "It was where I was planning to send you as well. So perhaps if you'd just been patient, the two of you would have been reunited."

I feel a chill run through me from head to foot. Everyone knows about the colonies. Prison colonies for the unwanted, run by companies that buy and sell their inmates as merchandise. Companies like Faraway Trades. There is no coming back from these places.

And that was where he had put my mother? And was about to put me?

I come very close to pressing the knife right through Crinksee's loathsome neck and putting an end to him. The urge to do so is enormous, but somehow—I will never entirely understand why—I resist.

But I have to make sure about Florin and Tryn. "What of my friends, the young man and the girl with him? They would have come in here looking for me, and now they're gone."

He manages a weak laugh. "When I said you'd left, they left, too. I don't know where they went from there."

Another lie. I am sick of this—sick of him, sick of this city, sick of everything. And before long, his associates will return. I am out of time. I press the blade of my knife down harder. Blood pools and runs freely down his neck. "You are one-tenth of an inch away from being dead," I whisper to him. "Lie to me one more time, or attempt to be even a little funny, and see what happens."

Again, fear surfaces in his eyes. They are hard with frustration and hatred of me, but there is no disguising what he feels in those moments. "Fine, then. They waltzed in here, demanding answers, so I sent them to the same place I sent your mother. Like I said, it is where I send all my problems. Well, those I don't just drown!" He attempts a laugh. "Maybe they'll become roommates! Maybe they'll . . ."

Then he sees the look on my face and goes still.

Abruptly, he bucks under me again, attempting to throw me off. But his sudden, desperate movements cause my knife to jerk sideways, and the blade cuts deep into his throat. Blood squirts everywhere. He thrashes momentarily, emits a single gasp, and the life goes out of him.

I am not sorry that he is gone. I have seldom been forced to kill a man, and I don't like how it makes me feel. But I didn't do it on purpose. I didn't actually do it at all. He did it to himself.

I rise and stand over him, thinking about what he has done to Florin and Tryn and how much I hate him for it. Do I have time to reach them before they're gone? Do I still have a chance to set them free?

I rise from Crinksee's lifeless body and hasten out the back door and into the night before his associates return.

ONCE OUTSIDE AND SAFELY AWAY FROM THE TAVERN, I CONSIDER the possibility that Crinksee was lying to me about Tryn and Florin. But no, he sounded too pleased with himself—not to mention that my instincts tell me it is the truth. I find myself wondering how many of those Trinch sent his way ended up with the slavers—or if that was the intended purpose all along. Did Trinch hope, by sending us to Crinksee, that Florin and I would end up in his clutches? Was that part of his revenge for forcing the information out of him? It feels entirely possible.

Regardless, I now have a lead on my mother. Even if Tryn and Florin are being sent to join her—an act I still intend to stop.

Sending anyone south by land is a long and dangerous expedition, so they must be going by boat—probably with other slaves. Meaning I must find the dockyard slips out of which the slaver ships would operate and discover if any sailings are planned.

I start running for the docks. It is late in the evening and there are few people about—and most of those I come across are not people I want to engage with. I push on, feeling increasingly desperate. How much time has passed since they were taken? I can't be sure. They probably won't set sail before morning—and perhaps not even for another day or so. Crinksee wouldn't dispatch a boat just to carry away two slaves. He would want a larger number before setting sail. So there is a good chance I can get my friends back before that happens.

I finally reach the shores of the Roughlin and the dockyards. I scurry along them for a time, but they are extensive and mostly deserted. I don't even really know how to find what I am looking for. Until a last-minute sighting of a Faraway Trades insignia brings me about for a closer look.

At this point, I force myself to slow down. This isn't a place where you just walk up and start asking questions. Besides, I don't want these people to know that I'm poking into their business.

I start walking the dockway, just seeing if anything presents itself. Like in Pressia, the Faraway Trades buildings are tightly sealed—likely to hide the fact that the bulk of their gains are made on the sale of slaves, weapons, and contraband.

After a time, I spy a solitary oldster engaging in fly fishing off the docks and walk over to see what he might know.

"Mind if I join you, Grandfather?" I ask him.

"Not so's long as you keep quiet and let me fish," he declares. "You ain't one of them women who talks all the time, are ya? And don't be giving me any more of that 'Grandfather' stuff. I ain't nothing of the sort."

I sit down quietly and stay silent for a long time. Behind us, around the Faraway Trades buildings, everything is still.

"You come here often?" the old man asks after sufficient time has passed for him to determine I don't intend to talk. "You look like you know your way around a boat."

"I have some skills. You?"

"Had some. Don't use them much anymore except like this here dockside stuff. Bad back, knees, one arm. Old age."

"Comes for us all, I'm told."

"Coming quicker for me than you," he notes.

Quiet again. I am getting restless. "The workers in those warehouses bother you much?" I ask.

"Naw. Too busy finding bad ways to make money."

"Slave sellers, I hear."

"That's them. Watched them send off a boatload this very night, not half an hour back."

My heart sinks. "They let you watch?"

"They wasn't paying attention to me. I come here all the time. They know me. Leave me alone, long's I leave them the same way."

"I suppose you don't frighten them much?"

"You suppose right. I'm an old man."

"Did you see the slaves they loaded?" I press.

"Some. One sure made a fuss. Young girl; Fae Water Sprite. She put up a whale of a fuss. Thought she was gonna break away at one point, but they tied her up. Had spunk, she did."

No question in my mind as to who we're talking about. I stay a few moments longer and then bid him good night and set off for the boat my companions and I docked earlier.

I already know what I have to do.

TWENTY-THREE

I T IS NEARING MIDNIGHT WHEN I ARRIVE BACK AT THE BOAT TRYN, Florin, and I used to sail here, and I think right away about how tired I am and how much I would like to sleep. But sleeping in this port is dangerous. Although Crinksee is dead, too many of his minions remain at large.

So I am going to have to sail this vessel alone. It's possible, but it won't be easy. It means navigating, reading my directional instruments, minding the sails, and keeping to my compass setting—all with no help. If the weather turns or something goes wrong with the boat, I will be in trouble. It is one thing to know how to do something and another to actually do it.

I won't wait for morning. The night is clear and cloudless, and there are no indications of a pending change in the weather. Best to get out of here while I can. I know in general where I am going—the Southern Isles. I just have to find the specific site of the Swansong Colony.

The stars are blazing in sparkling curtains everywhere I look. I breathe in the smell of the ocean as I ease my craft away from land

and begin riding the winds blowing out over Roughlin Wake. I progress down the coast for perhaps ten miles, searching for a suitable landing place. Finally, I spy a heavily forested island with numerous landing sites and pull into a cove fronting a stretch of forested hill country, intending to sleep until morning. By now, even a little sleep is a welcome idea.

But even when I am anchored and stretched out in my bunk, sleep comes slowly and is troubled when it arrives. I find myself lost in dark thoughts of my mother's fate. As well, I spend long stretches of wakefulness agonizing over what it might require of me to find my friends and free them from their captivity—a situation brought about by my decision to face Crinksee alone.

When those dreams and nightmares run their course, I begin wondering about my future, and how I will choose what part of the world and which form I will reside in. I am both Fae and Merrow, and both parts have equal claim on me. I love the freedom of my aquatic form, but to choose that life would mean giving up both my family and Tryn. Yet to choose a life on land would be denying my Merrow heritage. Apparently Tryn has discovered something of his Water Sprite heritage that would enable him to live in or near the water. He hasn't said much about it, but then he hasn't said much of anything about his Water Sprite self.

My thoughts then shift to my mother. Was this longing for the ocean what tormented her? Was this what made her leave me behind? And was she, as I suspect, a Merrow-shifter, or was she a full Merrow who was somehow able to live on land because someone "stole her tail"? And if so, how do you steal a tail? These are all mysteries that are yet to be answered.

I toss and turn, half asleep and half awake, moving from thought to dream and back again, longing for a peace I cannot find. I wake feeling tired and less than pleasant. But I dress and feed myself a little breakfast, then set sail once more.

I have not concerned myself with trying to catch up to the Faraway Trades transport, because I have no hope of catching it now. The transport will be engine-powered and virtually impossible to board while at sea. The best I can hope for is finding its destination and locating Florin and Tryn then. Any journey to the Southern Isles will take at least two days—especially relying on just the sails. But there is a hard wind blowing down out of the north, and it should provide me with what I require.

Once settled back down, well out in the waters of Roughlin Wake, I begin plotting my course. The islands I seek are several miles offshore, so approaching with any stealth will prove a challenge. I know from the details on my maps that they are heavily forested and mostly unoccupied—save, it seems, by the Swansong slave colony. It will be difficult finding the island, but not impossible.

I put up all my sails to make the journey swifter. I swing my vessel heavily into the wind, flying across the waves with remarkable speed.

For the first half of the day, my passage is hard but swift. Then the wind dies off a bit, and my speed with it. I slouch against the starboard railing, my gaze wandering out across the ocean, and find myself growing frustrated. I feel as if I am crawling toward my destination. But I have no choice but to push on as best I can.

Then I start to grow sleepy as the rocking of the boat continues and the day warms, and I find myself drifting off to another place entirely. There is such a sense of peacefulness in the sea that I give myself over to it. I can smell the ocean with its busy life and hear the rhythm of its urgent currents. I can sense the movements of schools of fish swinging this way and that. The backs of whales reveal themselves, sleek with water, dusted over with crustaceans, shellfish, and mollusks. Here a swarm of dolphins navigates a path, leaping and splashing in playful taunts. There stingrays' wide fins ripple as they glide. Above, seabirds soar and swoop as they hunt for food. Activity everywhere, and none of it even remotely dependent on the land.

I drift off now and then, but never for long, and I manage to hold my course. Eventually, the sun goes down and I find a new place to anchor for the night. The sea air is calm and balmy, and the sounds of the ocean are soothing. I am sleepy and warm, and I stay on deck this night, content to be exactly where I am. I feel a momentary twinge of betrayal when an unbidden memory of Brecklin arises, but it is there for only a second, then gone again. By now, Brecklin feels like someone I knew in another life.

Eventually, I close my eyes and sleep until dawn. And wake feeling very much at peace.

I set out again early. Crinksee said the colony I am seeking is called Swansong, and is at the edge of the Human side of the Southern Isles, but exactly where it lies within the wider chain remains uncertain. I sail all day and arrive at the northern end of the island chain just as the sun is descending. I make my way through the waters at a slow, steady pace, searching each island I pass for signs of habitation. There are dozens of small islands of all shapes and sizes, but only the larger ones would hold such a place. Many are heavily forested and deep enough that it is difficult to tell much about what lies within. Few are large enough to contain compounds of the size I am seeking, and some of those are virtually barren, lacking anything more than trees, underbrush, and rocks. There are obviously no colonies settled there, which makes my job much easier.

The wind is muted inside the island chain, so I sail more slowly now, searching for signs of habitation, but I see nothing.

I am reluctant to take the boat any closer for fear of being seen, and there is no way to maneuver my way nearer to any of these islands on sail power alone—at least not for a sailor of my limited experience. I have to get closer for a more in-depth examination, but I cannot do that by boat.

I maneuver the sailboat to the backside of an adjacent island too small to usefully serve as a colony, anchoring out of sight. I can make the swim with no problem and take a quick look around. I can do this as many times as I have to.

I know what's needed.

I will find Florin and Tryn, then determine a way to bring them to safety. And, if possible, I will find out what has happened to my mother.

I can do this.

I know I can.

TWENTY-FOUR

I CLIMB DOWN THE HATCHWAY TO WHERE OUR GEAR IS STORED and pull out a change of clothing. I shove it into a waterproof backpack and strap it over my shoulders, testing its weight, then add two short spears with carry straps that I loop over my back. I hope I am wrong, but I cannot think of a situation where I will not need weapons. I know I may be overdoing it, but I can at least start out fully equipped and hope for the best. I climb back on deck and strap on my knives, paying special attention to the one I was given by Auris.

I take a moment to strip off my pants, and then I go over the side of the boat and into the ocean waters.

I feel the change begin immediately. It happens more quickly than I expect, and I sense I am becoming steadily more comfortable with letting it happen—so much so that I no longer even have to think about it. I go from Forest Sylvan to Merrow in less than a minute, my physical appearance shifting, my breathing altering, and my bodily functions switching over. I don't have to think about it; just entering water makes it happen. It is mind-boggling.

I luxuriate momentarily in my double identity—the way I shift so smoothly from one body into another. When the change is complete, I begin to swim toward the nearest of the islands, keeping to the ocean depths as I do so.

The waters are empty and dark, the night sky's starlight reflecting off the waters from above while providing a rippling mirror of light from below. I glide through the ocean's currents toward my destination, looking for lights, listening for sounds that do not belong, surfacing now and then to be certain I am traveling in the right direction. The nearer I draw to the first island, the more tense and watchful I become. I am aware of the danger I am in. I am aware of what will happen to me if I am caught.

But I mostly stay beneath the surface of the water, lifting myself only long enough for a quick glance at what might be waiting farther ahead. And still I see nothing. The islands remain as vacant and empty as they first appeared, with only a few isolated lights visible and no other evidence of life. I maneuver closer to the shoreline for a better look, but nothing reveals itself. The only way I can be certain is to go ashore.

I swim closer still, then use my tail to squirm up onto a small beach, where I become my Fae self once more. There are no obvious trails or signs of usage, so I have to make my way blind. I proceed into the forest but find nothing. No buildings, no people, no signs of any life or evidence of any sort of occupation. The interior of the island is boulder-strewn and rugged, and there are no signs of established pathways or passages.

I abandon my search, reenter the ocean waters, transform once more to Merrow, and swim to the next.

My search continues through the night. It takes much longer than I had expected. I must take time enough with each island not only to be certain that there is no evidence of colony occupation but also that there is no evidence of anyone making use of the island even on a temporary basis. In each case, I start out hopeful and end up disappointed. On some of these islands there are signs of fires having once been built, but nothing to tell me how long ago this was or for what purpose the fires were used.

I work all night, but when dawn begins to reveal itself, I abandon my search and return to my boat. By now I am exhausted, and I strip off my damp clothes, drop into my bunk, and fall asleep.

When I wake again, another sunset is on the horizon and darkness lurks. I tell myself I have to find a more efficient way to do things. This search is taking too long and requires too much effort. There must be a way to make it more efficient. At the rate I am going, my search will take all week. I can't leave Florin and Tryn in the hands of the slavers for that long.

This night is darker and the skies more cloudy than what I encountered yesterday. What I need to do is look for docking platforms. If there is a colony on this island, it will require regular shipments of supplies and materials. And for that, there needs to be a way to load and unload whatever goods are required.

And to contain their prisoners, so they cannot escape.

Silently, I sail past the islands that I have already explored, find another hidden anchorage, and begin the search anew.

I search all night but find no evidence of anything useful. I am running out of options and islands, and I am beginning to wonder if I have been mistaken about this being the right location. Maybe Trinch or Crinksee lied to me. Maybe I am mistaken about where the Southern Isles are situated, and there are other groupings. Could it be that I am in the wrong place entirely?

By the third night, I am growing a bit desperate. But on this night I finally find what I have been searching for.

After anchoring the boat anew and conducting a few more fruitless searches, I discover the colony and its occupants entirely by accident. I am in the midst of searching the remaining islands that look large enough to house such a colony and not finding a sign of anything. But then I arrive at an island surprisingly close to the mainland shores, which is surrounded by strong underwater currents. I am swimming when I encounter the choppy flows and only barely escape being caught up in their rush. After backing off, I consider skipping such a dangerous place when it occurs to me this might just be the sort of concealment that Faraway Trades would prefer, given the illicit nature of their activities.

I make a semicircuit of the island, staying well out of the heavy flows, until abruptly I spy something that intrigues me. At the island's south point, away from the direct flow of the rapids, a heavily forested landscape seems to form a sort of natural tunnel through a mass of ancient cedars and firs. I cannot tell where the tunnel leads, but it is so well maintained that it looks as if taking a smaller craft through its opening might be possible.

I hesitate for a moment, trying to decide if this means something or is just another peculiarity. In the end I decide I need to find out. Swimming underwater, I work my way around to where I can bridge the currents. The crossing is swift and at times unpredictable, but my Merrow abilities make it possible for me to master the challenge and arrive at the mysterious opening. The trees have shaggy and ancient boughs covered with moss and lichen, and the whole of the forest beyond looks impenetrable.

Except that, once you get inside the tree tunnel, the waters seem to widen, and the inland passage to open up further. I can't tell much from under the water, but I think this might be what I am looking for.

So I abandon my caution and swim right in.

Several hundred yards farther on, I find what I have been looking for. The inlet widens but remains deep and passable enough for a medium-sized hauler or similar carrier of goods. It twists and turns to take advantage of the forest cover—no longer a natural feature of the island, but clearly manufactured. I travel along this until it widens again into a large, semicircular bay. To one side, dimmed, canopied floodlights reveal the loading docks I have been searching for. A set of them front an expansive yard where a mix of hauling machines and wheeled carts serve to carry goods farther inland to two large warehouses and what looks to be housing for the island's staff. Off to one side, a mix of iron-railed and barbed-wire pens form holding arenas and chutes that I know at once are not meant for animals. Their passageways direct occupants through cleaning machines and various loading ramps to count and process bodies, and from there run farther back into the trees and darkness to a jumble of low-roofed housing stables. It is clear, even from where I stand, that this is where the inmates are quartered. The exterior lights reveal the nature of the buildings and their clear purpose, maintaining a circle of brilliance that prevents anyone from sneaking away unseen.

I am horrified—yet also grateful that I have found this monstrous place and am done searching. But razor wire prevents entry except through guarded gates and well-lit open yards where nothing can pass unnoticed. I note now how many watchtowers and guard stations overlook this facility and quickly realize there is no easy way to reach the pens where Florin and Tryn are undoubtedly imprisoned.

I find a place where I can emerge from the waters of the inlet and stand upon the shoreline unseen. I am relieved to see only a scattering of weapons on the walls. Humans generally love to defend themselves, but my guess is that, in this situation, they are counting more on their isolation to save them. After all, unless you know the place is here, you can sail by and be no wiser, as I almost did.

If I stay on the outskirts of the colony, I can walk about unnoticed. While I do not intend to proceed far, I would like to see if I can find a way into this monstrous place. I move along the inner harbor toward a series of buildings that, judging from the sounds that issue from them, appear to house the machinery that allows the island to function. I proceed cautiously and reach my destination unnoticed. These buildings are razor-wired as well, but I notice that the largest of them is fronted by a concrete docking platform with heavy metal loading doors, drawn down and locked, and with two chutes that descend back into the water.

I don't hesitate. I go into the waters for a look around.

Partially submerged access grates block off everything but the waters that the pumps are drawing inside. If these are intakes, others must exist to provide discharge. But they would not be situated side by side or even very close to each other, would they? Especially if these pumps are what cause the heavy currents around the island's base.

Diving down for a closer look, I find that each grate extends downward a good fifteen feet, and the surge of water creates a powerful current. The force is sufficient to yank me right up against one set of metal bars and hold me fast. It is only with some effort that I am able to free myself and slip to one side, where the intake is decidedly less powerful. I pause there to look and listen more carefully. It becomes clear from the sounds of the pumps and the surge of the waters that the machinery is working at a steady pace, and any attempt to enter this way would probably end with me being yanked into the engines.

But just as I am about to swim out of the inlet and around the island proper to look for outflow pipes, the engines stop on the right-hand pipe, and the influx of the ocean's waters ceases.

I swim to that grate and examine it carefully. There are hinged fastenings on one side and locks on the other. Together, they fasten the grate to massive pillars. I take a closer look at a place where it appears to be the weakest—its upper edge is slightly ajar—and find something odd. At some point, the lock on that side of the portal has given way sufficiently that the gate does not seal tightly. It gapes almost four inches wide. I study the lock for a few moments, but I cannot tell anything about what caused this. In any case, I am able to break it open in seconds. How long it has been this way and why no one has fixed it troubles me, but at least I am inside the tunnel.

My Merrow strength has surprised me once again, but I am pleased to be able to rely on it.

I work the grate away from the opening far enough to allow myself to slip through. It is completely dark within, but I push ahead, feeling my way along the wall. I am submerged for nearly two minutes before I reach my destination.

Then I catch sight of lights ahead.

The machinery remains silent, but a sudden sense of urgency prods me. My instincts surface in a rush, sharp and insistent. Something is not right.

I surface long enough to spy a docking platform just ahead—its surface wide enough for unloading and storing equipment and supplies from the mainland. A few crates sit to one side, either recently delivered or awaiting transport. A wall lies behind the platform, and a wide-spaced pair of closed doors at the center suggests passages leading to the upper levels.

I study the space for a moment, and then decide to swim close enough to hoist myself up and resume my Fae identity. This might be the best chance I have to get into the complex and have a look at whatever's hidden inside.

Only just as I am about to move away, something soft brushes up against my tail.

I wonder suddenly what else is down here. The grate was forced wide enough to allow passage for smaller fish and other sea life, even before I widened it further, so it seems strange that nothing lives down here when access is so easy.

Troubled, I dive downward and resume swimming underwater toward the dock. This time, I am studying the water more carefully, searching for movement. If something really is down here, how does it manage to survive?

That's when I see the bones.

There are dozens of them, scattered all over the cavern floor, perhaps two dozen feet down—sometimes alone, sometimes in vast heaps. A large number of creatures have died down here—and not just fish. Many of these bones are either Fae or Human.

I am almost to the far wall when I see something moving. It sits off in a far corner where the dock beddings join with the cavern wall, all of it in shadow, barely visible. I catch just a glimpse of it and immediately start to back away.

Too late.

A tentacle snaps out and fastens about my arm. I remember the feeling of something brushing up against my tail earlier and recoil, but the tentacle has a tight hold on me and I cannot pull free. Suckers fasten to my skin and clothing, grasping so hard that I am held fast. Whatever it is that has grabbed me is trying very hard to drag me down to where it waits.

I can see it clearly for the first time, and I am both terrified and repulsed. It is some sort of giant octopus, but one that has become misshapen and distorted. Its arms have been damaged, and its body is rife with lesions and boils and gaping wounds. Dozens of small sea worms crawl all over its body, feeding on its wounds.

I don't want it touching me, but it just draws me closer.

I manage to free one of the spears I wear fastened across my back and bring it about. I spear the beast with my weapon, and it shudders in response but does not let go. Twice more I spear it, but the wounds do nothing to make it release me. Instead, it pulls me closer.

Now I know the reason for all the bones. I know why the grate was damaged and left unrepaired. I know why there is no other life in this cavern.

The creature must have arrived when it was small and has been here since, feeding and growing.

I know I am in serious trouble.

This monstrous aberration has a solid hold on me and no intention of letting go. It will make a meal of me if I do not do something to stop it.

In a flash of memory, I recall something Ronden once told me, how sometimes it is better to attack than to try to fight free.

Immediately, I embed my spear in the monster's skull and, using my tail to gain momentum, lunge right at it. My favorite knife is in my hand, slashing and ripping into the beast's body. Two more tentacles snake out to fasten on me, but I ignore them as I continue to attack. If I can cause it enough damage, I tell myself, it will cease its attack and look to escape.

But that doesn't happen. Instead, three more tentacles appear. My tail and my left arm and much of my torso are ensnared, and my second spear has been knocked away. My knife-arm is still free, but that alone is not enough. I manage to fend off the two remaining arms that seek to fasten about my neck and head, but I know I won't be able to hold them off for long.

Before me, a beaked mouth opens to reveal teeth and a dark throat. I am being drawn steadily closer.

Desperate now, I decide to go after its eyes. There are two of them—one on either side of its bulbous head. I suddenly go limp and let the creature draw me closer to its maw. I have to trick it; I have to get close enough to do the damage that is needed. It takes everything I have to give way like this, but my instincts tell me it is my best chance. I let the beast pull me to within a foot of its mouth, and then I strike so quickly that it has no time to react.

Slash! One eye is gone.

Lunge! The second one is badly damaged.

It all happens so fast that, for a moment, I am not sure I have succeeded. Then I feel the monster shudder. Stricken and nearly sightless, its arms loosen from around me and the beast pulls back, thrusting me away. Recoiling into its corner, it thrashes wildly, its arms tearing at the waters, its body heaving as if out of control. I do not try to give pursuit; I want nothing more to do with this monster. I hurtle toward the surface, my tail ripping at the waters to give me the power I require, and I launch myself onto the loading dock. Exhausted and shivering from the memory of those tentacles fastening about my body, I lie gasping on the empty platform as my body changes.

As I resume my Fae identity, I keep an eye fixed on the waters from which I have escaped. The surface bubbles and surges, as if this cavern has become a cauldron heated by a fire. The turmoil is extensive, and I half expect the octopus to come surging out to drag me down again. The fear is so great that I scoot my body backward until I am as far from the edge of the dock as I can manage to get. And I worry, further, that this much commotion will summon guards or other staffers to the cavern.

Finally, everything goes still and no one arrives to investigate, so I pull myself to my feet, take off my backpack, and bring out the change of clothing I brought. I am dressed again in moments, looking once more like a Forest Sylvan—though I am covered with sucker-marks, and the feeling of those arms fastening about me lingers. I am sore and welted all over, but I am alive. For the moment, at least, it is enough.

I have lost all of my weapons save for the specially crafted knife Auris gave to me, so I slip it back within my clothing, out of sight, and turn for the doors.

As I do, the doors release and start to open.

I lunge through the opening—fully expecting to encounter guards that have arrived to investigate the commotion—but no one is there. It takes me a moment to realize that the doors have released automatically in response to my approach, and I breathe a sigh of relief.

Now I am facing into an open area crammed with shipping pallets and stacking racks. To one side are doors that look to be elevators. To the rear is a stairway. What do I do now? How far am I willing to go to find out more about this place? I don't know. Farther than this, I tell myself. Far enough to find out what has become of my friends.

I choose the stairs and begin to make my way toward the upper levels.

I have no idea where I am going or what I am going to do once I get there. I am in the wrong building for finding Florin and Tryn, who will be housed somewhere in the prisoner quarters and not this warehouse. But I have come this far, and I might as well go a little farther. Maybe there is a way to get from this building to the prison quarters. But the truth is that, once again, I have not bothered to think this through. Florin and Tryn would be quick to tell me so, if they could, but I brush my uncertainty aside and I push on.

I reach the top of the stairs and find myself at a landing that fronts a single narrow door. This time the door doesn't open automatically, although I give it sufficient time to do so. I wait as long as I can stand to, then find and release its latch.

As I ease the door open, I see a massive chamber filled with machinery—no doubt the ones responsible for pumping the water. The machines hum and chug, so big that they block my view of almost everything else. I walk into the room and stand there staring at them, wondering where to go from here.

The decision is made for me as a sudden blow to my head sends me hurtling into a dark oblivion.

TWENTY-FIVE

I FLOAT IN DARKNESS.

Voices, broken and disjointed, reach out to me.

". . . have to wait, if you don't want . . . because injury is an irreparable form . . . don't think she . . ."

They are speaking of me. Whoever is talking. Whoever is there. What's happened to me? I remember a sharp blow to my head and then nothing. I want to open my eyes but cannot seem to make myself do so.

". . . just want her awake . . . how hard can it be to . . ."

I drift away, my focus loosening, my concentration fragmenting, my sense of self-awareness fading. I drop into a dreamless darkness. I sleep, and then I sleep some more, tucked away from everything.

Am I dying? The question nudges at me. I wonder if this is how it feels. Have I suffered a killing blow? Fear surfaces, and I am momentarily frozen. But I am stronger than that. I have never, for an instant, thought I was incapable of doing whatever it took to survive, so I will not give way now.

I drift some more.

". . . damn it, do your job . . . get her back . . . ask her what sort of . . ."

Visions haunt me with their demon whispers and savage taunts. Fears rise to challenge me in droves so vast I cannot see their ends. Some I understand, but many I don't. It seems as if their only purpose is to bury me under the oppressive weight of threats that are meant to crush me. I do nothing to encourage this, nothing to invite it, but it comes for me anyway.

My thoughts scatter.

I am a seventeen-year-old girl who is not who—or even *what*—she thought she was. I am a halfling—a mix of Forest Sylvan and Merrow. I am a creature of both land and sea. I am a mix-and-match sort of creature who does not really have a clear idea of which sort of being I wish to be.

Faces wash past me in brief flashes that attach themselves to words and voices but reveal little.

"You have to do something!" someone shouts angrily.

Slowly, I come awake.

I am in a dimly lighted room, bedded down in warmth and comfort. I am on my back, wrapped in sheets and blankets, my head resting comfortably on a soft pillow. All around me are machines that beep and hum in soft cadence and are attached to me by wires and tubes and cuffs. A single dim light reveals various electronic readers and recorders—all of them somehow monitoring my physical condition.

I attempt to move one arm and find I can't. Gently, I test the freedom of my other arm and my legs, and find no room for movement there, either. It doesn't take much for me to discover that I am fully restrained.

Abruptly, I realize what has happened. I have been found and seized by the people who run this place.

For a moment, I panic and almost scream, but I manage to stop myself. All I have left is whatever courage I can muster while I wait to discover exactly what these people have in store for me.

I think on it for a long time, forcing myself to stay calm, believing that self-control and confidence in my innate abilities will be enough to see me through. Foolish to think this way, but for the moment it is all I have to work with.

I consider what my enemies will attempt to do with me. They captured me in my Fae form, so they don't know my secret; they don't know about my Merrow side. That gives me at least a small advantage. None of them will know that I can change from one body to another, because they will not have witnessed it happening.

I lie quietly for a time, thinking things through. I am in great danger, I know. I am likely to be regarded as little more than a trespasser or spy. But I am at least a mystery they will want to understand, so they are unlikely to kill me right away.

For now, I must bide my time. I must delay for as long as it is possible, until I am recovered.

I must sustain my resolve.

I must be brave.

I DO ALL OF THIS TO THE BEST OF MY ABILITY BEFORE THE MEN I NOW recognize as Dr. Renwick and the Faraway Trades representative called Alcoin arrive—the same man I once held a knife to, all those months ago. The door flies open, crashing back against the wall with such force that the cart beside it crashes over. Alcoin reaches out, seizes my gown, and shakes me as you might a troublesome kitten.

"Listen to me, you ugly, little green-skinned freak!" he screams. "Enough of this pretense! You are well enough to talk, and if you aren't, you are no longer worth my time. So tell me the truth about how you found this place, or I'll cast you overboard attached to enough weights that this time you won't escape. Yes, I can see you recognize me. I was the one who had you bound and thrown off the docks in Jagged Reach. Then I was transferred here after you escaped as punishment for my failure. I don't know how you managed it, but this time you're going to tell me how you managed to escape that rack, and why and how you are here."

I meet his furious gaze, worried three times over and dizzy from the shaking, but determined to stay calm. "About the rack, friends saw what happened and came to my rescue." Close enough to true.

He shakes me again, and the room spins around me. "Those were *chains* that bound you!"

"My friends broke them."

A quick, furious intake of breath follows. "Who are you? And how did you find this place?"

I say the first thing that comes to mind. "Where's my mother?"

Laughter, long and loud. "We didn't hit you that hard, little girl, but I can assure you that you are no longer safely at home with your mommy. You have trespassed on Faraway Trades property and gotten caught for your trouble. The only question is if I pop you in the pens right now and sell you at our next market—though if you tell me the truth about how you found this place, I might let you heal up first. Or I can put out the word that we're holding you, and lure in that troublesome pirate and his crew. Would he come for you, do you think? You certainly went out of your way to rescue him."

I feel a jolt of despair. He recognizes me as the girl who freed Brecklin.

For the first time, I notice that he has my knife tucked into the belt of his uniform. Auris's knife, that she gave me. My best weapon, in the hands of this madman. Immediately, I wonder how I can get it back.

Then a third man steps forward—another who wears a Faraway Trades uniform, but one I haven't seen before. He must have been standing at the back of the room in the shadows. He is dressed in the same way as Alcoin, his countenance every bit as grim as his companion's as he regards me.

"Stop shaking her," he snaps, and Alcoin is quick to obey. The man addressing him is clearly his superior. "No need to be so rough."

This intervention should be welcome, but it isn't. The strange calmness of his voice only reinforces my belief that I am in a lot of trouble.

He leans close, and I can clearly see the dislike in his eyes. "Before we pen you up or dangle you as pirate bait—both equally acceptable plans, as far as my companion is concerned—I will give you a chance to redeem yourself. Tell me how you found this place, and I might consider letting you go. Perhaps, too, I could tell you something about your mother."

I am still half drugged with whatever medication they are using, tightly secured by arm and leg bands to the bed on which I lie. I cannot afford to dismiss the offer, but I cannot do anything to help, either. I wonder momentarily what Auris would do, and my instincts provide an answer almost immediately.

"Is my mother here? She's probably pretty easy to remember. She would have claimed she was a Merrow."

He shows no interest in what I am saying. "How do you know about this place?"

"A man named Crinksee told me. A man named Trinch sent me to Crinksee."

"Which led you here?"

"Yes."

"So you broke into our safehold? That didn't work out so well, did it? A worker saw you and knocked you down. What has that gained you?"

I say nothing.

"You seem very capable, but you also seem very young. Why should I believe you?"

"I don't know. Maybe because we both know lying won't help me at this point?"

"It won't."

"Good. Because I am not lying. Where is my mother? Crinksee sent her here, thirteen years ago."

"Thirteen years ago?" he scoffs. "No one stays on this island that long. A couple of weeks at most, and then off to market. She either died here or got sold. Do you really think to find her after thirteen years in this place?"

"I . . ." I squeeze my eyes shut and then open them again. "I am feeling sick to my stomach. Can I sleep now?"

In the background, Alcoin snorts. The one questioning me leans close once more. "You may. But once you are rested, into the pens you go. And you won't like that, I promise you."

He motions toward a nurse I haven't noticed before. She is standing at the back of the room, organizing bandages and medicines. A sharp word and she turns. She is older than the others and her bland face reveals nothing.

"Clean her up. Give her something to sleep."

Then both the speaker, Alcoin, and the doctor leave the room.

A FEW MINUTES PASS AS THE NURSE WIPES DOWN MY ARMS, BACK, and legs, then dresses me in a fresh shift. She says nothing as she works, but every so often she glances over at the closed door. She is clearly waiting for her superiors to check on her progress. She is also clearly nervous.

Finally she leans over me and whispers. "Keep your mouth shut and just listen. I heard what you said. I think I know about your mother."

I startle, but stay silent.

"She claimed to be a Merrow who had lost her tail. She had found a life on land with a man she thought she loved, but she still longed to return to the sea. Only she found that she couldn't; that she had been on land too long to return. Her husband died, and her daughter was taken away from her, so she was seeking her people in the hope of finding her tail and reclaiming her daughter. But she trusted the wrong people, and so was sent here instead."

The nurse glances again at the doorway. "She told me all this while she was in my care. She talked about living in the ocean and breathing the water. She talked about losing her tail when she came up on land and not being able to get it back."

"My mother," I breathe softly. "That was my mother. I was the child who was taken away."

The door opens, and another nurse appears carrying a stack of laundry. The two talk for a few minutes, their voices so soft I cannot hear what they are saying. How much of what I am hearing do I trust? How much faith can I put in this nurse?

The second nurse leaves once more and the first comes back over to me.

"Your mother was weak when she arrived and almost hysterical. Everyone in charge thought she was mad, but I believed her. But they knew they would have little luck selling a madwoman, so they just locked her away and eventually forgot about her."

Though I already know the answer from the nature and tenor of the conversation, I ask the question anyway. "What happened to her?"

The nurse shakes her head. "She died. Worn down and worn out."

I find myself in tears, hard as I try not to be. I am devastated. After all this, my mother is dead, and I never got to talk to or see her again. I close my eyes for a few minutes, trying to steady myself.

When I open them again, I ask, "What is your name?"

The nurse shakes her head. "Best if you don't know. If you don't know, you can't tell. I can only do this."

She reaches down and unfastens my restraints. "There, now you at least have a chance at getting free. Get out of here, and don't come back."

She starts to leave, then stops and turns back. "I am sorry again about your mother. She was a sweet woman."

Out the door she goes, silent and swift. She does not look back.

———

I AM EXHAUSTED, AND MY DESPAIR IS OVERWHELMING. MY MOTHER IS gone forever, and I cannot bring her back.

But there is no time to grieve now. What I have to do is find a way to escape. Because even though I cannot save my mother, I can still help Florin and Tryn.

I have to get out of here. Now.

I am still nauseous and dizzy from the blow to my head and all the shaking, but I force myself to rise. Still clothed in nothing more than my hospital shift and shivering with the cold that penetrates the room, I hobble about until the blood begins to flow freely through my limbs and body once more. I am still unsteady, but I have to continue. I know the best I can hope for at this point is to escape my imprisonment. I cannot help Florin and Tryn in this condition; they will have to wait. If I don't get free, we all will be lost.

But how will I get out of here?

I move to the entry door and stand there for a long time, listening. I hear nothing, but I am reasonably sure that there are guards stationed without. I have to find a way to get past them.

Then I notice the sealed window inserted high up on one wall. The glass is clouded so that, while light can penetrate, vision is obscured. Also, it provides only a narrow opening. But if I can manage to reach up and open it, I might be able to pull myself through. Pushing a wheeled medical cart across the room and placing it up against the wall below the window, I lock the wheels in place and heft myself onto the cart. Standing there, I search for release latches.

There are none. The window is a solid, immovable pane.

I climb down again and begin searching anew. I find medical uniforms in various sizes and shapes, but disguise seems unlikely to succeed, given my decidedly Fae-looking skin and hair. I need something else.

Unless . . .

I strip off my shift, then don fresh shoes and the medical clothing. It doesn't fit well, but it doesn't need to do more than cover me up. I fit myself with a tightly laced-up cap and mask and smear what remains of my face with some sort of white cream I find. I put on surgical gloves and belt myself together.

Then, loading blankets and pillows onto the cart, I form them into the shape of a body, strap them down, and wheel the cart out the door and out into the well-lighted hallway beyond.

Two guards are standing watch, one to either side of the doorway. Giving them a commanding wave, I shout. "Summon Dr. Renwick, immediately!"

I am hoping that the barked order will confuse them sufficiently that they will do as they are told and not question me.

And indeed, one produces a device and begins speaking into its receiver. I turn to the second. "Watch over the patient. And no touching; she's very contagious. I'll find help!"

I stride away, the last of my fading strength keeping me upright, fighting to make it appear that I am walking in a normal way and not lurching. The guard not on the intercom calls out to me, but I brush him off with a gesture and he chooses to let me go.

I reach the end of the hallway, pass through a doorway marked with an EXIT sign, and find a stairway. I have no idea where I am in this building and no idea of how the building is laid out. I have to get out, but which way should I go?

A siren sounds, blaring and raw, a clear warning that my escape has been discovered. I go down the stairs, rushing faster in spite of my weakness, forcing down my sudden nausea and loss of balance, knowing that this is my last chance to be free of this place. I tear off my clothing as I go, intending to shift back into Merrow as soon as I am back in the water. There are shouts and cries now coming from down below, mixing with the slamming of doors and fastening of locks. I have to hope that no one really knows what is going on yet. I have to hope I can figure something out for myself.

I burst through the door at the bottom of the stairs and slam into a guard who is standing just outside. With a cry, he goes down in a heap. I keep running, searching for a door leading out of the building. I pass through one section of the building into another and find what I am looking for: a heavy doorway marked with an EXIT sign. I don't pause to consider; I simply charge through and find myself back outside. I hear shouts and the sounds of automatic weapons fire. Someone is shooting at me.

I dash for the inlet waters and plunge in. Immediately I begin to change back into my Merrow self. There is an unexpected shock when it happens, and I nearly black out. I am still recovering from the blow to my head, but I have no choice in the matter. The change is not something I can control once I am in ocean water. I close my eyes and try to steady myself, but the effort is beyond me. I sink slowly downward, my body changing as I do, gills forming, legs merging into my powerful tail, water filling my lungs and providing me with life.

All at once, I am so tired, I just want to sleep.

At this point, my strength gives out completely, and I begin to drift until I come to rest on the ocean floor, dazed and weak. I know I should swim away to a safer place. I know I am too close to the Swansong compound and the Faraway Trades guards. I know they will be searching for me and likely find me, and I will be back in their clutches.

But even fully reverted to my Merrow form, I cannot seem to muster the strength I need to act. I just lie there, helpless, growing weaker, feeling myself slipping away.

TWENTY-SIX

I DON'T KNOW HOW MUCH TIME PASSES. I DON'T KNOW MUCH OF anything except how helpless I feel. Thoughts of what needs doing swirl through my head, but I fear I am not equal to the task. I drift helplessly, nothing more than another piece of detritus lying on the ocean's sandy bottom. Visions swim before my weary eyes.

Perhaps I sleep for a time. When I wake, my head hurts less, and I realize that I am not alone anymore. Shadowy figures are swimming all about me, come seemingly from out of nowhere. Supple bodies with fins and gills and powerful fish tails that propel them through the waters with ease—I know them at once.

The Merrow have found me.

They materialize as if by magic—at least a dozen of them gathered around me. They swim in slow circles, examining me. They take their time, sometimes moving swiftly, sometimes just suspended in the water like statues. For a long time, they do not approach but only observe, taking my measure while allowing me to take theirs.

Eventually one approaches—a woman of considerable age, if I am correct. Her scaled skin is worn and wrinkled, but her eyes are bright with curiosity and humor. She comes up to me and lays her finned fingers on my arm.

Are you not a beautiful creature, she observes—a statement and not a question—and I am pleased that I understand her with no trouble. Perhaps all Merrow language is the same, or perhaps my *inish* is working better now on translating her words. But whatever the cause, we are communicating freely.

My name is Charlayne, I tell her, *and I am pleased to be here with you.*

You are most welcome. You are a wondrous mix of Merrow and Fae. Are there more of you?

No. I am alone.

Are you seeking a home? Do you wish to live with us?

I smile. *I am seeking a refuge. I have only recently discovered my Merrow side. I am new to the sea and to life within it. I was raised on land, unaware of my Merrow blood. But I want to stay with you awhile. Is that permitted?*

Of course. All Merrow are welcome here, and it shall be so for you. Come with us and tell us your story. Tell us how you came to be as you are.

I go with them willingly. I am excited to find more of my people who wish to know about me and will in turn reveal things about themselves. I have not forgotten about Florin and Tryn, but perhaps here I can find allies to aid in their rescue—as well as learn more about my heritage.

To my surprise, we swim not toward the outer reaches of the islands but toward the shoreline of the larger landmass that constitutes the wastelands. Enough time has passed that the sun has risen, and under its bright rays, the tone and feel of the water change dramatically. Instead of turning colder as it would in deeper waters, it warms. We are nearing a massive cliff wall that forms a promontory to a deeply submerged collection of underwater islands fasted to both the cliffside and the ocean floor. Many are riddled with caves and caverns, and there is life all about them—fish and crustaceans and tentacled anemones and worms of all sizes. It is very different here than it was in the Helles, and I am reminded anew of how much I still have to learn. But I want to, so I pay attention to everything around me. Now and again, we come across predators of considerable size, but they show little interest in the Merrow.

I have entered an underwater village—not so huge and daunting as a city, or even as immediately recognizable as those places that both Humans and Fae require for shelter. Mostly, the homes and buildings have been formed of rock chiseled either by the ocean's flow or by the hands of the inhabitants, and openness is their defining characteristic. Unlike Winnis and Douse's people, these Merrow are tenders of vast stretches of gardens, farmers who raise and cultivate underwater crops. Their homes and habitats are spread out wide, their residents able to swim into and out of them freely, and all of them are conjoined and sheltered by reefs and barriers.

I have entered another world, a habitat of a people I am only just beginning to know and understand. The differences between these Merrow and those I encountered before are immediately apparent. These Merrow are larger and less agile, better equipped for farming than for hunting, and their colors are deeper and more muted, better suited to their less tropical environment. Homes are settled comfortably amid larger and more productive gardens and small crop farms than the few I remember from the Helles Merrow. They nurture penned fish in vast numbers, as well as other species that I don't recognize. There are playgrounds filled with Merrow children entertaining themselves. Everything is so spread out and open, and I am thoroughly enchanted.

I study everything as I swim. I am awed by the size and sweep of the world through which I pass. It is clear from the numbers of Merrow that appear ahead of me that this is a major enclave—a place where these people have lived for a long time. In the shallower waters, an array of colors glimmers in patches in rocks, sand, and shell life. It is immeasurably lovely.

I look over the bodies and faces of young and old, men and women, large and small members of this extended family. There must be several hundred of them, and all share a clear bond of community. They all come to look at me—some closer than others, some more boldly, some not, all with clear interest. In the background, there are men at work building a wall, and in the foreground dishes of food are being set out on tables.

My first acquaintance swims over to guide me toward the tables. *Come eat with us, young one. Share a meal. Meet some of those who show so much interest in you.*

I follow her lead and soon find myself at a table piled high with raw shellfish—different in appearance yet similar in concept to what I ate among the Helles Merrow. I take a handful, and find them delicious. I wonder how much of my hunger for this food is determined by my Merrow heritage, but in the end, it makes no difference. I am starved, and I eat heartily.

I am called Torasun, my guide tells me. *I am a Dom Som to this fine family—the wife of the Profar and the mother of his eldest children. He will come to you shortly and converse.*

How many of you are there? I ask.

Well over three hundred. Many are out working the fields and harvesting the crops; you will see them later. For now, you have me. I will answer your questions if you answer mine.

Seeing no reason not to, I tell her virtually everything—about how I discovered my Merrow nature, how I befriended the Merrow who live in the Helles, how I traveled back home in my Fae form to my family in Viridian Deep, and finally, how I found my way here. I deliberately do not speak about Florin and Tryn, or the Faraway Trades slavers, just yet. I am still new to these people and this place, and I do not want to scare them off with demands for help. My needs can wait until later.

Torasun listens carefully and does not interrupt once. When I have talked myself out, she laughs.

Such a grand tale! You must tell it again to the Profar when he comes. But now that you are here, do you plan to stay? Do you wish to be one of us?

Do I? I do not dismiss the possibility, but it is entirely too early to decide what I wish to do next. Despite my fascination with this new world and its people, I have not forgotten that I cannot move on with my life until I have rescued my imprisoned friends. At some point, I must speak of this and of my mother's fate, but I know better than to rush into things too quickly.

Instead, I pepper Torasun with questions about her people and how they live. I learn how the various communities of Merrow who inhabit the vast stretches of Roughlin Wake are all unique in how they live and quite different from one another. They live as their ancestors lived before them, and the lives they pursue are in large part determined by how they grew up and what their elders taught them. But all share the same dislike of land people—particularly Humans—and all are tribal by nature and heritage. Their knowledge of the upper world is minimal and focused mostly on avoidance.

Then, finally, the Profar appears.

He is a giant—twice as big as I am, and all muscular power—though verging on elderly, his face is stern within a webbing of seagrass beard and uncut hair. His presence is unmistakable. He goes to each of perhaps a dozen Merrow women and kisses them gently in greeting before coming at last to Torasun and doing the same with her. He spies me at once and reaches for my hand. I extend it, and he bends to kiss me as well. Torasun is already talking about me, explaining who I am and how I appeared. The Profar listens to her but never takes his eyes off me.

When Torasun has finished, her partner gives me a nod. *A story worth telling. But what brings you here, young one? You are too far from your home to be off by yourself.*

I have been by myself for more than three years now, I tell him. *I know how to live that way. But having found out the truth of my bloodline, I feel the need to know more. If I am Merrow, I need to understand more about what that means.*

It is so, he acknowledges. *But how did you learn about us?*

Because you came to find me, once I appeared in your waters. But there is something more I need to tell you.

Now I reveal the story of my search for my mother and my discovery of her death in the slave camps of the Faraway Trades Company. I tell him of the fates of my companions, Florin and Tryn, and how I must find a way to free them. I tell him, finally, of how the Humans have constructed a slave camp on one of the islands, and of my desire to set all those slaves free. I confess, as well, that I lack the means to do so.

The Profar frowns. *You would seek our help if we were willing to provide it?*

I would beg for it, I confess. *But I do not think I have the right to do so.*

He is a big man, stern, but when I say this, his face warms in a smile.

Begging is not appropriate, he says. *Begging is for supplicants, not guests.* But then he becomes serious again. *What you ask is difficult to provide, but it could be done. How important is this task to you?*

I don't hesitate. *There is nothing more important. My friends are there, and I cannot forsake them. I cannot leave them to a life of misery and slavery. Do you know of a way that I can free them?*

Torasun looks sharply at the Profar, and there is a long silence, during which I am certain they are speaking privately. By her facial expressions and gestures, she is clearly trying to convince him of something. His frowns grow deeper, and at one point he shakes his head emphatically. My heart sinks.

But as the silent conversation continues, I find myself wondering instinctively if I have been doing the same thing. Or even if I can learn how. Can I somehow master the ability to convey my thoughts privately to some, while broadcasting other speech more openly to others? Do I have the ability to pick and choose?

There are subtleties to the Merrow speech I had not considered before, and I want to know more.

The silent dynamic has shifted a bit, and now it is the Profar who looks determined and Torasun who looks wary. Finally, she gives him a long look, then nods slowly. The Profar looks at me and smiles.

There is a way, child, he tells me, *but it could be risky.*

I sense that I am missing something. *What is the price of this help?*

His smile is reassuring, his eyes kind. I smile in return as he reaches for my hand, takes it in his own, and holds it fast. *All is well. Let us resume eating for now. When we are finished, I will reveal everything.*

I sit quietly for the remainder of the meal, uncertain despite his reassurances. I cannot think of a way that the Profar will be able to help me with a colony on land when his people are confined to the sea.

Eventually, the meal concludes. The Profar, with Torasun beside him, swims over to my side of the table and holds out his hand once more. *Please come with us.*

I take his hand, and together the three of us swim away from the festivities and into a vast garden of brilliant azure sea flowers that borders a shell-encrusted walkway. We swim without speaking for a long time, and then the Profar turns to me.

The help you seek cannot come from us directly, you understand, he confirms. *We are not land people; we are people of the water. To fight these loathsome Trades creatures ashore would be impossible for us. For that, you need help from your own kind. Would you be willing to seek it if I were to show you where it could be found? There is risk involved, however.*

I nod back. *To save my friends, I would risk anything.*

Well and good then. Because in order to succeed, you have to seek the assistance of a band of pirates. And of one pirate in particular.

My heart lurches. I stare at him, my mind spinning. Is it at all possible that he is talking about *Brecklin*? It can't be, can it? Why would Brecklin Craile be involved in this matter?

This pirate? I quickly ask. *What is his name?*

The Profar gives me a long, steady look. *His people call him the Silver Blade.*

Just like that, I start grinning.

TWENTY-SEVEN

THE PROFAR TELLS ME THAT I CANNOT MEET WITH THE BLADE right away; first, he must send out a signal, to bring the ship closer. Tomorrow or the next day, he is certain, Brecklin will be here.

I hate leaving Florin and Tryn in captivity for any longer than I have to, but as long as no ships are coming in to take them away, sail them on to someplace where I cannot find them, and sell them as slaves, I will force myself to wait.

The Profar promises me his people will keep watch for ships either coming or going, and warn me if any should arrive. Then Tora-sun takes my arm and steers me away silently. Yet I sense her displeasure.

This matter is not yet settled, she says finally. *I will speak with him again.*

About what, I wonder, as she draws me onward. Is she worried somehow about Brecklin? Did she not believe me when I told her that I know him? At this point, I hardly know what to expect. I cannot believe that Brecklin Craile is somehow involved with these Merrow.

How does the Profar know Brecklin? I ask, unable to quell my curiosity any longer.

That is the Profar's story to tell, not mine, she says.

Though I would rather ask Brecklin directly than rely on the Profar, I wonder if even *he* will tell me.

In any case, there is nothing more to decide right now, so I allow myself to be led to a small crevice freshly laid with seagrass and fronds. Torasun tucks me into them as if I were a child, then caresses my arms as a reassuring mother might and kisses me on the cheek.

Sleep well, she whispers as she rises. *And do not despair. At the very least, the Blade will help you free your friends. All will be well.*

I believe her. Not that I am particularly worried about asking Brecklin for anything—particularly when it comes to taking down the Swansong Colony. He's been fighting the slave trade—and the Faraway Trades Company—for most of his life. One of his greatest desires was finding and taking down a slave colony, but he'd never been able to uncover the location of one before.

No, my biggest worry is not getting him to agree, but putting him back within Faraway's clutches. After all, it was freeing him from their grasp that got me into this mess in the first place.

I watch Torasun as she goes, wondering all the while what is going to happen on the morrow. But finally I close my eyes and fall asleep.

I sleep later than almost everyone save a few of the children, and wake to a turmoil of activity. Food has again been set on the tables, and mothers and children are settling into their daily routines. I rise, still wearing my clothes from yesterday, straighten them out as best I can in the ripple of the ocean currents, then brush out my hair with a comb left next to my bed. I take momentary note of the way my skin color darkens in these cooler waters. Instead of remaining a soft beryl, it is now a darker emerald. My hair, already tousled, has become a nest of wildness—still as green as ever, but now leafless once more. But there is not much I can do about it, so I let it float around me the way it wants. Like my life, it is subject to conditions beyond my control.

I have breakfast with a few of the other Merrow women and their children—late risers, just like me. While at first no one talks to me, eventually a tiny girl asks me who I am, and from that point on, everything opens up. The questions come hard and fast, and I feel like I am making new friends. Torasun and two of her daughters come to sit with me, and I grow steadily more comfortable in their presence. We speak of my experiences on land versus theirs in the water, of our different peoples, of the dangers and risks we occasionally face, and of our different histories.

In the midst of all this, the Profar suddenly appears and announces it is time for us to depart. A clutch of other Merrow men and women—all of them younger than the Profar and Torasun, and most bearing a resemblance to one or the other—stand nearby, waiting. A few of their sons and daughters, I presume. I do not miss the fact that, in this world, men and women share an equal voice.

The Profar turns back to me, his expression intense. *Listen to me, young Char. We swim now to find the Silver Blade. We will be staying under the water and not surface until we find him. My son Valcheris will lead us, and only on his signal do we reveal ourselves. If we are cleared to proceed, I will explain to you what is needed once you surface. Are you ready?*

I smile and nod.

Off he swims, with the rest of us following, working our way south through the island chain. Our pace is quick and steady, but I find myself able to keep up with even the largest Merrow without difficulty. I feel encouraged by this. Still, swimming alone with these Merrow warriors makes me feel a bit wary. These are seasoned Merrow, and I am but a new hatchling. I should be wary of being overconfident, but I think I am nothing of the sort. I have spent my life taking risks and acting when others would hesitate. I do no less now.

I have no idea about where we are going. But before long, we are close to the southern end of the island chain and almost into open water. We stop in the shadows of the last island, keeping hidden below the surface, while Valcheris swims on ahead. He is gone for a long moment. When he returns, he speaks to his father directly, and again I cannot hear him. Truly, it seems that these Merrow rely on a form of mind-to-mind speech that can be channeled both broadly and narrowly, and I find myself wondering again how I can master this skill.

Especially if it can be used to communicate over distances where vocal efforts would fail, as perhaps the Profar might have done with Brecklin.

The Profar's thoughts reach out to me and the others in our group once more. *It is safe. Charlayne and I will go on alone.*

I am eager to proceed, eager to see my old companions once more. Though having met Tryn, I find myself wondering how I will react to Brecklin. Will it be for us as it had been, or have I been cured of my infatuation? I cannot be sure.

Together, the Profar and I swim on. He chooses our way carefully, always staying in the shadows and out of the light—though we are deep enough that, even if someone on the surface is looking down, we would be difficult to detect.

In minutes, we reach the southernmost of the Southern Isles and move around its circumference at a slow, steady pace, always staying close to its protective mass, far down and well hidden. I have no idea where we are going or what we are going to do once we get there, but I follow the Profar's lead without question. He seems to be searching for something, but I have no idea what it is.

Finally, he stops. He drops down a bit farther and indicates a huge iron link chain that stretches downward until it disappears into shadows. He gives me a questioning look, as if asking whether or not I understand what it is. When I shake my head, he uses his mind voice to speak a single word.

Anchor.

He beckons me upward, and we swim toward the surface of the ocean. Overhead, a huge dark shadow looms, and it appears to me that the island is supporting a substantial overhang.

Do you understand? he asks.

This time I do.

What I have mistaken for an overhanging part of the island is in fact a huge ship lying at anchor, its lines familiar, its width and breadth and shape instantly recognizable.

After all, I have scrubbed her down, pried away her barnacles, and repainted her boards on a regular basis over the past three years.

This is Brecklin's ship, the *Wayward Bound*.

He's waiting for you aboard, the Profar declares, *with his crew down belowdecks. He knows you want to speak to him, but not why. Come back when the talking is done and a decision has been reached. Do not let yourself be seen anywhere off the ship. Is it true you know him from before?*

Well enough, I think, as I nod in affirmation.

I shove away from the anchor chain and swim for the surface.

I REACH THE PLACE WHERE THE ANCHOR CHAIN BREAKS THE WATER and hang there for a few minutes, peering up at the vessel's sides. I neither see nor hear anyone moving about, so I pull myself out of the water and hang from the chain while my body sheds the waters of the Roughlin and I revert to my Fae self. It takes only a few minutes. Then I am climbing the chain all the way up to the anchor storage port, and from there levering myself to the ship's gunwales and over the deck railing.

Unfortunately, pantsless once again.

But no one sees me coming, and no one challenges my approach. I spy a lookout in the mainsail crow's nest, but he is facing out toward the open sea and not down to where I scramble up. The deck remains clear, and all signs of life are absent. I wonder why Brecklin has ordered my former shipmates belowdecks, but perhaps it is just to maintain the secrecy of my coming aboard.

In a crouch, I scurry along the deck railings and gain the entrance to the aft cabins, including the captain's quarters. Nudging open the doors, I slip inside. I am in luck. No one sees me enter. I move all the way down the passageway, past all the cabin doors of the officers' chambers, to Brecklin's rooms.

I knock once and, without waiting for an invitation, enter.

Brecklin Craile is sitting at his desk, paperwork strewn in front of him. He looks up, blinks once, then leaps from his chair and rushes over to greet me with a warm hug.

"Little Scrapper," he murmurs, hugging me close enough that I don't want him to stop. "Such a pleasure to see you once more! I was worried about you."

I hold on to him the way one might hold on to a lifeline in a drowning sea. I am besieged by memories, and in those few seconds, I remember why it is I loved him.

"I've missed you, Captain," I say as he releases his embrace.

His laugh is soft and comforting. "Not nearly as much as I've missed you. Who would have thought it possible?"

Exactly the words I had hoped to hear for so long.

He smiles. "I can tell you've lived through more adventures than you thought you would since rescuing me from those Faraway thugs. You must sit down and tell me everything. But, first, let me get you some pants."

He winks, moves over to a closet, and selects and hands me a spare pair of his trousers, which I put on with a flaming face. They are too loose, but he lends me a belt and I cinch them tight.

"Now, I want to hear everything," he says, "good and bad and otherwise. Come! Sit!"

He steers me over to a pair of deck chairs that flank his desk, and we sit facing each other. Then abruptly he leaps up again without explanation, walks to the bar, pours us each a glass of whiskey laced with a bit of water, and returns. We toast and drink deeply. I don't like whiskey, but I don't pause a moment before consuming it.

"Now tell me everything," he urges. "Where you've been and what you've done. Leave nothing out."

So, I do—everything from the moment I rescued him from the Faraway Trades people until our current reunion. He listens raptly, hanging on my words, and I find my heart beating faster.

It takes me quite a while to complete my tale, and I have more than enough time to savor his undivided attention. Never has he listened as fully or for as long as he does now, and I am so enthralled by his attention that I find myself resurrecting all the old fantasies: that he loves me in turn, that we could have a life together.

Until finally I rein myself in and remember the reality of my situation. And Tryn.

"Such tales!" Brecklin concludes. "So, now you are part Merrow—which explains your ease on the water, lass—and I am given to understand from that old rascal Profar that you are in need of aid. How so?"

"How do you know the Profar?" I cannot help asking. "Are you friends? And how do you even know about the Merrow?"

"We've known each other for more than ten years. He saved me when I was very young, still a cabin boy on the *Rush Water's Song*. I was washed overboard in a storm, and he fished me out, carried me back to land, and put me ashore. We have been friends ever since. We have actually become rather good at saving each other. We have done so a number of times. The last time we met, I scared off a bunch of explorers who were too close to discovering his colony. Flying a pirate flag has its advantages."

I shake my head, smiling. "You're full of surprises. I didn't know about the connection between the two of you. I didn't even know you were familiar with the Merrow people. You never mentioned it."

"I mention it only to those who need to know. Now you are one of them. Tell me what you need."

I launch into a short but thorough tale of my mother's sad history and my search to discover the truth about her. I tell of how my father died and how she tried to bring out my inner Merrow, but how those who witnessed it thought she was trying to drown me and took me away, placing me in an orphanage instead. And how she went to Trinch, who sent her to Crinksee, all in an effort to find her people and regain her tail so she could get me back, and how she was betrayed by Crinksee and sold to the slavers of Faraway Trades and eventually died in their keeping.

"I know you've wanted to find one of their colonies for ages," I say. "Well, as I've told you, there's one hidden here, and I know how to find it. We can strike a huge blow against the slave trade if we take it down—but we need to get all the people they've imprisoned out in the bargain—especially my friends."

Brecklin grins. "I always knew you would bring me good luck one day, Little Scrapper. Not only rescuing me from Faraway clutches, but now giving me a chance to avenge myself on those bastards who took us both by destroying one of their enclaves! Not to mention freeing more than a shipload of people. You're my good-luck charm, indeed."

"So you are ready to help?"

"Of course I'm ready! Tell me all about this Swansong Colony, and together we'll come up with a plan. But first, are you prepared to see your former crewmates? I had ordered them all belowdecks, save the lookout, because I wasn't sure you wanted to be seen. But I know they will be delighted to see you again."

"No more so than I will be to see them," I respond with a grin.

It is a joyous reunion, and I am hugged and pounded on the back by all my former crewmates, who declare themselves delighted to see me alive and well. Many ask where I suddenly appeared from, out here in the middle of the water, but Brecklin just deflects that, saying he sent me off in secret to try to locate a slaver colony. Now I have done that, and we are about to attack it, and that raises enough general cheers that the mystery of my appearance is forgotten.

And then we all settle down to plan our attack.

TWENTY-EIGHT

I WANT NOTHING TO DO WITH ANY OF THIS, THE PROFAR DE-
CLARES.

I have just returned to the Merrow colony after Brecklin rowed
me far enough out of sight of the *Wayward Bound* that no one would
see my change, and have finally finished outlining the details of the
plan the Silver Blade and I have crafted for attacking the Swansong
Colony.

I stare at him in disbelief.

This was your idea! I exclaim.

He points a forefinger in the direction of my nose. Nothing was
said about Merrow involvement. *This is not a matter in which the
Merrow should be engaged. It is a land people problem, for land people to
solve.*

*So you would condone slavery simply because it is not your own
people who are enslaved?* I fire back. *You would leave any resolution of
the problem entirely to your friend and his crew and lend no hand at all?
Weren't you the one who sent me to talk to the Blade? Didn't you encourage me to find an answer through him? And all the while you had no in-*

tention of helping? I find that more than a little disturbing—especially since my mother, one of your own people, died in their care!

Your mother had abandoned her Merrow life—by choice! It is not my problem to address. It never has been. It is a problem that belongs solely to the Humans and the Fae.

You are wrong. It is indeed our problem—a problem for all of us to address, I respond as calmly as I can, filled with a mix of anger and disgust that I hope I am managing to conceal. I need the Profar's support. *You see what these people are doing. Do you think, if these slavers knew you existed, they would exempt you from their predations?*

Then it stands to reason that we must make sure they never learn about us, he says sharply. *Which they would, should we choose to attack them.*

But shouldn't all right-thinking people of the world stand up for one another when they see harm being done? I counter. *Shouldn't we all help one another?*

His face turns dark. *Help one another? How much have any of the land people ever done for us? Fae or Human—how much? How much care have you shown the water people? How hard have you worked to protect our lives? Almost none of you even know we exist. We are a myth, a fairy tale. Even those few who suspect we are down here make no real effort to earn our friendship. You do little to protect the ocean that is our home or to take care of the underwater lands in which we live. You have no concern for us. We are nothing to you. So why should we show any care for you?*

He gestures at me, finger pointing. *I know you are different, young Char. You are half Merrow, and one of us. You see the Merrow people as equals. But others are very different, and we do not answer to them.*

I understand his thinking—which I know from Winnis is likely the thinking of most of the Merrow—but still I am angry at the Faraway Trades Company for buying and selling people as if they were nothing more than merchandise. It is a sin to treat *anyone* in this fashion, and now here is this wise and powerful leader of the

Merrow telling me it is none of his concern because the people are not his own.

As if I have summoned it from out of the ether—as if time and distance mean nothing—I hear a small, quiet voice speaking familiar words.

Go save those who were stolen. They are waiting for you.

Parse said those words to me. But I know he would say something more, if he were here to do so. He would tell me to save them all—all the slaves stolen from all the peoples, no exceptions. And he would have the Merrow do the same.

As quickly as that, I know what I must do.

The challenges we face lie on both land and sea, I tell him. The Silver Blade has offered to face those on land—and he offers to do that because he knows the Merrow cannot. So will you do the same? Will you agree to match the courage and bravery of the pirates—who, after all, are in more danger from these slavers than you? Did you know that your friend the Blade has already been captured once by these people? And it was me— by myself—freeing him from their clutches, that led me to discover my Merrow side. Would you do less to help him? You, who have known him longer?

And what would that require of us, youngster? How can we manage to protect ourselves from these monsters? You mean well, but you should remember that you are only one small person facing a fortress manned by armed soldiers. Go ashore to meet them and you are embracing your own death.

Perhaps. But I don't think so. I have already infiltrated their compound once; I can do so again. In fact, I intend to. While Brecklin catches their attention from the outside, I will be working my way to the inside in order to break out the slaves. Then, together, we will cause as much damage as time allows.

If you are not caught and executed on the spot. You ask too much of yourself.

I nod. *And you, Grandfather, do not ask enough.*

A long pause marks the passage of the moments as we face each other wordlessly. Finally, he says, *Very well. I will take my soldiers into the waters, and we will do what damage we can to their vessels, should they try to escape that way. I will stand with you as long as there is reason to do so. I will pray for you to the Shades and the magics that ward us all.*

Then he turns and swims away, and I let him go.

Later, when I am alone, I think it all through once more. I wonder what Auris would have done in my situation. Once, I would have gone instantly to my big sister for help, but those days are behind me. She isn't here to help me anymore. No one from my family *is*.

There's still Florin and Tryn, of course, but what help can they offer? I wonder what's happened to them since they were taken and enslaved. Are they still within the confines of the colony, or have they escaped and found hiding places amid the islands?

I know that worrying about them now is pointless. More immediate problems require my attention. Such as breaking Florin and Tryn out of that colony, if they are indeed still there—as I suspect they are.

I have promised both the Profar and the Silver Blade that I will sneak into the Swansong slave colony under the cover of Brecklin's initial attack. Then, with the continuing attack still distracting the guards, I will find and free the slaves, and together we will sabotage whatever equipment and artillery we can locate. It will be our goal to cause as much damage and disruption as we can from within while Brecklin attacks them from without. Fighting a battle on two fronts will split their attention and hopefully enable us to prevail.

Given the fortress's hidden location on the interior of the island, Brecklin will have to sail through the inlet to reach the fortress, which will doubtless alert the Faraway Trades minions to his presence. But he has faith in his vessel's cannons to breach their

walls—especially since their main defense seems to be their reli-
ance on the secrecy of their location. Why bother to over-defend a
place that can't be found, save by those who know the path?

Yet even as I review the plan, it still seems mad, filled with too
many holes and uncertainties. They will still have cannons and
similar artillery on their walls that can harm his ship. They will
undoubtedly have more and better weapons than the pirates can
bring to this fight. I can barely believe we are doing this, but we
have no other option. I need to do what Parse has asked of me and
I now ask of myself: free the slaves, especially Florin and Tryn,
whom I have put in their present position, and this seems the best
way to achieve it. The only way, if I am being honest.

I am in the same position that Auris was in not all that long ago,
when she broke into the Goblin prison to rescue Harrow. But in her
case, she had only herself to depend on. I have Brecklin and his
crew, and the Merrow. And, with a little luck, Florin and Tryn and
their fellow prisoners, once I let them out.

I just need to be careful and stay wary. I need to be brave.

WHEN OUR PLANS ARE SETTLED, I SWIM BACK TO MY SLEEPING SPACE
to find some rest. Our attack against the Faraway colony will begin
around midnight. I will go ashore while Brecklin and his crew navigate the inlet, then the Merrow and the pirates will place themselves and their equipment where they can do the most damage.
And under cover of their attack, I will find and free the prisoners,
while doing as much damage as I can along the way. We are ready.
We have only to wait.

I have been resting for only a few moments when I sense another presence entering the room. Through the shadows, I make
out the slender form of Torasun as she swims into view. *Can't sleep?*
she asks me.

I haven't really tried. I'm still thinking about everything.
Worried?

A bit. Okay, maybe more than a bit.

She smiles. *You will be fine. You're skilled and you're committed. Just don't act rashly. Think before you leap.*

I'll try. And thank you. For everything.

We are quiet for a time, listening to the movement of the water, tracking its flow, watching the shift of the light from above the surface. Darkness is growing, and the night is settling in. I think about home and family and wonder how long it will be before I see either. Or if the worst will happen, and I will never see them again. The possibility is there. I can't say I haven't had my fair share of risky encounters. I've survived them before, but there is no guarantee that this situation will be the same.

I am no fool, and I harbor no false illusions.

My thoughts drift. *Torasun, can I ask you a question about my mother? She always used to say that my father stole her tail and she couldn't get it back, but I still don't understand what that means. How can anyone steal a Merrow's tail?*

The older woman smiles at me. *It is only a saying. Someone's Merrow self can never be stolen, but it can be forgotten. Some Merrow have the capacity for change within them, able to become both Merrow and land-dweller. It is rare, but it happens. Your mother must have been one such.*

I nod. *I have suspected as much for a while. The Merrow I met in the Helles told me that some Merrow can change back and forth, but it is very rare. The last one from their colony left fifty years ago and never returned. But if they have the ability to change back and forth, won't they just retain that? Why did my mother lose her ability to change? Or is that also something that happens?*

Sadly, it is something that happens—or so I have heard. If a Merrow chooses to live on land—if they love a Human or a Fae enough to forsake their Merrow heritage—they can choose to undertake this change deliberately. But after a time, they can lose their Merrow self by deliberately resisting the urge to change back again. The more time passes, the more fixed the new identity becomes. And before long, they have lost the capacity to change at all.

I am suddenly worried. *Do you think this might happen to me? If I choose to live among the Merrow, will I lose my ability to live on land? Or if I choose to stay with my family on land, will I lose my ability to become Merrow? Or will my half-Fae blood change this?*

I don't know, child, Torasun tells me sadly. *I suspect that is something you will have to discover on your own. But know that it is hard for a Merrow to be away from the sea for too long—especially once they have lost the capacity to change back. Even in land form, we long to return. I wonder if that yearning was what finally drove a wedge between your mother and father. The resentment toward the one that caused the loss can become strong, and that is what we mean when we talk about "stealing our tails."*

To me, this is horrifying—that altering your physical form for love can result in a change that lasts forever—perhaps even longer than the love itself. I cannot imagine what that would be like. To make the alteration out of love, and then be forced to live with it, even if that love has died, seems a cruel fate for anyone.

Torasun is silent for a long moment, then adds, *Part of the reason the Profar was so reluctant to pledge his aid was because not all of his people are locked in an aquatic form.*

I startle visibly at this, and she gives me a twinge of a smile. *The other Merrow you spoke to were not wrong,* she says. *The trait is very rare. But at least two of us among the Merrow here have the use of it— myself, and my son Valcheris. It is not a form either of us uses often; we are content to live our lives under the water. But both of us have the capacity to operate on land for a limited time—and have undertaken the change enough that we have not lost the ability to do so.*

Now I indeed understand the Profar's reluctance, when he knows that the lives of his wife and son are at stake.

We have argued about this repeatedly, the Profar and I, she continues. *He does not believe either of us would be safe on land, especially since it is not a form either of us uses often. But I have told him that the cause outweighs his fears. Valcheris and I have spoken, and we both agree that you need allies on land. The Profar will not like it, but we will be there to aid you. The Merrow are good at avoiding notice—we have an extra sense when it comes to not being seen—so we will help you as we can.*

I would never ask that of you, I say, horrified, and Torasun pats my arm.

I know you would not, she says. *But it is not your decision. Nor even the Profar's—though it does not lessen his guilt in hiding this truth from you. It is a decision Valcheris and I made together, and we will stand by it. We will be going with you tonight. We will be standing by your side.*

After Torasun leaves, I lie there thinking over what she has told me for a long time, beginning to understand my own origins a bit better. My mother gave up everything that mattered for my father, and then found it wasn't enough.

Would I give up part of myself for the love of a man? For Brecklin or Tryn? I don't think so. Fortunately, it is not something I have to consider physically, as I can currently shift back and forth with ease. But if I found a life on land with either Tryn or Brecklin, could I give up my Merrow side forever and never return to the sea? Or, if I took up a life among the Merrow, would I be unable to return to the land to see my Fae family? And if I stayed too long in one form, would my body also lose the ability to recall the other?

Loving someone requires sacrifice, it is true. But surely not this much. I am not so young or naïve as to be unaware of this. I must never assume that I will not be tempted. I must never forget my mother's fate.

TWENTY-NINE

I SLEEP BUT A SHORT TIME AND COME AWAKE AT MIDNIGHT. AL-
ready, others are up and about. The Merrow who will fight beside me today are preparing. Somewhere up above me, riding the
currents of Roughlin Wake, the pirates under Brecklin's command
are doing the same. All of us face an enemy we intend not only to
defeat but to destroy. When we are finished, nothing of these men
and women who have traded in the lives of those less fortunate
should remain.

It is quiet and deserted enough in my little alcove that small
schools of fish swim past, slipping untroubled through the Merrow
encampment, finding their surroundings no more threatening than
the sands beneath us.

I lie where I am for a moment, then rise, fully awake. Today I
will risk everything to save Florin and Tryn—and to strike a blow
against Faraway Trades that they will find hard to recover from.
Maybe I can't take down the slave trade altogether, but if I strike
the first, crippling blow, then perhaps others will follow.

I dress in my protective clothing and strap on my weapons. On
this day, I wear a lightweight metal vest that Torasun has provided

me—a shield that wraps about my chest and back to protect my vital organs. She and her son will wear similar vests. That we will all be under fire is guaranteed. We must look to our safety and consider ourselves in mortal danger at all times. I know we will encounter wicked souls who will try to kill us.

But we will not die easily.

I leave my resting place and move out into the open spaces beyond. Others are engaged in eating, mostly in silence, so I also partake.

When the Profar gives the call, I respond at once. But matters have changed. Valcheris will continue to be my companion, but Torasun will remain behind. The Profar has put his foot down. It is one thing to send his son into battle; it is another to ask that he send his senior wife, too. I understand his reasoning and settle for what help I can get. I fear for Torasun's safety as well.

Valcheris swims with me from the depths to the surface near the island that houses the fortress. A handful of others from the Merrow clan will follow shortly and take up positions around and within the inlet, and will be responsible for disabling any boats on which the Faraway people attempt to escape.

I think we are strong enough to do what is needed. I will miss Torasun, but at the same time I will feel better knowing she is safe.

Valcheris and I reach our designated goal without difficulty. There should be guards at the inlet's entry and along its banks. But, as before, these people think their colony hidden enough that they keep such sentries confined to the perimeter of their fortress. There has never been a threat to their safety, and they do not yet see anything to suggest that one exists now. If they knew that the Merrow and the Blade and his crew were planning an attack, they would be taking a different approach. Their overconfidence will be their downfall. Even I, young as I am, have learned that lesson.

So Valcheris and I next swim the length of the inlet to the inland harbor. There are guards on watch, but they do little more than survey the harbor from their watchtowers and wall tops to reassure themselves that nothing is happening. Wrapped in shadows and gloom, we are all but invisible.

Armed with stronger forms of weapons than I possessed on my earlier attempt, we swim down to the underwater gates that will give us access to the inner wall loading docks and their octopus guardian. We spring the gate fastenings easily with wrenches and pliers and move inside. But this time the octopus does not come forth to challenge us and no other obstacles bar our way. I don't know what has become of the beast; maybe it died from the injuries I inflicted on it the last time I came through. But whatever the case, we reach the loading platform unchallenged.

Once surfaced and landed, we undergo the change. It happens swiftly enough, and Valcheris and I are courteous enough to look away as we regain our land bodies and slip into the extra pants we have brought.

From there, we go into the interior sections of the surrounding walls and make our way ahead silently until we find an exit door opening into the inner courtyards.

And there, we wait.

Our plan is simple enough. We are to hold back until we hear the start of an attack from the cannons and crew of the *Wayward Bound*, once it has sailed into the inner harbor and is within range of the fortress with their cannons. This is a formidable complex we have entered, with a sizable complement of guards and weapons, but it exists primarily to house slaves awaiting transfer to buyers or to market. It is essentially a way station and not a full-fledged fortress, so an attack from a heavily weaponized warship will cause serious problems. When the *Wayward Bound* opens fire, every available guard in the colony will run to man the walls and the protective cannons. When that happens, Valcheris and I will open the gates and free the slaves from their imprisonment so that they can aid us in the conflict.

Admittedly, the plan is risky and subject to any number of unknowns. But it is the best plan that the Silver Blade and I could come up with on short notice.

Valcheris and I will do what needs doing, as we are the only ones who could have made it inside the fortress in secret; no pirate would have survived the two-minute swim inside the airless tunnel. Besides, the pirates are fierce and skilled and much stronger physically than I am, but they lack both my instincts and my *inish*. They would be found out quickly enough once they were inside the colony, and that would be the end of all of us.

Valcheris I can depend upon; I have seen for myself how well trained and skilled he is. Secrecy and stealth are what we need in this matter, not numbers. The attack will succeed only if no one inside the walls of the colony discovers that anyone from outside has penetrated their defenses. A quick, hard strike by cannon from without should draw everyone to the walls, which gives the two of us already inside a way to release the locks on the gates from inside, and at the same time start freeing the prisoners to help with our attack.

If Auris could see me now, how proud she would be! And my sisters and Harrow, too. Little Char, always ready to fight, always ready to risk everything all by herself. And yet now here I am, with a plan and allies, moving with stealth and caution, using good sense and making an effort to protect myself. I have grown beyond the impetuous young girl they knew into someone they would not even recognize.

Time slows to a crawl as we wait, Torasun's son and I. We each know our roles in the fight ahead. We just have to be patient.

The thunderous roar of the warship cannons startles us both, but we are both quickly on our feet and out the door into the courtyard. Cannonballs strike the walls of the compound, smashing walls, ramparts, and wall cannons alike. Fireballs follow—explosive missiles that fall against roofs and shatter through windows, setting everything ablaze. The entire colony comes awake in response, guards rushing from their bunk rooms for the walls, shouts and cries rising up, shadowed figures rushing everywhere.

Valcheris is already running for the gates to release their locks, his passage swift and sure. I bolt for the slave pens, wire cutters in hand. The attacks from both sides of the colony walls have begun.

I reach the holding pens unchallenged, as no one sees me in the panic. The pens are a simple complex of two containers—one for men and one for women. There are only two watchtowers guarding the pens, but their minders are momentarily ignoring everything except the attack on the main walls, their heads turned away from where I stand. Most of the prisoners are still asleep, many just lying on the ground. There are so many inmates, I cannot begin to sort them out. How am I to find Tryn and Florin among so many?

But I have no choice; I have to. And I have to release everyone else locked away in here. Only freeing the entire imprisoned population will provide enough manpower to overwhelm the guards.

I will have to use speed and confusion to get this done. I use the cutters I have been carrying on the heavy wires that seal off the men's pen at a place where the shadows are deep and neither of the guards situated in the watchtowers is looking. Then I drop to my hands and knees and crawl through the mass of prisoners, shaking their sleeping forms as I go, whispering the same words over and over.

"Help is here. We're going to free you. Wake up!"

Most of those I wake only stare at me blankly. Almost nobody moves. Only a few try unsuccessfully to respond. All of them are heavy-eyed and barely functional. It seems the guards keep them in line by using drugs to dull their wits and slow their ability to react. I am horrified as I realize how dysfunctional they have become. There is no help to be found here, and no magical solution for making them spring to our aid. The help we were counting on from the prisoners is gone.

I abandon my efforts and go in search of Tryn, but I can't find him. The minutes slip by, and I am losing both time and opportunity. I start to feel the first nudge of panic as I realize that I can't waste much more time searching for my friends; I have to get back to the gates to help. All my pirate allies in this struggle must have burst through the open gates by now to stand with Valcheris in hand-to-hand combat with the colony guards. They must be barely holding on, as even a chaotic and disorganized counterattack will ruin us all. I have to go to stand with them.

Then I stumble over Tryn, who is lying sprawled amid a collection of prone forms at the far edge of the men's pen. His eyes are empty and his breathing slow. I cry out in relief when I find him and hold him to me. He barely responds. I blame myself. He would not be in this position were it not for me.

I cut my way out of the men's pen on the far side, and find Florin close to the borders of the women's pen. She, too, is barely awake. But she is able to recognize me, and she grabs my hand fiercely through the wires of the pen.

"Char," she whispers. "It's too dangerous. Get out of here!"

"You've been drugged," I whisper back, passing her the cutters. "Use these to get free, then crawl over to Tryn. Try to wake him. Do whatever it takes. I will come back for you."

Then, weeping with rage and frustration, I leave behind this tragic collection of men, women, and children. I am abandoning them, but what choice do I have? I cannot help them when they cannot do anything to help themselves—or to help any of those who were counting on their assistance.

Time is running out fast.

I break headlong across the courtyard for the front gates, unslinging my blades as I run. Lights are on everywhere I look—high-powered strobes that cut the protective darkness to pieces. Voices lift into shouts, and bodies are still breaking from their sleeping chambers and duty posts, converging on the struggle taking place at the gates. I am not immediately recognized for what I am because those who crowd out into the courtyards are charging about with no idea of what is happening, and I can hide myself easily in the chaos.

I am skilled and well trained in hand-to-hand combat. My

brother and my sisters saw to that. I take down the few who try to stop me so fast that they are gone almost before they realize what is happening. I race to join that battle taking place just inside the gates and find a handful of men blocking my way. I don't hesitate; I go right into them, cutting through them to reach the pirates who have come to my aid. Valcheris already stands among these new attackers, and all of them are fighting hard to hold the gates open against the defenders seeking to regain control.

I see the Silver Blade at the forefront of the pirates, blades in both hands, his expression fierce with determination and excitement. I charge over to stand beside him.

"Courage, Scrapper!" he cries. "Stand your ground, and we will stand with you!"

The remaining guards converge on us, but we quickly dispatch them. The gates open wider and more of Brecklin's crew pour in.

Then, out of the corner of my eye, I see something even more hopeful. Some of those imprisoned within the pens have risen and begun to break free. Many still stagger or lurch from the effects of the drugs, but there are others who have clearly regained at least a portion of their strength. Any show of force is better than none, I think. I see some of them snatching up makeshift weapons. I think I see Florin and Tryn, and rejoice.

But the resistance to our invasion is fierce and determined. Many of my pirate comrades have fallen and others are injured. I'm not sure how much longer we can last.

Suddenly, Brecklin Craile goes down. Without warning—without a sound—the Silver Blade collapses. In response, the rest of us close about him protectively, beating back the attack that instantly follows. I have never fought so hard or so desperately in my life. I force myself not to look at him. I keep my eyes on the enemies trying to reach him and place myself in their path at every turn.

Valcheris and I stand at the forefront of the remaining pirates, refusing to be driven back or cede ground, determined to stand to the last. Maybe the colony guards can sense this. Maybe they simply have lost interest in continuing a fight that they have decided they cannot win, for I can feel their defenses wavering.

At almost the same moment, Tryn appears beside me—haggard and bloodied, his face an intense mask of determination—bearing a weapon he must have seized from one of the guards. He gives me a look, and with an exhilaration I cannot explain, I scream to those who fight beside me, "Take them! All of them! Let's end this!"

With my companions beside me, I rush into the faltering colony defenses and throw them back. I leave Brecklin and those who tend to him behind. No time for them now. I look ahead, searching. I have not seen Alcoin, the doctor, or the commander since breaking into the compound, but I look for them now.

Then I spot them. They stand near the entrance to the commander's quarters, a handful of guards in front of them. I shout to my companions to follow me and charge toward the colony leaders.

We are on top of them almost immediately. Both the doctor and the commander take a step back as we rush them, but Alcoin steps forward, lifts his automatic pistol, and discharges it several times at point-blank range. Tryn goes down without a sound and, on instinct, I go down with him. When Alcoin attempts to point his weapon at me, I am no longer where I was, and that proves his undoing. I have already seized Tryn's weapon, and now I discharge it.

Alcoin falls, his life ended.

Burning with renewed fury, I turn on the commander—the one who threatened me, the one whom I hold responsible for everything—but he is already disappearing inside his headquarters, slamming and locking the doors behind him. I follow after him, and as I pass the fallen Alcoin I notice the knife that Auris gave me stuffed in his belt. I yank it free. It belongs to me.

When I try the door, the lock holds firm. I wish I still had my lockpicks, but I do not. I rush around the side of the building, searching for another entry. Nothing. I go all the way to the backside, and here I find a door I can open. I do so carefully, giving my instincts time to warn me of what is waiting beyond, paying attention to where I step and what I sense might be waiting that would threaten me.

I search the entire first floor and find nothing. I climb to the second. Again, nothing. Where is the Faraway Trades leader? I go up to the third and final floor and stop while still in the stairwell, trying to get some sense of where my enemy is. This time, my instincts find him. He stands off to one side, hiding from me, waiting. Does he know who pursues him? I can't be sure, but I hope so. I hope that just the thought of me terrifies him. I think of Tryn and Brecklin Craile, fallen along the way. I think of all the men, women, and children who have died in his slave camps. I think of all the harm this man has caused over the years, and I detest him more than ever.

I rush up the final three steps and spin toward where I sense he will be waiting. My *inish* does not fail me; he is exactly where I think he should be. But he carries a handgun, and he fires it. I feel the bullets strike me twice—once in my leg and once in my side. The first bullet wound is superficial and the second does nothing but dent my armored waistcoat. Auris's knife is already in my hand and I fling my blade at him with as much power as I can muster.

My aim is true. The knife takes him in the throat and leaves him gasping for breath. In mere seconds, he bleeds out.

I hobble over to make certain of his fate and can tell instantly that he is gone.

I GO BACK DOWNSTAIRS AND JOIN MY COMPANIONS.

All of the Faraway forces are either dead or have been made prisoners.

Tryn lies amid a scattering of other bodies. I kneel beside my friend, my almost lover, my hope for the future, and I take his hand in mine. I know he is dead. Three bullets have struck him in the center of his chest. But he looks so peaceful—almost as if he might still wake up if given a few more moments. I stay with him for much longer than that—not to give the time to him, but to give it to myself. I do not want to leave him. I do not want to admit that he is gone. He came here to help me, and now he is dead. I cannot stand the thought of letting him go.

I kiss him one last time and cry until I think my heart will break.

THIRTY

I T IS HERE THAT FLORIN FINDS ME. SHE IS ALIVE AND WELL, AND rushes to me when she sees me stricken and on my knees. She hugs me to her in that same familiar way, my oldest and truest friend, my always brave companion. When she sees Tryn, we cry together. She tells me how his companionship got her through the early days of their capture and imprisonment, and I sense that she might have fallen a little bit in love with him, too.

I find myself wondering, if he had lived and the choice had been his to make, which one of us he would have chosen.

Brecklin has survived the battle. He took a bullet to the knee, which collapsed him instantly, but his people have gotten him to safety. And though he may never walk again without a limp, he is alive. When I finally see his face, grinning back at me, I fly toward him and kiss him so hard and deep that he finally has to pry me loose and hold me away from him.

"Hey, there, Little Scrapper," he says. "I'm glad to see you alive as well, but . . . ah . . . I think we should set the record straight here."

"What . . . what do you mean?" I ask—confused enough that I am not thinking it through. Clearly, something isn't right. I can feel it. Kissing him was not like kissing Tryn at all. There was no spark, no passion. And having experienced the real thing . . .

"Scrapper," he tells me, leaning close enough to give my cheek a gentle kiss, "listen to me. We shall be companions and friends forever but we won't be anything more. That kind of love isn't there for you. It isn't what I want. It never has been."

Oh. I blush. "I understand," I say, and unfortunately I do.

"And I owe you an apology, too. I suspected you saw me as more than just your captain and should have said something earlier, but I kept hoping you would see the truth of things on your own. You're like a little sister to me, Char. I admire your fighting spirit and love you dearly. But just . . . not that way."

I find myself smiling. "Well, at least we *both* understand now. And you've more than paid me back for saving your life in Pressia, so I'd say we're even. Now, what are we going to do about them?"

I gesture toward the former slaves, most now milling about in the growing dawn. "Is *Wayward Bound* big enough to get all of them someplace safe?"

He puts his hands on my shoulders, reassuring touches that mean more than he will ever know. "I'll make sure of it."

I LEAVE BRECKLIN AND HIS CREW TO SEE TO THE CARE OF THE former slaves while Florin and I deal with Tryn. We bear his body into the jungles on the far side of the island, find a place that overlooks the ocean, and bury him there. Florin and I sit with his remains and exchange a few short words about things we remember about him and what he meant to us. We speak the way you do about losing someone who was special to you. I feel fresh hurt inside, remembering. I feel his loss so deeply. It is good to be able to share that with Florin. Both of us cry as we speak of him and what he meant to us.

Then Florin asks, "Did you find out what you needed to know about your mother, Char?"

I don't answer right away. Instead, I remember suddenly that the nurse who was so kind to me while I was imprisoned was among the slain. I manage a nod. "I think my mother was broken from the moment she gave up her heritage," I say. "I know she loved me, but I also know that by myself I would not have been enough to cure her unhappiness. Perhaps it was for the best that Ancrow adopted me, in spite of the manipulations she performed on me. I found a stable family with Ronden and Harrow and Ramey—and later Auris, too."

She hugs me. "I am so glad, Char. But what will you do now?"

I shrug. "Long term? I still have no idea. But in the short term, I have a few people I need to see, things I need to do, and promises I need to keep. What of you? Will you go home now? Back to Zedlin and your people?"

She grins, almost her bright self once more. "I don't think so. That isn't where I belong anymore. I was thinking of something else. The pirate life worked so well for you, I thought I might give it a try myself. I've spoken with the Blade, just briefly, about taking me on as a member of his crew, and . . ."

She trails off, and her face turns sober. "I know now how horrible it feels to be enslaved with no hope of rescue. Tryn was certain you would find us, but I wasn't sure how you could manage it, not even knowing where in the world we were. He was right about you, but I don't ever want anyone to feel the way I did when I was imprisoned. I was certain all was lost, and I felt all broken apart. I was just garbage to those people. So I'm going to help Brecklin find a settlement for those we rescued, and then maybe I can go with him to find more colonies, and hopefully help break apart Faraway Trades' slave business for good."

I can tell from the fire in her eyes that she has found a calling that means something to her—at least for now. And a pirate's life will be suitable to a spitfire like her. "And Brecklin has said he will take you?"

"He has. I've never sailed on a boat quite like his, but I've been on the water all my life, and I'm a quick study. I'll be fine."

I hug her again and wish her luck. With Florin on their tail, the Faraway Trades people will have some difficult times ahead.

———

WITH THE AID OF BRECKLIN'S CREW, WE TEAR DOWN THE SLAVE PENS and use *Wayward Bound's* cannons to reduce the Swansong's buildings, walls, and equipment to rubble. The next Faraway Trades ship to arrive here will find the ruins—and perhaps Brecklin, Florin, and an armed warship waiting for them.

As for me, I go down into the depths to thank the Profar for his aid, and seek treatment for my injuries. There I find a wounded Valcheris and his mother, Torasun, waiting for me.

I knew you would come back to us, Torasun advises me as she helps me bind up my wounds. *It was not only for you that this was necessary. It was for all those who were imprisoned in that Shadesforsaken place. It was for those who had no hope. We understood their suffering, my son and I. We knew what the Merrow needed to do to make things right.*

The Profar, who is watching us, nods—albeit reluctantly. *There was never any question as to the rightness of what you wanted done. I doubted that Merrow involvement would be wise, but I was wrong. We are pleased to have been able to help you in your efforts.*

Torasun looks at him—and perhaps says something privately to him as well—for he scowls again and growls, *Very well. I wasn't willing to allow my favorite wife and true love to enter into such madness. Nor was I happy to find that my son had gone against my wishes and risked his own life. But I am proud that they stood up for what was right. And in that, I speak the truth, lass. You should know that you are always welcome here to share our home and our friendship. Go home, if you must, but consider coming back to us. You belong here.*

I suspect he is right and that one day I will return. But for now, other matters need addressing. Rising back to the surface, I find my abandoned boat still moored behind a nearby island and return to Jagged Reach. My first visit is to Glad Jack, telling him of both Tryn's fate and the loss of the 520. He is deeply saddened by the first but shrugs off the second. There is always another boat to find, he suggests in his wry, no-nonsense, seaman's way. There is always another sailing to be made.

Then, on a whim, I return to find Portallis. But she has disappeared, perhaps gone off on another journey to find another shelter in another place entirely. I will never know. Although I try, I do not find her or ever see her again. But I will never forget her or the comfort she gave me when I needed it most.

I also visit Winnis and Douse, who are both delighted to see me, and again renew their offers to make my home among them.

Of the two Merrow offers I have received, this is the more compelling. This is the Merrow community that first helped me discover the truth about myself, and nowhere else has my sense of ease with my Merrow body been stronger. Plus, the waters here are warm and lovely—and though my Merrow body does not feel the water's coldness in quite the way my Fae form does, I am still most drawn to this tropical splendor.

But first, I must return to Viridian Deep and strengthen my relationships with my family—and Ramey in particular. I owe it to her, especially, to make amends for my selfish withdrawal from her life. I owe it to her to persuade her that I value her friendship and want it back. I owe it to all of them to let them know I am safe and that I have discovered the truth about my mother and my early life. I must find a way to do all of this.

I work my way back to Viridian Deep by crewing for several vessels going in roughly the right direction, and eventually end up back in Zedlin's village. I tell him of Florin's decision to fight the slave trade she so recently fell victim to, and take joy in seeing his eyes light up when he hears that his sister might have finally found something that matters to her.

Florin, at least, has found her place in life.

I wish I could say the same for myself. I am still at odds over what I should do next.

It is time to go back to my family in Viridian Deep.

———

It is early evening when I arrive at Auris's place, and Harrow is there, too. After we have greeted each other, Harrow suggests that Auris and I go for a walk while he looks after Parse and Safra. Trust Harrow to be able to judge what is best in any situation. He knows that Auris and I need some time alone. I smile at him in gratitude and whisper my thanks as he rises to come kiss me on the cheek and welcome me back. Auris is lucky to have him. But then, Harrow is lucky to have her. I hope one day I will have a relationship like this for myself, but I have years ahead of me yet.

I do take a few minutes to speak with Parse alone before taking my walk, though. I tell him of what has happened to me and how helpful it was to have his insights and advice. I have never seen him reveal much in the way of emotional response, but to my astonishment, he actually blushes.

Love you, Char, he manages, and I choose to leave it at that.

Auris and I walk the high tree lanes through the gathering darkness. We take our time and at first say nothing, but then I find I can stay silent no longer and drag her to a public bench, where we sit while I tell her everything.

In the silence that follows, I think I have said more than I should. But I don't want to keep back any part of what has happened and what I have learned just because it is difficult to admit. I need to tell someone, and there is no one I would rather tell than my big sister.

By the time I have finished, I am in tears. Auris moves close and takes me in her arms, holding me while I cry. If those passing by notice me, I do not notice them. There is only Auris. I find such comfort in the strength of her arms and the softness of her voice.

"There, there, little one, no more tears," she whispers. "It is over and done with. You have come home to us, and you are safe. You must give whatever pain or sadness remains time to heal. It will not be easy, but you have us to help."

She rubs my shoulders as she holds me, and I feel the warmth in her words. Eventually, the tears diminish, and feelings of peace and renewal begin to filter through me. Finally, I draw far enough back from her that we are face-to-face again.

"Parse told me something before I left," I say. "He told me to save those who were stolen, by which he must have meant the slaves imprisoned in the Faraway Trades colony. I think he senses things we don't."

Auris arches an eyebrow. "I have thought the same more than a few times. He is a strange child, but he comes from a strange family, and magic is deeply seated in his *inish*. Was his guidance valuable?"

"Very much so."

"Then I am grateful for his intervention. Still, perhaps, I should keep a better eye on him. Tell me, what are your plans now? Where will you go from here? Or will you stay awhile with us?"

"I will stay awhile, if you will have me. I still have some reparations to make—especially with Ramey."

"Ramey needs you. She misses you terribly, even if it might seem otherwise from your last visit. She told me how bitter and angry she was. She told me how she hurt you. But she hurts, too. You should go to her, tonight. Tell her how you feel. She is alone; Atholis is away for a few nights. There is no better time."

I nod. "I will do as you suggest."

We rise, and she embraces me again. "Come back to stay with Harrow and me when you are finished."

We break apart and start to walk away from each other. She calls over her shoulder, almost as if mimicking her son. "Love you, Char."

I give her a wave. "Love you twice as much."

I WALK ON TO FIND RAMEY. SHE IS STILL LIVING IN ANCROW'S OLD house, where she has always made her home. I wonder how long she will stay there. She lives there now with Atholis. Their relationship has been strong from the start, and now they are partnered. But she is still living in her childhood home. I wonder how much longer she will want to stay in a house that carries such painful memories. Then again, Ramey has always been less judgmental about her mother than the rest of us and was never one to dwell in the past. So perhaps what she is doing is best, replacing old, troubled memories with happy new ones.

I walk slowly, debating what I will say to my sister, working through my thoughts, considering apologies and explanations. There is so much we need to share with each other, so much we need to set right. I am the youngest, and I have always been in awe of Ramey's ability to see and know things so clearly. She was always the smartest of us, the steadiest and most insightful, while I was wild and careless, always quick to charge and slow to learn. I should have been more like her. I might have been better off, if I had been.

I approach her house and take a deep breath to steady myself. But lights are on, so I know she is home. I go up to the door and knock firmly.

When the door opens, Ramey stands there staring at me, wordless and expressionless for a moment. She looks so grown up. Different even than when I saw her only weeks ago. When did this happen? Or did I just not see it when we were last together? "Hello, Ramey."

She turns away and stands with her back to me for a long moment.

"Ramey," I say. "I'm sorry . . ."

"No!" She cuts me off. "Please, don't say that."

I stare at her in shock and disappointment.

Then she wheels back to me, revealing the tears that she has been hiding, and embraces me fiercely. "Don't ever say that again. You and I, we shouldn't have to. We should just know it."

Her arms wrap tightly around me, and I bury my face in her shoulder. "I just want us to be like we were," I whisper.

I feel her nod. "Me, too. I love you, Char. Please forgive me for what I said before."

She holds on to me in a way that tells me what I really need to know. Everything is going to be all right.

A MONTH LATER—A MONTH OF REST, RELAXATION, AND RENEWAL, yet one that leaves me with the firm knowledge that it is time to stretch my wings once more—I set off in search of another adventure, with the blessing of my family and some cryptic guidance from Parse. There are more Merrow colonies to discover, some of which may house members of my mother's family. There is also a whole wide world to explore, with mysteries still unknown.

Someday, I may find the place where I belong, or the cause that gives my life purpose. Or maybe that sort of resolution is not for me.

Either way, I know I need to make the journey.

ABOUT THE AUTHOR

TERRY BROOKS has thrilled readers for decades with his powers of imagination and storytelling. He is the author of more than forty books, most of which have been *New York Times* bestsellers. He lives with his wife, Judine, in the Pacific Northwest.

terrybrooks.net

Twitter: @officialbrooks

ABOUT THE TYPE

This book was set in Goudy Old Style, a typeface designed by Frederic William Goudy (1865–1947). Goudy began his career as a bookkeeper but devoted the rest of his life to the pursuit of "recognized quality" in a printing type.

Goudy Old Style was produced in 1914 and was an instant bestseller for the foundry. It has generous curves and smooth, even color. It is regarded as one of Goudy's finest achievements.

BY TERRY BROOKS